bird in hand

bird in hand

CHRISTINA BAKER KLINE

WM WILLIAM MORROW *An Imprint of* HarperCollins*Publishers*

FIRST EDITION

Designed by Joy O'Meara

branch illustration from iStockPhoto

Library of Congress Cataloging-in-Publication Data

Kline, Christina Baker, 1964–
    Bird in hand: a novel / Christina Baker Kline.—1st ed.
       p. cm
    ISBN 978-0-688-17724-9
    1. Marriage—Fiction. 2. Friendship—Fiction. 3. Domestic fiction.
4. Psychological fiction. I. Title
PS3561.L478B57 2009
813'.54—dc22

                                                              2008049966

09 10 11 12 13   OV/RRD   10 9 8 7 6 5 4 3 2 1

ISBN 978-0-06-182963-5 (international edition)

To David

It is a queer and fantastic world. Why can't people have what they want? The things were all there to content everybody; yet everybody has the wrong thing.

—FORD MADOX FORD, *The Good Soldier*

bird in hand

prologue

For Alison, these things will always be connected: the moment that cleaved her life into two sections and the dawning realization that even before the accident her life was not what it seemed. In the instant it took the accident to happen, and in the slow-motion moments afterward, she still believed that there was order in the universe—that she'd be able to put things right. But with one random error, built on dozens of tiny mistakes of judgment, she stepped into a different story that seemed, for a long time, to have nothing to do with her. She watched, as if behind one-way glass, as the only life she recognized slipped from her grasp.

This is what happened: she killed a child. It was not her own child. He—he was not her own child, her own boy, her own three-year-old son. She was on her way home from a party where she'd had a few drinks. She pulled out into an intersection, the other car went through a stop sign, and she didn't move out of the way. It was as simple as that, and as complicated.

Something happens to you in the moments after a car crash. Your brain needs time to catch up; you don't want to believe what your senses are telling you. Your heart is beating so loudly that it seems to be its own living being, separate from you. Everything feels too close.

As she saw the car coming toward her she sat rigid against the seat. Shutting her eyes, she heard the splintering glass and felt the wrenching slam of metal into metal. Then there was silence. She smelled gasoline and opened her eyes. The other car was crumpled and steaming and quiet, and the windshield was shattered; Alison couldn't see inside. The driver's door opened, and a man stumbled out. "My boy—my boy, he's hurt," he shouted in a panicky voice.

"I have a phone. I'll call 911," Alison said.

"Oh, God hurry," he said.

She punched the numbers with unsteady fingers. She was shaking all over; even her teeth were chattering.

"There's been an accident," she told the operator. "Send help. A boy is hurt."

The operator asked where Alison was, and she didn't know what to say. She'd taken a wrong turn awhile back, gone north instead of west, and found herself on an unfamiliar road. She knew she was lost right away; it wasn't like she didn't know, but there had been nowhere to turn, so she'd kept going. The road led to other, smaller roads, badly lit and hard to see in the foggy darkness, and then she came upon a four-way stop. Alison had pulled out into the intersection before she'd realized that the other car was driving straight through without stopping—the car was to her right and had the right of way, but it hadn't been there a moment ago when she had moved forward. It had seemed, quite literally, to have come out of nowhere.

Alison knew better than to explain all this to the operator, but in truth she had no idea where she was. Craning her neck to look out the windshield, she saw a street sign—Saw Hill Road—and reported this.

"Hold on," the operator said. "Okay, you're in Sherman. I'll send an ambulance right away."

"Please tell them to hurry," Alison said.

She called her husband from the hospital and told him about the accident, about the car being totaled and her injured wrist, but she didn't tell him that all around her doctors and nurses were barking orders and the swinging doors were banging open and shut, and a small boy was at the center of it, a small boy with a broken skull and a blood-spattered T-shirt. But Charlie knew soon enough. She had to call him back to tell him not to come to the hospital; she was now at the police station, and there was silence for a moment and then he said, "Oh—God," and whatever numbness she'd had was stripped away. She flinched—told him, "Don't come"—and he said, "What did you do?"

It wasn't the response she'd expected—not that she had thought ahead enough to expect anything in particular; she didn't know what to expect; she didn't have a response in mind. But her sudden realization that Charlie was not with her, not reflexively on her side, was so profoundly shocking that she braced for what was next.

"Do we need a lawyer?" he said when it was clear she wasn't going to answer, and she said, "I don't know—maybe. Probably."

"Don't say anything," he said then. She could tell he was flipping through scenarios in his mind, trying to lay things out in a methodical way. "Just wait until I get there."

"But I already said everything. A boy is—a little boy is—they don't know yet—hurt." She said this, although they'd already told her there was swelling on the brain. The police weren't wearing uniforms, and they didn't handcuff her or read Alison her rights or any of the other things she might have expected. The boy's parents were weeping; the mother was wailing *I let him sit on my lap; he was cold in the back and afraid of the dark,* and the father was slumped with his hands over his face. The walls of the lobby vibrated with their sadness.

"Jesus Christ." Charlie breathed. And she thought of other times he'd been exasperated with her—on their honeymoon, when, after two days of learning to ski, she suddenly froze up and couldn't do it; she was terrified of the speed, the recklessness, of feeling out of control; she was sure she would break a limb. So she spent the rest of the time in the lodge, a calculatedly cozy place with a gas flame in the fireplace and glossy ski magazines on the oak veneer coffee tables, while Charlie got his money's worth from the honeymoon. She tried to think of an experience comparable to what was happening now, some time when she had done X and he had reacted Y, but she couldn't come up with a thing. Eight years. Two children. A life she didn't plan for but had

3

grown to love. Friends and a hometown and a house, not too big but not tiny, either, with creaky stairs and water-damaged ceilings but lots of potential.

Potential was something she once had a lot of, too. Every paper she wrote in college could have been better; every B+ could have been an A. She could have pushed ahead in her career instead of stopping when it became easier to do so. She hadn't known she wanted to stop, but Charlie said, "C'mon, Alison, the kids want you at home. It's a home when you're home." But after she quit he complained about bearing the heavy load of responsibility for them. There was no safety net, he said; he said it made him anxious. He wanted her at home, but he missed the money and the security, and she knew he missed seeing her out in the world, though he didn't say it. He saw her at home in faded jeans and an old cotton sweater, he saw her at seven o'clock when the kids were clamoring for him and strung out and cranky and he had just endured his hour-long commute from the city.

And yet—and yet she thought she was lucky, thought they were lucky, loved and appreciated their life.

But tonight she was living a nightmare. Her friends—some of them, at least—would probably try to comfort her, provide some kind of solace, but it would be hard for them, because deep down they would think that she was to blame. And it wasn't that they couldn't imagine being in her position, because every mother has imagined what it would feel like to be responsible for taking the life of someone else's child.

But worse, every mother has thought about what it would be like to have her child's life taken from her.

Alison could hear Charlie asking for her, out at the front desk. Polite and deferential and panicked and impatient—all of that. She could read his voice the way some people read birdcalls. She almost didn't want him to find her. As she looked around at the dingy lights, the dirt-sodden carpet, heard the clatter from the holding cells down the hall, she wondered what it would be like to stay here—not here, perhaps, but in prison somewhere, cut off from other people, penitent as a nun. Or in a convent, a place with stone walls, small slices of sky visible through narrow slits, neatly made narrow beds. A place where she could pay for this quietly, away from anyone who had ever known her.

You might expect that she'd have thought of her children, and she did—peripherally, like a blinkered horse looking sideways; when she tried to think of them straight on, her mind went blank. Her own boy's brown curls on the pillow, her six-year-old daughter's twisted nightgown, her covers on the floor . . . Alison saw them sleeping, imagined them dead—just for an instant. Imagined explaining—and stopped. The only thing she seemed able to do was concentrate on the minute details of each moment: the cold floor, hard seat, dispassionate officers tapping on keyboards and shuffling papers. The tick of the wall clock: 11:53.

part one

At a four-way stop every vehicle must come to a complete halt before proceeding one at a time across the intersection, regardless of whether there is any other traffic in sight or not.

If two or more vehicles draw up to one of these junctions and stop, waiting to proceed across it, then they should proceed in the same order in which they arrived. If two vehicles arrive at one of these junctions at precisely the same time, so that it is impossible to tell which arrived first, then in theory the vehicle on the right has priority. However, many drivers are unaware of this rule and there are complications due to all the possible permutations of turns.

—JOHN CLETHEROE,
Driving in the USA and Canada
www.johncletheroe.org/usa_can/

It had been a rainy morning, and all through the afternoon the sky remained opaque, bleached and unreadable. Alison wasn't sure until the last minute whether she would even go to Claire's book party in the city. The kids were whiny and bored, and she was feeling guilty that her latest freelance assignment, "Sparking the Flame of Your Child's Creativity," which involved extra interviews and rewrites, had made her distracted and short-tempered with them. She'd asked the babysitter to stay late twice that week already, and had shut herself away in her tiny study—mudroom, really—trying to finish the piece. "Dolores, would you mind distracting him, please?" she'd called with a shrill edge of panic when three-year-old Noah pounded his small fists on the door.

"Maybe we shouldn't go," she said when Charlie called from work to find out when she was leaving. "The kids are needy. I'm tired."

"But you've been looking forward to this," he said.

"I don't know," she said. "Dolores seems out of sorts. I can hear her out there snapping at the kids."

"Look," he said. "I'll come home. I have a lot of work to do tonight anyway. I'll take over for Dolores, and then you won't have to worry."

"But I want you there," she said obstinately. "I don't want to go alone. I probably won't even know anybody."

"You know Claire," Charlie said. "Isn't that what matters? It'll be good to show your support."

"It's not like she's gone out of her way to get in touch with me."

"She did send you an invitation."

"Well, her publicist."

"So Claire put your name on the list. Come on, Alison—I'm not going to debate this with you. Clearly you want to go, or you wouldn't be agonizing over it."

He was right. She didn't answer. Sometime back in the fall, Claire's feelings had gotten hurt—something about an article she'd submitted to the magazine Alison worked for that wasn't right, that Alison's boss had brusquely criticized and then rejected, leaving her to do the work of explaining. It was Alison's first major assignment as a freelance editor, and she hadn't wanted to screw it up. So she'd let her boss's displeasure (which, after all, had eked out as annoyance at her, too: "I do wonder, Alison, if you defined the assignment well enough in the first place . . .") color her response. She'd hinted that Claire might be taking on too many things at once, and that the piece wasn't up to the magazine's usual standards. She was harsher than she should have been. And yet—the article was sloppy; it appeared to have been hastily written. There were typos and transition problems. Claire seemed to have misunderstood the assignment. Frankly, Alison was annoyed at her for turning in the piece as she did—she should have taken more time with it, been more particular. It pointed to something larger in their friendship, Alison thought, a kind of carelessness on Claire's part, a taking for granted. It had been that way since they were young. Claire was the impetuous, brilliant one, and Alison was the compass that kept her on course.

Now Claire had finished her novel, a slim, thinly disguised roman à clef called *Blue Martinis*, about a girl's coming-of-age in the South. Alison couldn't bear to read it; the little she'd gleaned from the blurb by a bestselling writer on the postcard invitation Claire's publicist had sent—"Every woman who has ever been a girl will relate to this searingly honest, heartbreakingly funny novel about a girl's sexual awakening in a repressive southern town"—made her stomach twist into a knot. Claire's story was, after all, Alison's story, too; she hadn't been asked or even consulted, but she had little doubt that her own past was now on view. And Claire hadn't let her see the manuscript in advance; she'd told Alison that she didn't want to feel inhibited by what people from Bluestone might think. Anyway, Claire insisted, it was a novel. Despite this disclaimer, from what Alison could gather, she was "Jill," the main character's introverted if strong-willed sidekick.

"Ben will be there, won't he?" Charlie said.

"Probably. Yes."

"So hang out with him. You'll be fine."

Alison nodded into the phone. Ben, Claire's husband, was effortlessly sociable—wry and intimate and inclusive. Alison had a mental picture of him from countless cocktail parties, standing in the middle of a group with a drink in one hand, stooping his tall frame slightly to accommodate.

"Tell them I'm sorry I can't be there," Charlie said. "And let Dolores know I'll be home around seven. And remember—this is part of your job, to schmooze and make contacts. You'll be glad you went."

"Yeah, okay," she said, thinking, oh right, my *job,* mentally adding up how much she'd earned over the past year: two $50 checks for whimsical personal essays on smart-mommy Web sites, $500 for a parenting magazine "service" piece called "50 Ways for New Moms to Relieve Stress," a $1,000 kill fee for a big feature on sibling rivalry that the competition scooped just before Alison's story went to press. The freelance editing assignment with Claire had never panned out.

"The party's on East End Avenue, right?" he said. "You should probably take the bridge. The tunnel might be backed up, with this rain. Drive slow; the roads'll be wet."

They talked about logistics for a few minutes—how much to pay Dolores, what Charlie might find to eat in the fridge. As they were talking, Alison slipped out of her study, shutting the door quietly behind her. She could hear the kids in the living room with Dolores, and she made her way upstairs quietly, avoiding the creaky steps so they wouldn't be alerted to her presence. In the master bedroom she riffled through the hangers on her side of the closet and pulled out one shirt and then another for inspection. She yanked off the jeans she'd been wearing for three days and tried on a pair of black wool pants she hadn't worn in months, then stood back and inspected herself in the full-length mirror on the back of the closet door. The pants zipped easily enough, but the top button was tight. She put a hand over her tummy, unzipped the pants, and callipered a little fat roll with her fingers. She sighed.

"What?"

"Oh, nothing," she said. "Listen, Dolores will feed the kids, you just have to give them a bath. And honey, try not to look at your BlackBerry until you get them in bed. They see so little of you as it is." She yanked down her pants and, back in the closet, found a more forgiving pair.

When Alison was finally dressed she felt awkward and unnatural, like a child pretending to be a grown-up, or a character in a play. In her mommy role she wore flat, comfortable shoes, small gold hoops, soft T-shirts, jeans or khakis. Now it felt as if she were wearing a costume: black high-heeled boots, a jangling bracelet, earrings that pulled on her lobes, bright (too bright?) lipstick she'd been pressed into buying at the Bobbi Brown counter by a salesgirl half her age. She went downstairs and greeted the children stiffly, motioning to Dolores to keep them away so she could maintain the illusion that she always dressed like this.

She went out to the garage, got into the car, remembered her cell phone, clattered back into the house, returned to the car, remembered her umbrella, made it back to the house in time to answer the ringing phone in the kitchen. It was her mother in North Carolina.

"Hi, Mom, look, I'll have to call you later. I'm running out the door."

"You sound tense," her mother said. "Where are you going?"

"To a party for Claire's book."

"In the city?"

"Yes. And I'm late."

"I read her book," her mother said. "Have you?"

"Not yet."

"Well. You might want to."

"I will, one of these days," Alison said, consciously ignoring her mother's insinuating tone. Then the children were on her. Six-year-old Annie dissolved in tears, and Dolores had to peel Noah off Alison's legs like starfish from a rock. Alison made it out to the car again, calling, "I'll be home soon!" and madly blowing kisses, and realized when she turned on the engine that she didn't have a bottle of water, which was annoying, because you never knew how long it would take to get into the city, but fuck it. There was no way she could go inside again. Half-way down the driveway she saw Annie and Noah in the front window, frantically waving at her and jumping up and down. Alison pressed the button to roll down her window and waved back. As she pulled the car into the street she could see Noah's cheek mashed up against the glass, his hand outstretched, his small form resigned and motionless as he watched her drive away.

EAST END AVENUE was quiet and damp in the shadows of early evening. Several blocks over, traffic swished and rumbled, but here Alison was the only one on the street. After easily finding a parking spot—just in time for the changing of the guard from metered to free, a rare lucky break—she locked the car doors and pulled her coat tightly around her. It wasn't raining now, but the air was chilly; bare trees creaked in the sharp wind like old bedsprings. The avenue, the build-ings, even the cars parked along the street, were washed in dull tones. Early March—not yet spring, though not still winter. A purgatorial season, Alison thought, when the manufactured cheer of the holidays has worn off, and desolation feels palpable. Or maybe just to her. She wasn't sure, and had so little confidence anymore, in ascribing opinions to other adults. She seemed to have lost the ability to gauge what they might be feeling and thinking. (Children were a different story; she had developed an uncanny ability to decipher their moods—even those of the ones that weren't hers.) She wondered if such an ability, which she used to pride herself on, was a social skill you could lose without practice.

The doorman, dressed in a navy blue uniform and standing just inside the small vestibule leading to the lobby, inclined his head and said, "Good evening, miss," as Alison approached. "Miss"—she liked that.

"Apartment five-twelve?" she asked, waving the invitation.

Holding the door open, he ushered her in. "Elevator straight ahead."

"Thank you." She nodded, thinking, Oh yes, it's like this; it's this easy, and walked through the gleaming, harlequin-tiled lobby, past marble columns and inset mirrors, glancing at her reflection as she passed. Her hair was windblown; she was wearing last year's coat—or did she buy it two years ago? It hardly mattered—the cut was conservative, tasteful, unexceptional, made to last for years without drawing undue attention. Under the coat she wore the loose black pants and a heather gray ribbed turtleneck she'd bought at the Bendel's end-of-season sale on a rare foray into the city a few weeks earlier. At home, in front of the mirror in the bedroom, she had toyed with a scarf, a Christmas gift from her mother in the luminous shades of a medieval stained-glass window, but ultimately decided against it: too . . . suburban. She'd tucked it back in the drawer.

When Alison had lived in the city and worked as a magazine editor, she'd observed the fashion editors for ideas about what to wear. She'd never been particularly creative herself, but their example wasn't hard to emulate: a wardrobe of black basics, with several fresh pieces mixed in each season to keep it current. A short pleated plaid skirt, a plum-colored poncho, round-toed satin shoes. But now that she no longer knew which trends to follow, even these small flourishes were risky. And besides, the person she'd become had little use for them. When was the last time she'd worn a short pleated skirt or satin shoes? Now she dressed in clothes that didn't gap or expose too much, that absorbed mess and fuss and a child's handprints, that could as easily be worn at a playdate as at a meeting of the planning committee of the preschool fund-raiser. After they'd moved to the suburbs she'd added a little color to her wardrobe so she wouldn't come off as too "New York"—unfriendly, severe—but she balked at the bright costumes some women wore, holiday-themed sweaters and socks, matching headbands. These women scared her as much as the trendiest New Yorkers did, at the opposite end of the spectrum—possibly more. She was less afraid of being judged by them than she was of becoming them. She didn't know how that might happen, but she feared it could be as simple as prolonged exposure, a wearing down of discernment and a fun house–mirror questioning of her own judgment. It was happening already, in so many ways. Here she was, at the threshold of this party, doubting the drab cut of her coat, her risk-averse turtleneck, whether she had a right to be there at all.

As the button flashed and the elevator doors finally opened—it had taken forever; she might as well have walked up the stairs—Alison heard the clickclickclick of high heels on the tile floor of the lobby. She turned to see a woman striding toward her, her flapping coat exposing a lime green lining. "Hold it!" the woman commanded.

Alison stepped into the elevator and pushed the DOOR OPEN button. The clicking sped up, and then, in a staccato clatter, the woman was inside the elevator, too. "Thank you," she said without looking at Alison, one polished fingernail poised over the panel of small circles designating the floors. She paused over 5, and then, seeing that it was lighted, dropped her hand. Out of the corner of her eye, Alison watched the woman compose herself. Like a preening bird, she made fine adjustments: she touched the back of her head, unfastened the buttons of her quilted silk jacket. She slipped a finger into the waistband of her skirt and smoothed it. Alison observed all of this with a benign curiosity. So this is how a woman prepares for a party, she thought; these are the small modulations that give her shape and identity.

Since she was a child, Alison had made these kinds of minute assessments of other females, searching for clues that would show her how to act, how to carry herself, how to pull off being a woman. Her own mother was uninterested in social niceties; when Alison was growing up her mother wore paint-spattered T-shirts for days in a row and tied her hair back with rubber bands. She went barefoot all summer and wore sneakers when it got cool. It was almost worse that she was effortlessly beautiful; she had no tricks or techniques to pass along to a shy and insecure daughter. In fact, it puzzled her that Alison was interested in learning those things she so assiduously avoided. "Why do you buy these trashy rags?" she'd ask, pausing over a stack of *Seventeen*s and *Glamour*s on the floor of Alison's bedroom. "They perpetuate such absurd stereotypes."

"I like them," Alison would say, snatching the magazines from under her mother's inquisitive gaze. "There's a lot of information—"

"About the crap they want you to buy."

"Not only that," Alison would say, without the tools or the fortitude to make a reasoned defense. Her mother was right, but it wasn't the point. However unrealistic or unattainable, the paint-by-numbers makeup guides and ugly-duckling before-and-afters gave Alison a sense of possibility. They made her feel that she might one day transform herself into the kind of woman she dreamed of being—confident, savvy, sure.

How ironic, she thought now, fleetingly, as the elevator ground to a hesitant stop at the fifth floor before it settled into the right notch and its doors lurched open, that for a while, when she lived in New York, she actually was that woman—or a reasonable imitation—and now she was feeling as vulnerable and insecure as she had back in high school. It takes so little to strip the gears, she thought, to find yourself pedaling in place when you thought you were moving forward.

"Are you a friend of Colm's?" the peacock said suddenly, turning around as they stepped out into the hall.

Colms. Colm. Alison panicked for a moment; the word sounded made up, like the name of a *Star Trek* alien. Oh, yes, Colm—the name on the invitation, Colm Maynard; it was his apartment. "No," she said. "I'm an old friend of Claire's."

"From Bluestone?"

Alison nodded.

The peacock narrowed her eyes and gave Alison a once-over. "Fascinating."

Even from halfway down the hall, the buzz of the party was audible, with an occasional shriek of laughter rising above the din. Pushing open the door to 512, the peacock exclaimed, "Darling!" in the general vicinity of a cluster of twentysomething publishing types, throwing up her hands and disappearing into the crowd.

In the long entry corridor, people were juggling drinks and business cards. They barely acknowledged Alison muttering "Excuse me—pardon—excuse me" as she nudged past, inching her way into a large, dimly lit room. Stepping back against the beige linen-covered wall, she looked around. The apartment was enormous, rooms leading into other rooms, all of which seemed to be filled with people. She could see a bar at the far end of the living room, set against the panoramic backdrop of the East River, with a young man in a starched white shirt with rolled-up sleeves mixing drinks. Several fresh-faced women—moonlighting college students, Alison suspected—were circulating trays of teeny-tiny brightly colored hors d'oeuvres. The crowd was dense and animated, densely animated; for a moment Alison saw it as one breathing organism. She shook her head, dispelling the illusion. That was an old trick from childhood, a way to transform an intimidating situation into something remote and featureless that she could observe from a distance.

Claire's hardcovers were piled in stacks on tables around the room. The cover, hot pink with white letters, featured a slightly blurry photo of a martini glass, tipping sideways, splashing droplets of blue liquid around the spine and on the back. This wraparound style was, Alison knew, the signature of Rick Mann, a graphic designer whose book jackets were everywhere this season. Sidling over to a table, she flipped the book open to see the author photo. Claire was half in shadow, her molten hair as timelessly sculpted as an Irving Penn landscape, her expression a pensive gaze into the middle distance. The photographer, Astrid Encarte, was another trendy name. Evidently the publisher had spared no expense.

Turning the book over, Alison skimmed the names on the back cover—a roster of young, self-consciously renegade authors delivering a predictable staccato of lush adjectives and arcane phrasings— "Nebulously brilliant wanderings of an incandescent mind over the pitted minefield of an American childhood," one said. Another exclaimed simply, "Wow. Yes. Hello!"

Across the room, Claire was holding court. Wearing a sheer lace dress over a spaghetti-strapped black sheath that accentuated her toned biceps, the toes of her pointy green heels poking out from under the hem like the snouts of baby crocodiles, she bent forward with the flat of her hand across her stomach, her other hand flapping theatrically in the air. "Oh, behave!" she exclaimed. The man who'd provoked this admonishment whispered in her ear, and she looked up at him flirtatiously, in that flagrant way that is only possible with a gay man, and said, "Trevor, you are *terrible*."

Despite their long history, Alison was hesitant about approaching her. Several months ago she had extended an olive branch by inviting Claire and Ben to dinner in Rockwell, but Claire remained as distant as ever. It occurred to Alison that their falling-out was somehow bigger than she'd realized; it seemed unlikely that a trivial magazine assignment alone could have ruptured a lifelong friendship. But Alison was afraid to ask.

For years, growing up, the two of them had spent much of their time together exploring provocative questions and ambivalent answers— about the world, about other people, about themselves. But the better you get to know another person, the more you risk with each revelation. More than once, as teenagers, when Claire was passing along gossip about somebody else, Alison wondered if all this time spent together might be insurance against Claire's hating her someday. At the time, Alison didn't know why she even imagined it—she just had the feeling, deep down in some barely acknowledged place, that Claire's friendship might be provisional.

Why are you so distant? Sometimes, Alison thought, you don't ask the obvious question because you don't want to know the answer. And it's not only that she might not tell you—it's that the truth is layered and complex; it is no single thing. Perhaps she does believe, as Claire had said, that you don't have much in common anymore; she doesn't want to intrude in your busy life; your children are so present and take up so much of your energy. But what she means by saying that you don't have much in common is that you are inconvenient to get to and clueless about the latest movies, and you hold your child over your head to sniff his diaper. She means that she is ambivalent about having children, and the simultaneous mundanity and chaos of your life repels her. She finds your daughter's constant questions tiresome; she is sick of those dinners in the city when you become skittish and distracted around ten-thirty and start looking at your watch because you have to get home for the babysitter's midnight curfew. The truth is, she can sense your impatience with the details of her life, too—her quest to find the best dim sum in Chinatown, her exhaustion from jetting off to Amsterdam for the weekend, her analysis of the latest off-Broadway play. What good did it do to articulate the ambivalence? In therapy, maybe a lot. In real life Alison wasn't sure.

Claire had a glamorous future to look forward to, at least for the next few months, and she also had an intriguing, and now very public, past. Alison was just an anonymous suburban housewife who'd grown up in a small southern town—nothing special about that.

It wasn't that Alison wanted to be Claire—she didn't. But she admired her tenacity and clarity and single-mindedness, particularly compared with her own indecisiveness. Alison had been living for other people for so long that she could barely identify what she wanted for herself anymore. She'd find herself paralyzed with indecision in the strangest places—the grocery store, for instance, where she roamed the aisles with a rising panic, even as she clutched a list in her hand: What would her kids eat? What would her husband want? She rarely asked herself what she wanted. It seemed irrelevant.

In front of Alison, now, was the drinks table. Martini glasses stood in rows like cartoon soldiers; on the other side of the table stood the second unit, ordinary wineglasses for the spoilers who weren't in the spirit. Alison wasn't at all sure that she was in the spirit, and she'd never really liked martinis; but to ask for a chardonnay or, worse, a club soda, seemed cowardly. She watched as the bartender poured a midrange Swedish vodka, in its distinctive ink blue bottle, into a large shaker of ice. He added Curaçao and shook it, then strained the liquid into a martini glass and added a twist of lemon peel.

"One of those, please," she said, and the student-bartender, more charming than experienced, flashed her a grin and sloshed blue-tinted alcohol all over the tablecloth before handing her the sticky glass. She took a sip. The martini tasted lemony, with a medicinal aftertaste, mouthwash fresh. The next sip was sweet; the taste of the Curaçao melted away, overwhelmed by the alcohol. She was beginning to like it.

Emboldened now, holding her glass out like a calling card, Alison made her way over to a group of strangers and introduced herself.

Where is Charlie? Claire scanned the room for a glimpse of his sandy hair and broad shoulders, but no one remotely resembled him, not even from the back. Out of the corner of her eye she'd seen Alison wandering alone through the crowd a few minutes earlier, but that didn't necessarily mean Charlie wasn't there. Maybe he'd been waylaid in the foyer.

That morning he had called Claire from work. "It's your big night," he said. "Excited?"

"A little nervous. I'm glad you're coming."

"I want to. I'm going to do everything I can."

"What do you mean?" she said, struggling to keep the irritation out of her voice. "This is important to me. Why can't you just say you'll come?"

He sighed. "It's complicated. The kids, Alison . . . I'll try. I'm just not a hundred percent sure."

"But I'll be really disappointed." She knew she sounded petulant, but she didn't care.

"Me, too."

"It won't be any fun without you."

"Oh, come on, Claire—you're going to have a great time, whether I'm there or not."

"No, I won't," she said stubbornly.

"Claire," he said. "I do want to come. I want to be there for you. But I'm no good at hiding my feelings; you know that better than anyone. With Alison there, and Ben . . . Frankly, it seems dangerous."

"Don't be so dramatic, Charlie. It's a big party, with lots of people."

"But I won't be able to keep my eyes off you."

"That's okay; I'm supposed to be the center of attention."

"Not to mention my hands."

She laughed. "Stop. Promise you'll come."

He had promised, but she wasn't sure she believed him. This would be the first time the four of them would be in a room together since that night out in Rockwell, three months ago. Once or twice in the past few months Ben had remarked that they hadn't seen much of Alison and Charlie; but everyone was busy, and it didn't seem particularly strange. The falling-out with Alison, Claire had to admit, made it easier to do what they were doing.

"Claire, this guy's important," her publicist, Jami with an *i*, said sotto voce, startling Claire out of her musings. Jami motioned toward a man with wolfman sideburns who was bearing down on them, snagging a martini from a waiter without breaking his stride. "Jim Oliver. He's a reviewer for *People*."

"Hello," Claire said as he joined their small group. "I'm Claire."

22 "I deduced that," he said. "Though I must say you look livelier in person than in that ice-princess author photo."

"Thank you. I guess."

"We're all so proud of her." Jami beamed, squeezing Claire's waist. "Did you hear we made a hard/soft deal with Japan today? And her agent is talking to Dreamworks? And she got a great review in *EW* this week? It's all happening so fast!"

Claire felt ridiculous, standing there listening to Jami inflate the facts. She had a mental image of her 230-page book literally puffing up and floating away on its own hot air. The Japan deal was for a paltry $5,000; Claire's agent had managed to slip the book to Dreamworks because her neighbor was a minor executive there; the "great" review in *Entertainment Weekly* was actually an okay B+. But this, Claire knew, was the game.

"It's at the top of my pile," Jim Oliver said, taking a swig from his glass. He held it aloft and squinted at it, as if contemplating a toast. "So what's with the blue martinis?"

Claire held up a copy of her book and wagged it at him.

"Well, that clears it up," he said. Jami, whom Claire had gotten to know well over the past few weeks, elbowed her in the side.

"It was my mother's drink," Claire said. "Curaçao is like heroin to her."

"And she was—you know—depressed," Jami interjected with a meaningful nod.

Claire looked across the room at her mother, Lucinda Ellis, there in the flesh, chatting amiably with Martha Belle Clancy, the safety blanket she'd hauled up from North Carolina. The two of them, wearing floral dresses and beige pumps and Monet pearls, looked like stage props for Claire's book. Every now and then Ben would bring someone over to meet Lucinda, and she'd gush in a way that tended to startle New Yorkers but that came as naturally to her as breathing.

As she looked around, Claire's gaze fell on Alison, standing at the drinks table, accepting a blue martini from a boy with a tattoo of thorns ringing his forearm, and looking around for someone to talk to. She seemed unsure of herself, out of place. In Claire's former role, the role she'd played all her life, she would have rushed over to introduce Alison to someone, but now she decided to let her be. Claire's therapist was helping her to separate, to stop feeling responsible for other peoples' feelings at the expense of her own; it was part of her decision to write the book, to put off having kids, to take time to figure out what she wanted in her life.

To get involved with Charlie.

Claire glanced at her watch: 8:44. "Will you excuse me for a moment?" she said to Jami. "I'll be right back. It was nice meeting you," she added to the *People* guy, who tapped the book and grinned.

In the bathroom, with the door locked, she pulled her cell phone out of the little bag she was carrying and pushed number nine, speed-dialing Charlie's cell phone.

"Hi," he said, picking up after several rings. "This is a surprise. Aren't you—?"

"I escaped," she said. "I'm in the bathroom."

23

"Who's that, Daddy?" she heard a child say, and Charlie replied, in a muffled voice, "Nobody, honey, just—work."

"'Nobody'?" The word stung, even though Claire knew she was being irrational. She sighed. "You're not here."

"I'm sorry," he said. "I should've called. At the last minute—"

"I knew you weren't coming." He didn't say anything, so she continued. "It's okay. It's just . . . boring without you."

"I don't believe it. This is your moment."

"It doesn't feel like my moment. It all feels very—removed, somehow."

"It's a damn good book. You know that, don't you?"

"What book?" Claire could hear Annie asking in the background.

"Nothing, sweetie," he answered, his voice muffled again. "Just something I read. Go help Noah with the train tracks. I'll be there in a minute."

"You finished it already?" Claire asked.

"Just this afternoon, on the train." He paused, and Claire guessed he was waiting for Annie to leave. Then he said, "It's an incredible story. It makes me—oh, never mind. We'll talk about it later."

"Tell me."

"Honestly—it makes me like you even better."

"Oh." She smiled into the phone.

"So relax. Enjoy this."

"Urrr." She groaned. "I'd rather be with you." She held the phone to her ear, listening to the static between them. "When can I see you?"

"Soon."

"When?"

"It's the weekend," he said. "I don't think I can get away."

"Before I leave on tour? Monday?"

"Yes," he said.

"Charlie . . ."

"What?"

"I just . . . I want to be with you."

"Yes," he said again.

When the call was done she clicked off and held the warm phone to her chest for a moment, as if it were a piece of him. Then she slipped it back into her bag and opened the door. Surveying the room, she watched as Alison caught Ben's eye and he nodded and held one finger out—wait—so that the person he was with couldn't see. After a moment he extricated himself with a deft turn and started to make his way over to her. Claire saw Alison's features soften and her shoulders drop. Now she could relax—Ben wouldn't desert her until she found her footing.

All evening, Claire had watched Ben work the room as only Ben could, seeking out the uncomfortable and the socially awkward, refilling drinks and matchmaking commonalities. Every now and then he'd look over at her and lift his glass, offering to refill hers, or raise his eyebrows in a bid to rescue her if she needed it. More than once, feeling the warmth of his gaze, Claire wondered how it could be possible to love someone as much as she loved Ben, and yet no longer be in love.

Ben needed a drink. For the past fifteen minutes he'd been listening to Martha Belle Clancy, Claire's mother's best friend, talk about her hobby—a series of needlework dioramas she was making of major Civil War battles (she'd completed six already, through Fredericksburg)—and for at least twelve of those minutes, his glass had been empty. Feigning interest in Martha Belle, a challenge to begin with, was getting harder by the second. Ben had already chatted pleasantly with Claire's mother about all the things she disliked about New York—the weather, the traffic, the noise—and by now he figured he had just about fulfilled his husbandly obligations.

Surreptitiously, he glanced around the room—wasn't a waiter supposed to be circulating? He'd settle for another blue martini, though what he really wanted was a Scotch. Where might Colm have hidden the hard stuff? If Ben could somehow extricate himself, maybe he could hunt it down.

Just then Alison emerged from a crowd in the hall, and Ben was momentarily distracted. He watched as she moved across the room to the drinks table, where the bartender poured her a martini. My God, she's lovely, he thought—those fine features, bright inquisitive eyes. She seemed flooded with quivering energy, like a doe standing in a clearing. The gray sweater and black pants she was wearing reminded him of how she'd looked in England ten years ago. With faint creases around her eyes, her slim body softened slightly by motherhood, she was still, he thought, gamine, with an Audrey Hepburn–like grace.

Why was she alone? Why hadn't Charlie come? Being present at these kinds of events was the sort of thing the two couples always did for each other, expected of each other. It was Claire's first, perhaps only, book, as important to her as the births of Alison and Charlie's children (and hadn't Ben and Claire come to the hospital as soon as they could, hadn't they brought flowers and gifts even as Ben's heart was aching with longing for a child of his own as he held the astonishingly light bundle in his arms, looking down at its curranty face?). Clearly it had something to do with that falling-out between Claire and Alison, which Claire refused to discuss with Ben in any kind of rational way but also refused to get past. What was that all about, anyway? It was so unlike Claire to hold a grudge. Ben attributed it to prepublication jitters and maybe some unresolved childhood issues. It did make things awkward for the four of them. Ben didn't feel that he could call to make plans, and even his friendship with Charlie—which he'd thought of, perhaps näively, as separate from the couples' friendship—had suffered; Charlie stopped calling. Ben picked up the phone several times to dial Charlie's number at work and then . . . put it down.

Ben and Charlie used to meet for lunch twice a month at least, at the Harvard Club (if Ben was paying) or a hole-in-the-wall Chinese place called Kung Pao (if Charlie was). More often they'd send each other e-mail arcana—a funny video clip, an absurd real-news story, a link to someone's noteworthy blog or an obscure band's Web site. Sometimes they'd get together to listen to live music in the Village. Over the past few years, what with Charlie having kids and moving out to the suburbs, it had gotten harder to see each other, particularly without spouses. Their jobs were demanding; their interests had diverged. Amiable, affable Charlie had become a bit tense and distracted. He spent weekends, now, changing diapers and puttering around the house. His life had taken on the gravity of responsibility, which trumped petty outside interests. When Ben talked about a play he'd seen or a book he'd read or even an article in *The New Yorker*—anything more taxing than the sports page—Charlie would shake his head. "I'm living under a rock," he said once. "I can't think of the last time I went to a show or finished a book. It's all-work, all-kids these days."

Not that there was anything wrong with that. Ben envied Charlie's transition to parenthood, the way he talked about his children with wonder and puzzlement and something verging on awe.

Ben caught Claire's eye across the room and raised his empty glass in a tacit offer to refill hers. She smiled and shook her head, almost imperceptibly, then gave him a playful grimace no one else could see— Here I am, soldiering through.

"You and Claire simply must get down to Bluestone to visit," Martha Belle was saying. "I know y'all have a lot going on, but it has been a while, hasn't it?" She nudged him with her elbow. "And Lucinda is dying to have some grandchildren. She says she doesn't want to put pressure on you, but I think a little pressure can do wonders."

"Martha Belle, you are too much," Ben said. "But you don't have to convince me. Claire is going down there on her book tour, so you might raise it with her then."

"Well, maybe I will," she said, raising her eyebrows with a significant pause, as if all had become clear.

Ben clasped her hand. "It's been a pleasure. I want to see those dioramas one of these days."

"I look forward to showing them to you," she said, beaming. "I know you need to mingle. Go, go!" She shooed him away with plump, fluttering fingers.

Ben made his way over to the bar, in search of the elusive blue martini and the ill-at-ease Alison Granville. He found both.

"Oh, Ben!" Alison said, with obvious relief. "It's lovely to see you."

He took a martini from the bartender and kissed Alison on the cheek. "Lovely to see you, too," he said. "I've been trying to get over here since you walked in."

"I saw you with Martha Belle. She always scared me a little when we were kids. She's so—energetic."

Ben nodded. "She's the manic to Lucinda's depressive. Have you heard about those dioramas?"

"Oh, yes. In fact, I've seen one or two. They're quite impressive."

"I'm sure they are." Though Ben and Alison had little in common, and he couldn't remember a time he'd ever been with her alone, having a shared knowledge of Claire's world gave their exchanges an easy familiarity. "You look wonderful," he said.

"Do you think so? I feel a little—dowdy," she said. "It's hard to keep up with you city slickers. And I'm sure I have kid goo on my pants somewhere."

"So that's what that is," he said. "Everyone was talking."

She gave him a smile. "It wouldn't be the first time."

"Where have you been lately? I haven't seen you in months."

"I know," she said.

"Anything new?"

"I've been doing some freelance work. Not much, to be honest. I know it sounds ridiculous, but with the kids and everything—"

"It doesn't sound ridiculous," he said. "It sounds nice, actually."

"It is. It is nice." She tilted her glass to take a sip, but it was empty.

"You need another drink," he said. He took the glass out of her hand and set it on the table.

The bartender handed her another martini. "Thanks," she said. She took a sip and turned back to Ben. "It's so funny that Lucinda's kitschy cocktail has spawned all this."

"The next big fad sweeping the nation," Ben said in a radio announcer's voice. "Bluuue martinis."

"I doubt Claire would mind."

"I wouldn't either," he said. "We have big plans, you know. We want to open a Blue Martini theme park, for adults."

"No roller coasters, I hope."

"Oh, definitely roller coasters. Cocktails and roller coasters. How great would that be?"

She laughed.

"So did you come alone?" he asked. "Where's the ball and chain?"

"He had to stay home," Alison said. "A minor domestic crisis."

"Nothing dire, I hope."

"No, just . . ." She shook her head. "It doesn't matter. He wanted to come."

No point in belaboring it, Ben thought. "Well, tell him he was missed."

"I will," she said. "Who are these people?"

"Let's see," he said, looking around. "Editorial assistants, publicists, media types, relatives. All here for the free drinks."

"Do you know everybody?"

"Just the relatives."

"I used to love these parties," she said. "I guess I'm out of practice."

"It's all publicity, anyway. We're just stage props for the marketing team."

"No, we're here to celebrate Claire's achievement."

"It's only an achievement if it translates into sales," he said.

"That's a little cynical, isn't it?"

"Is it? You know the business better than I do."

"All right," she said. "So—I assume you've read it?"

"Of course. Have you?"

She shook her head.

"It's pretty good. There is this annoying character named Jill, but other than that . . ." He grinned. "Look, it's a novel and all. But you don't come off too badly. In case you're wondering."

Was it his imagination, or was Alison blushing? She took a sip of her drink and cocked her head to the side, as if she were trying to decide what to say. "Ben, can I ask you something? Do you . . ." She stopped. Her cheeks were flushed. "Do you know about this—this thing Claire and I had a few months ago? It wasn't a big deal—or at least I didn't think it was. But we haven't really spoken since."

He nodded. "I heard something."

"I guess I really hurt her feelings. I must have."

"Don't assume that. Frankly, I wouldn't take it personally. She's been crazed with this book stuff. We've barely had a conversation in the past few weeks, and I live with the woman."

31

"Well, okay," she said. "It's just not pleasant to be—estranged, you know?"

In that moment he sensed Alison's vulnerability, as deep and raw as a wound. It wasn't just being alone at a party, or being at odds with Claire; it was something more. She might not have known it yet, but it seemed to Ben that she was deeply unhappy. And in some way, impossible to articulate, even to himself, Ben felt linked to Alison in this, as if his fortune and hers were entwined.

"I do know," he said.

By the time Alison did, finally, talk to Claire, the party had thinned and the bartenders were loading dirty stemware into plastic rental crates.

"I've been trying to get over to you all night," Claire exclaimed, an obvious lie that Alison was content to accept. Claire pushed the hair out of her face and exhaled, blowing air across her lower lip, as if now, finally, she could relax. "Have you talked to my mother? Does she know you're here?"

"We said a quick hello," Alison said. "We've both been . . ." She waved her hand around to indicate a flurry of activity. In fact, she had been avoiding Claire's mother all evening, and she suspected that Claire's mother had been avoiding her. Lucinda's quiet diffidence had always depressed her; Alison rarely knew what to say. Alison had always thought that they recognized in each other certain personality traits, such as timidity and passive aggression, that neither of them particularly admired. Their orbiting Claire this evening only accentuated their similarities.

"Did you have a good time?" Claire asked suddenly. Her eyes were glassy and unfocused. She reminded Alison of a birthday kid after blowing out the candles, exhausted from being the center of attention for too long.

"It was a great party," Alison said, with genuine feeling—it had been a great party. "Did you enjoy it?" This was where their relationship was now—somewhat formal, and yet still, somehow, intimate. Alison didn't know if Claire had had a good time, but she felt entitled, even obligated, to ask.

"I did," Claire said, as if she were surprised to say so. "Though it's weird for things to be so . . . so public, after all that time scribbling away in a room by myself."

"Dear God, yawn. Isn't that what all writers say when they finally get published?" Ben said, coming up behind them. "We're going to have to think of something more original for you to say when you go on tour, you know."

"My husband, my press agent," Claire said.

"By the way," said Alison, "Charlie's sorry he can't be here. We had a babysitting situation."

"Oh, that's all right," Claire said.

"We should all have dinner again one of these nights, after Claire gets back," Ben said. "Maybe you two could come into the city." He touched Alison's back with the flat of his hand. "We miss you guys."

"We'd love that," Alison said. She took a sip of her drink. (As one of the bartenders was packing up, he'd handed Alison a half-full glass of blue liquid. "The end of the martinis," he said. "I'd hate to see it go to waste.")

"Mmm," said Claire.

"So when are you going on tour?" Alison asked.

"In about a week. Just a few towns. Nothing major."

"Are you going, Ben?" Alison asked.

He shrugged, and Claire shook her head. "It's going to be so tedious," she said. "One obscure radio station after another."

"She says I'd be trailing after her like Prince Philip. Though I think that could be fun. I've got the stance down." Ben clasped his hands behind him and rocked on his heels, then added, "I did point out to her that the queen rarely makes appearances at chain stores in strip malls."

Two women, the peacock from the elevator and a fresh-faced girl with a Marc Jacobs bag, whose proprietary manner with Claire implied that she was either her new best friend or her publicist, joined the group.

"Fabulous! Party!" declared the peacock. "Everybody wants to know when you're writing a sequel."

Claire laughed uncomfortably. "Let's just get through this, shall we?"

"You know, if you push another one out right away, it increases your selling power exponentially," said Peacock.

"But I've said everything I have to say," Claire said. "What's left?"

"Well, for one thing, sex," the fresh-faced girl said, her voice dropping to a coy whisper. "There's not a lot of it in this book."

"Wait a minute," Ben said. "Aren't you billing it as 'a young girl's sexual awakening'?"

"Sure, to sell copies," said Fresh Face. "But it's really pretty tame. The book ends when she goes off to college—just think of all the material Claire's got saved up from the past ten or fifteen years!"

All at once Alison realized that Claire was becoming agitated. Her cheeks were pink and her eyes hard and bright; her hand fluttered at her neck. "First of all," she said in a strained voice, "remember, this is fiction. And second . . ."

Peacock and Fresh Face exchanged glances. They were clearly accustomed to dealing with sensitive authors; this was part of the deal.

"Second . . ." Claire's voice trailed off. She looked at Ben beseechingly.

"Second," he jumped in, "if this novel were, in the slightest way, based on her life, the sequel would be dreadfully boring. Prince Charming, happily ever after, end of story."

Claire reached over and pulled Ben toward her, kissing him on the cheek.

"Aw," said Fresh Face, "sweet. A love story."

Peacock glanced at her watch. "Well, time to go. Fabulous party," she said again. "Congratulations, Claire."

"Thank you," Claire murmured, air-kissing them both.

"I'll call you tomorrow," Fresh Face said, holding one hand out like a phone receiver, pinky and thumb extended, as they walked away. "You get some rest!"

Alison watched them head toward the door, grabbing the leftover books from side tables along the way. "I guess I'd better be going, too," she said. "See what I can scrounge up at home for dinner."

Claire nodded distractedly.

"Well," Ben said, trying and failing to catch Claire's eye, "why don't you come and grab a bite with us? We're going to a little bistro around the corner on Second."

Claire snapped to attention. "Ben," she said abruptly, clutching his arm. "I'm—I'm really tired. This might not be the best night."

"It's okay—I can't, anyway," Alison said quickly. "I need to get home. Let's do it another time."

"I'm sorry if that sounded bitchy," Claire said, turning toward her. "It's just . . . my mother and everything . . . You understand."

"Of course, of course."

"I'm so glad you came," Claire said. "Honestly. It means a lot to me."

Something about this irritated Alison. Perhaps it was the earnest tone, at once overly formal and grandiose, the celebrity thanking her audience for its support. Perhaps it was bigger than that: Claire's appropriation of an inheritance of stories and memories on which both of them had claims—an archive of secrets, a library of shared experiences. Their childhood together was Claire's childhood now, defined by her interpretation.

Alison took the elevator down to the lobby alone. Stepping outside, she gazed at the street in front of her, glistening like an oily river. The air smelled, improbably, of damp soil. Alison fumbled for her keys, feeling around in her bag for the smooth silver Tiffany's ring Charlie had given her for her birthday (the little blue box had held such promise, and then it held . . . a key ring). As she opened the car door and slipped into the driver's seat, Alison realized that she hadn't missed Charlie, the way she'd expected to, at the party. Instead she'd felt a small thrill at being alone in the city—even as her mood turned cloudy. Being alone and anonymous might be preferable, she thought, to being alone and observed—which was how she felt most days in the fishbowl of Rockwell. She started the car. As she drove north on East End Avenue, the multicolored lights of the city refracted through the raindrops on her windshield.

When the phone rang, Charlie was in a deep sleep. It took a moment for him to realize that the ringing was not inside his head, somewhere in his dream, and then, all at once, his brain collected itself in a rush—late night—Alison gone—and he lunged for the telephone, fully awake. He heard her voice and could tell right away that something terrible had happened. Alison was, by nature, calm. Charlie had seen her break down only twice: the day her father had a heart attack, and the time Annie, as a toddler, got lost in a mall.

Alison wasn't crying, but there was a hysterical undercurrent in her voice, as if on the other end of the line someone were holding a gun to her head and she wasn't supposed to let Charlie know. As she spoke, Charlie cradled the phone on one shoulder and pulled a pair of khakis over his boxers, grabbed two random socks out of the laundry basket and put them on, fished his sneakers out from under the bed. As he yanked an old Izod over his head he realized that she was asking him a question.

"What?" he said.

"Jesus, are you listening?" Alison breathed. "I asked if you can come right away."

"Sorry, I'm getting dressed," he said. "I'll be there as fast as I can."

Their next-door neighbor, Robin, didn't hesitate when Charlie called and told her there'd been an accident and the car was totaled, and asked if she could come over and stay with the kids. The only thing she wanted to know was whether Alison was all right. He said she was. Then he remembered that Alison had said she had hurt her wrist, and he told Robin that, too, thinking it might mitigate the inconvenience if she knew it was serious. He didn't say anything about the boy.

The streets of Rockwell were quiet and wet and dramatically lit, like a stage set. Driving like this, in a rush of adrenaline in the still of the night, felt strangely familiar, and after a moment he realized why: Charlie and Alison had taken predawn trips to the hospital for the births of both of their children. Alison used to joke that she was physically incapable of going into labor unless she was in a deep sleep; Charlie joked that the kids were considerate to give them a taste of the nocturnal schedule they'd be keeping. How ironic, he thought, that his associations were with hope, with promise, and now. . . .

He felt a great weight descend on him; he almost couldn't breathe. She might have been killed—it was impossible to fathom. Emotions sloshed around inside him like conflicting pronouncements in a Magic 8 Ball: I should have gone with her. She's hurt. In pain. How the hell did this happen? Was she drunk? The car must be totaled; we can't afford a new one. Jesus, what if there's a lawsuit? This is going to completely fuck up my life.

Claire—

He took a deep breath. Alison, with whom he had fallen in love and married, who had borne him two children, would now carry a burden of guilt and remorse. And he, who was no longer in love with her, who was, in fact, in love with someone else, would have to help her get through it, would have to be the good husband for—how long?

He didn't know.

Was he up to it? He didn't know.

He was the one who had talked Alison into going to that damn party. He knew she wasn't comfortable driving at night, in the rain, in the gnarl of traffic moving to and from the city. Why was he so invested in her going? What did he think it would prove? Claire had called him earlier in the day to make sure he was coming, and he hadn't called her back to tell her he wasn't. It was complicated; his chest had felt tight all day. The truth was, Charlie wanted Alison to go to the party because these days when he allowed himself to feel anything at all for her, he felt overwhelming sadness and pity, and he didn't want to feel that anymore. If only for a night, he wanted to nudge her back into the world she had been a part of, the one she'd given up for him, for the children. He wanted her to be happy.

And maybe in some small, terrible way, he wanted her to get used to the idea of being alone.

He turned on the radio to keep from thinking. He stared at the road ahead. For some reason what came to mind were generic moments from his childhood: smacking a ball with his wooden bat high and hard and rounding the bases on a hot afternoon, kicking up dust the whole way home; staring at a clock, portentous as a full moon, in a chalky-smelling middle-school classroom. Even when he tried, he couldn't remember much specific detail about his adolescence. In Charlie's memory his parents were always the same age, in their late thirties, his mother smiling and his father joking with his sister and flipping burgers on the grill, an endless family barbecue under a wide Kansas sky.

According to the radio station, 1010 WINS, the tunnel was as clear as the bridge. He got on Route 80 toward New York and took exit 7, as instructed, to the station house in Sherman where Alison was— waiting? Being held? He hadn't asked.

As Charlie drove along in the preternatural brightness he started thinking about how he'd responded when Alison called—how his reaction had been impatience, not empathy, and how differently he might have felt even a few months ago. You would think that two people who had built a life together over eight years, who'd seen each other at all hours of the day and night, who were raising two children together, might know each other better than anyone else in the world. But Charlie had the peculiar sense with Alison that he might never know her. She'd always been a kind of mystery to him. He could sit down next to a woman at a dinner party and feel, after thirty minutes, that he understood her better than he did his own wife.

Marrying Alison had been a slow-motion dive into an untested body

39

of water. He wasn't sure, he had never been sure, but then he had never really been sure about anything or anyone. Getting married seemed brave and important. But now he wondered if it was the opposite—a form of cowardice, a lack of ambition, a capitulation to his most conventional and conservative impulses.

Charlie's love for Alison was like a rubber band; it always snapped back to its original size. And now, when it mattered, he realized that it didn't stretch at all.

"Your husband is here," a female officer said, not unkindly. "How's that wrist?"

Alison looked down at it, this thing in her lap wrapped in a soft beige bandage and secured with two metal butterfly clips, and thought, with a strange sense of disconnection, that it actually was hurting a bit, throbbing even, though until the officer had asked she hadn't been aware of it. "It's okay," she said. "Thanks."

The officer hesitated a moment, as if she wanted to say something more. It was a response that would become familiar to Alison over the next few days and weeks. In that split second, she knew what the woman was thinking: she was repulsed by Alison and horrified at what had happened, but she understood that Alison would suffer for it, and she felt sorry for her. Alison looked at her, and she glanced away. "Well, I'll send him back," the officer said. "Then we'll need to get a statement from you."

"I think I'm . . ." Alison's voice faltered. She cleared her throat. "Getting a lawyer. He said I might need a lawyer."

The officer nodded. "That's probably not a bad idea."

After she left, Alison took a deep breath and let it out slowly. In the silence she could hear raindrops against the small windows set high in the wall. She rubbed the arm of the swivel chair and felt the rough wood, worn down to ribbons of grain. Her head was pounding, a low, throbbing pulse that had started at her temples and was spreading down her scalp, and she pressed her fingers against her skull to push it away. All of a sudden she felt a different kind of pressure on her shoulder, and it took a moment to realize that it was a hand—Charlie's hand, the one with his wedding ring. She looked up. He was pale and somber. He was wearing a Yankees cap and a faded navy blue tennis shirt, all three buttons uncharacteristically undone, revealing a thatch of light-brown curly hair.

"Alison," he said, and she heaved forward, a sob rising from her stomach into her throat like a wave that has been gathering underwater. He crouched down, and she pulled him toward her, clawing his shirt, wanting to climb into his lap, to hide herself there. "Easy, easy," he whispered, but he didn't move, and she burrowed closer. She gulped and choked and a noise came out of her, a low whine. In a distant part of her mind she could see herself as she must have looked to him: rodentlike with panic, scrabbling and desperate. She could sense him flinch, but it only made her cling tighter. She wanted to reassure him that she was all right, she would be fine; but she couldn't speak. She felt poised on the edge of something deep and terrifying, vertiginous with fear and regret and anger—at herself, at the slick carnival of the evening, at the parents of the little boy who let him sit in the front seat. "This can't be happening," she sobbed, clutching at Charlie, and he stayed still for a moment, then reached up for her hands and held them firmly in his own.

"It is happening, Al," he said quietly. "It is happening. And you need to pull yourself together."

It was a rebuke, and it stung. She searched his face for any sign of compassion, but his expression was unreadable. She felt a creeping annoyance, like a teenager with a scolding father. "I know," she said.

"So how's your wrist?" He touched the bandage tenderly, as if to mitigate his harsh words.

"It's just a sprain."

"That's good. How does it feel?"

She shrugged. "It hurts a little."

He nodded, then rubbed his whole face with his hand. "Do you know anything—the boy . . . ?"

"They haven't told me anything."

"Jesus." He filled his lungs with air and breathed out slowly. At a desk across the room, a clerk was typing on a keyboard, her eyes steadfast on a computer screen. The room had the claustrophobic feel of an underground bunker. Everything was gray: the carpeting, the desks, the computers and chairs. The room even smelled gray—fungal, with an overlay of disinfectant. Mildew and ammonia. The fluorescent lights overhead were encased in cages. Alison could not quite comprehend that it was almost midnight on a Friday, and they were there in that room.

All at once she thought aloud: "Where are the kids?"

"I called Robin," he said.

Alison winced. Robin was a good neighbor, but not a close friend; Alison hated that she was involved. But who else could he have called?

"What did you tell her?"

"That there'd been an accident. That you hurt your wrist." For the first time, he looked in her eyes.

The clerk got up from her desk and riffled through a file. She picked up the phone and dialed, waited a moment, and began talking quietly. Alison heard her say, "Not much. An accident report. Yeah, one. In surgery. A three-year-old male." She shook her head. Then she caught Alison looking at her, and turned away.

"So what now," Alison said to Charlie, trying to keep her voice even.

"I suppose you should tell me what happened."

"I think you already know," she said. "Don't you?"

"Well, I know some things," he said. "I know that your blood-alcohol level was just over the limit. Point oh-nine percent."

Her skin prickled. "I didn't know that."

"And that a little kid is. . . ." His voice trailed off.

She nodded helplessly, trying to shake herself into believing it and not wanting to believe it at the same time. Pushing, pushing the horror away. She tried to look in Charlie's eyes, and he wouldn't look at her. "Charlie, I had two drinks the whole evening, I swear. Two—two and a half. They were making these martinis—"

"You don't even drink martinis."

"I know," she said miserably. "They were . . . blue. You know—the title of the book. Claire's mother drinks these blue martinis, so. . . . And there wasn't really any food; I didn't eat dinner—"

"Do you realize how fucking irresponsible—?" He shook his head violently.

There was no point in responding. It didn't matter anyway. Nothing she could say was going to change what had happened.

ON THE WAY home from the police station, they were mostly silent. Charlie drove, deftly finding his way along back roads, through small towns, to the Garden State Parkway. Sitting in the passenger's seat, Alison looked out the window at the passing cars and exit signs. Halfway home, she realized that her fingertips were numb; she was gripping the hard plastic of her seat belt buckle. A fluttery feeling in her chest made it hard to catch her breath. Charlie glanced over at her a few times, and once he asked if she was okay. She nodded, not trusting herself to speak.

"There's something I don't understand," Charlie said after a while. "Why didn't you just pull off somewhere when you took that wrong turn? Why in the world would you just *keep going*?"

She tried to remember why. *Why?* She had driven up the East Side of Manhattan and sliced through the park to the West Side, all the way over to the river, and then she had snaked up to the George Washington Bridge. She knew that she was not quite sober—but sober enough to be in control; she felt in control, if she thought about each movement carefully as she did it. Recently she had taken Noah and Annie to the Big Apple Circus, where they'd seen clowns spin plates in the air, keeping them balanced and steady at the end of long poles, and she thought of this image as she drove. Before she knew it, just over the bridge, she had to make a decision. She passed signs with too many letters and numbers; her brain was foggy, and she seemed to have forgotten which way to go, how to choose among all the options. Ordinarily, at night, on the way back from the city, Charlie would have been driving. Now the dashboard clock said 9:41, and she had no idea how to get home.

In a panic, she veered right with the traffic. Instantly she knew she'd made a mistake. The road was unfamiliar; she was clearly driving away from her sleeping children and quiet town, toward points unknown. She kept driving because she didn't know how to get off; there didn't seem to be an exit. She kept driving because she had turned right instead of going straight, and she began to wonder, somewhere in a place that wasn't rational or even fully conscious, whether this might have happened for a reason. Perhaps there was something out there that she might not otherwise have gotten a chance to see. She was driving at night with two and a half strong martinis in her, and suddenly she began to feel that an unplanned detour might be exactly what she needed.

It was the first time in a long time she had done something unexpected, something that defied common sense. And maybe, in that brief moment between making a wrong turn and a critical miscalculation, it felt good.

45

Not so many years ago, she had been a single girl living with friends from college in a small apartment in the city. Now it was as if that life had happened to someone else. Now she made grocery lists and tyrannosaurus-shaped pancakes and the children's beds. She kept the house and car running smoothly; she ran the 5K race for a cure, which the Junior League sponsored every spring; she organized the fall harvest bazaar at Noah's preschool. She hired people to clean the house twice a month, to tend the yard, clear the gutters, paint the sunroom. She took the kids to school, Charlie's shirts to the dry cleaner, took care of all the myriad details that gave her life, in some vague, intangible way, direction and meaning. In her former life, she had seen herself as one small part of a large and complex organism. There was freedom in that view. She was not responsible for, or to, anyone. Now she was at the center of a complicated universe of her own; she kept the planets spinning.

But sometimes a small piece of her rebelled against the way her life had evolved. She wondered if maybe she should have tried harder to work out a balance. She knew women who did, who stayed at the magazine and had full-time help and lived in two-bedroom apartments in the city. Sometimes she envied their choices and their freedom, their ability to slide in and out of identities, to be different people at different times of the day. But she hadn't wanted that life, the stress and conflict of it. She didn't want the feeling of being yanked in several directions at once. Sometimes she wished she could lead two lives at the same time, or perhaps consecutively—one with children and one without, one in the city and one in the suburbs, one married to Charlie and one . . . Alison pulled up short. No—Charlie wasn't part of the dilemma. She would want to be married to him, wouldn't she, no matter what?

They arrived home in the yellow-gray light of early morning. Stepping out of the car onto the familiar driveway felt strange and wrong, the way it feels, Alison thought, when you know you are dreaming and imagine that you could wake yourself at any time. Her head was clear, now, and she had a faint ache behind her eyes. She hadn't really drunk enough to be hungover. The officer they'd spoken with at the station said that from what he understood about the accident, Alison didn't appear to have been at fault. "We don't normally charge people for not getting out of the way quick enough," he'd said, looking down at the report and stroking his black mustache. "If that is, in fact, what happened. We'll have to wait for the full report to find out."

As Charlie and Alison reached the back door, Robin pushed it open. "I heard you drive up," she said, ushering them inside. She gave Alison a quick, gingerly hug and exclaimed over the bandage on her wrist.

"It's nothing," Alison said. "It'll be fine in a few days."

"Well, thank goodness. I'm sure it could've been a lot worse."

The compassion in Robin's voice made tears spring to Alison's eyes. She bit her lip and turned away.

"It's been a long night. We need to get this girl to bed," Charlie said in what struck Alison as an actor-y voice. "We appreciate your coming over, Robin."

"Of course. Anytime," she said as she turned the door handle, stepped outside. "What are neighbors for?"

The kitchen was gloomy and shadowed, but they didn't turn on any lights. A hazy glow from the motion-sensor floodlight in the backyard washed over the countertops. On the fridge the day before, Alison had posted a drawing of Annie's with a teacher's prompt—"I am happy when"—above Annie's response: "Mommy and Daddy are hugging me." In the drawing Annie was a blond-ringleted smiley face wearing a triangular pink dress, with two jellyfishlike giants looming over her, misshapen red hearts rising from their skulls. Noah was out of the picture.

As Alison gazed blankly at the drawing, Charlie came up behind her. "She wanted me to sing lullabies tonight," he said. "'Bye Baby Bunting' and 'Mockingbird.' I couldn't remember all the words, but she knew every one of them."

"It's funny that she wanted baby songs."

"She was missing Mommy."

"Did she say that?"

"No," he said. "She didn't want to hurt my feelings. But I could tell."

Alison knew what Charlie was doing—chiding her for being gone (though he'd encouraged it), suggesting that if she'd stayed home none of this would have happened, and letting her know that she was needed and loved, all at the same time. They often spoke in this kind of code, by way of discussing the children. Anecdotes were crafted with an instructive purpose, like Bible stories, and meant to be interpreted on several levels. At an elemental level, these stories were a way of connecting when they felt most alienated from each other. There was always something to say about Annie and Noah. And they both knew that they were the only two people in the world who could sustain this degree of minute interest in them.

Alison nodded slowly. "Well, I'm going upstairs."

"I'll lock up," he said. "Be there in a minute."

When Charlie opened the bedroom door she pretended to be asleep. In the darkness she could hear every sound of his undressing: the muffled clink of his buckle and the whoosh of his belt as he pulled it off, the soft buzz as he unzipped his pants. He hopped on one foot to take off a sock. He drew in his breath and mumbled, "Fuck," and she had to stop herself from sitting up to ask what was the matter. It might be something physical, like hitting his shin. Then again, it might be something else.

The bed groaned slightly as he eased onto his side. He sat there for a moment, then glanced over at her. "Alison," he said. It wasn't quite a whisper. She stayed still. He pulled down the covers and slid in.

Even from the other side of the bed, she could feel him. He emanated heat like some large animal, a dog or a bear. When he was asleep she thought of him like that: as a big slumbering mammal. But he wasn't asleep now. She could hear his shallow breathing. "Al," he said, and touched her arm.

A marriage hinges on these moments. Does she answer, or does she lie still? All Alison could feel was an overwhelming dread. She did not want to know what he had to say. She remained quiet; the moment passed, and she drifted into sleep.

part two

Confusion is perfect sight and perfect mystery at the same time.

— JANE SMILEY, *The Age of Grief*

February 2009

"Welcome back, Mr. Downing. Will you be paying in cash today?"

Charlie was stunned: he'd only been to this small Midtown hotel four or five times in the past two months, but the desk clerk not only recognized him; but he also remembered his alias and preferred form of payment. "Uh—yes. Thanks." He pulled out his wallet and extracted four fifties, laid them on the counter.

The clerk took the crisp bills with a deep nod. "Room 1121, as usual?"

It was the cheapest room in the hotel—as cramped and dark as a closet—but it suited their needs. "Yes."

The clerk handed Charlie two key cards. "Have a nice day, sir."

Slipping the cards in his back pocket, Charlie glanced toward the revolving door in the foyer. No sign of her yet. She'd said she might be a little late; she was meeting with her agent several blocks away to discuss details of her upcoming book party. He didn't mind; he was happy enough to have a moment. To anticipate. He settled into a boxlike white leather chair and closed his eyes.

Charlie didn't know how, exactly, but for the time being he seemed to have figured out how to make it all work. The key was concentration. As long as he was fully engaged in the activity of the moment—working on an account, meeting Claire at the hotel, coming home to see his family—he was amazed to find that he could pull it off.

He felt a strange kinship with those men you see on *Dateline* who have hidden lives that their families only learn about after they die. He'd always wondered how they did it, how they found the time and summoned the energy to deceive so many people. Now he knew. It didn't take much energy, just sheer will. You had to compartmentalize each discrete part. It was surprising, when you thought about it, how little people really knew about one anothers' lives anyway, and how easy it was to lie.

Charlie had never thought of himself as a particularly good liar; his father had always told him he was terrible at it, transparent as glass. Now it occurred to him that this was psychological bullying, typical of the old man. His father told him he was a bad liar so he wouldn't lie. But he wasn't actually a bad liar. As it turned out, he seemed to have a knack for it.

Of course, Charlie had always had a remarkable ability to shuffle his thoughts so as to avoid certain subjects altogether. It was a skill he'd acquired long ago, way back in his Kansas childhood, and it had served him well. It was what enabled him to excel in high school and then in college while his mother was undergoing treatment for cancer and his father was driving the family business into the ground. It was what propelled him to graduate magna cum laude and with a fellowship to Cambridge, as far away from the mess of his family as he could manage.

Charlie thought about his parents' bland insistence that his father's company was fine, until the day they announced that it was going under. Of course he'd suspected there was trouble—they all did. But nobody had said anything about it. And then, when his mother got cancer for the second time, though Charlie knew about the chemo and the radiation and the lymph nodes, it was months before anyone acknowledged how serious it was. She was dying by the time Charlie's sister called and urged him home.

Charlie felt a hand on his shoulder and opened his eyes. Claire was leaning over him, her auburn hair brushing his face. She kissed him on the lips.

"Were you dreaming about me?" she whispered.

"Of course," he said. "I only ever dream about you."

The morning after the book party, Ben was yanked into consciousness by the ringing of the phone.

"You get it. Probably your mother," Claire groaned, turning over into her pillow and pulling the covers over her head. His mother, it was true, had an irritating habit of calling early in the morning. "I just assumed you'd be up by now," she'd chirp with surprise when they complained. "The morning's half over."

"Hello," Ben said flatly into the receiver, not bothering to check caller ID.

"Ben, it's Charlie."

"Oh, hey." Ben shook his head to clear it. "What's up?"

"Well, I'm—I'm—aah . . ."

Something in his voice made Ben sit up. He pushed Claire's shoulder, and she rolled over and looked at him, sleepy-eyed. "What is it?" he said into the phone.

"Alison was in an accident last night coming home from the party," Charlie said.

"Oh, Jesus," Ben said.

"What? What?" Claire demanded.

"Alison was in a car accident."

"Oh my God," she gasped.

"She's all right," Charlie said.

"She's okay," Ben reported.

"Is she . . . ?" Claire sat up, pressing against him. "Wait, I'll get another phone." She jumped up and ran into the living room. "Hi, Charlie, I'm here," she said, her voice loud and breathless on the line.

"She's all right," Charlie repeated. "It's just . . . somebody—in the other car . . . there was a boy . . ."

"Oh, no," Claire said, getting it before Ben did.

"We just got a call. As it turned out . . . he didn't make it," Charlie said.

"Oh my God."

"My God," Ben said, thinking even in that moment how inadequate their words were—how inadequate any words would be.

"Charlie," Claire said, her voice strangely calm. "Oh my God. Charlie. What are we going to do?"

Her response was odd—the "we" too familiar, Ben thought. Why did she always have to go inserting herself into the center of other people's dramas? For a moment no one said a word. Ben could hear them all breathing, as if they were trying to figure out what to say next. There was so much to say—there were so many questions—but it seemed both too soon and vaguely prurient to ask.

"We want to help," Ben said finally. "Do you need—what do you need?"

"I don't know. Thank you. Nothing."

"Is—was—Alison at fault?" Claire asked suddenly.

"Umm—no. Not exactly. She's being charged with DWI. We hope that's the extent of it. We're waiting for the police report."

Ben lay back against his pillow, shaping it with his left hand into a hard pallet under his neck, holding the phone with his right. How many martinis had Alison had last night? One—or two—and was there another just before she left? "Does she need a lawyer?" he asked.

"Yeah," Charlie said. "Yep."

"Hey. My college roommate," Ben said, leaping into the idea with relief. "This is what he does. Practices in Ridgewood. Let me call him."

"Okay. I appreciate it."

"Good, good," Ben said, glancing at the clock, calculating what time Paul Ryan might be in his office, trying to remember where he'd stashed his number.

These things happened to people, Ben knew. They happened all the time. Every morning, over his cup of coffee, he read about scenarios far worse in the Metro section. Ex-husbands bent on revenge, half a dozen kids killed in a fire, construction workers plummeting to their deaths, carloads of teenagers in head-on collisions. But they didn't happen to him or to anyone he knew. And now Alison had been in an accident, and a child was dead. It didn't seem possible.

"She's at home now?"

"She's asleep. Took an Ambien. Two, in fact," Charlie said. Then he blurted, "I should've gone to the party. I knew she didn't want to go alone."

"It's not your fault," Claire said. "It was raining, wasn't it," as if the rain were to blame. "I'm. So. Sorry, Charlie," she breathed.

"We're both sorry," Ben said with annoyance, acutely aware in that instant that Claire's empathy had shut him out.

And with a jolt he realized that this feeling—separated from Claire, by her choice—wasn't unfamiliar. An almost imperceptible rift had developed between them, he thought, since her miscarriage several months ago—he wanted to try again and she didn't, he was sure and she wasn't. Claire had always been, by nature, somewhat moody and unpredictable, but after she lost the baby she was alternately withdrawn and overly solicitous. She often seemed to have something on her mind, but when he asked, she said she was simply tired, or thinking about a scene in her book. Ben had let these vague denials suffice, afraid of confirming what he suspected: she was becoming emotionally detached. She was pulling away.

But he told himself he was being silly. They were both caught up in their work; that was all. Truth be told, Ben had been so preoccupied with a project at his architectural design firm that he'd had little time to think about much else. Sloane Howard had gotten a new commission, a big one, in Boston, right on the harbor, and Ben was working hard to meet both the client's mercurial needs and the arcane structural codes and limitations of downtown Boston. He wanted to create a structure that would put his small boutique firm on the map.

Sloane Howard made most of its money designing second and third homes for the very rich—homes that the next owner would likely as not tear down in pursuit of his own grandiose vision, a "bash and build" trend that Sloane Howard benefited from as much as it decried. But Ben, wooed to Sloane Howard from a larger firm as a junior partner a year ago, had greater aspirations. So when the chance came to bid on this ambitious, high-budget arts complex, with its large and small performance spaces, restaurants, offices, and conference center, Ben didn't hesitate.

He hired two new associates, fresh out of the M.I.T. graduate architecture program, who hadn't yet been seduced by the boldfaced names on the Sloane Howard client list into bowdlerizing their talent. He wanted unconventional thinkers whose designs were so radical as to be unworkable, bold ideas that would inspire him to greatness. As it turned out, the boy he hired was smug and pompous, and the girl so dismissive of Ben's peers at "Drone Coward," as she and the boy quickly nicknamed the firm, that Ben felt duty-bound to stick up for the other partners, a position he'd never dreamed he'd find himself in. At one point Ben came across an e-mail the boy had sent the girl in which he complained about Ben's pedestrian taste. Talk about biting the hand! But Ben didn't say anything. He knew that the two of them would move on in a few months, and he was determined to extract what he could out of them before they left.

The three of them stayed late into the night, took field trips to look at pioneering buildings, studied other architects' models, sought inspiration in museums and theaters around the world. The design Ben submitted three months later was original but not radical: huge panes of glass sloping toward the water, creating the illusion of a continuous liquid surface, joining in a series of connected cubes, the largest of which contained a magnificent concert hall. When the design was picked as one of the four finalists, a *Boston Globe* headline asked, "Sloane Who?"

The other finalists were suitably pedigreed: the best-known Boston firm, a major New York powerhouse, and a New Haven group fronted by a big-name guru. But to the surprise of virtually everyone, including Ben, the Sloane Howard design was chosen. "This structure will be a beacon of light and beauty," declared Philippa Boyd, the eighty-three-year-old philanthropist whose name would be on the building, in her reedy, wavering voice at the press conference: "a clear symbol of hope on the harbor for the noblest aims of humanity." A little overwrought, Ben reflected, standing behind her at the podium—but certainly preferable to "stylish." He'd taken a huge risk on his vision, his dream—and now it looked like that risk was actually paying off.

In the meantime he hadn't been home much. He felt as if he were back in grad school, working on a term paper—the hours spent focusing on a single topic, trying to understand it, to create a thesis that would hold up under scrutiny from experts in the field. He didn't think of eating until he was ravenous, and then he grabbed whatever was close by; he didn't go to bed until his bones ached with fatigue, or until he realized he was reading the same sentence over and over because he was drifting in and out of sleep.

Claire had been understanding—incredibly so, he thought. She'd always called herself "high maintenance," though he wouldn't have said that, necessarily. Anyway, he liked to take care of her; he took deep pleasure in it, a pleasure that only intensified as he got older without children. He needed some object for his paternal feelings, and they both agreed they didn't have the lifestyle for a dog (though he would have liked a dog—he'd always wanted one, even as a kid, a Boston Terrier, maybe, or a beagle—a scrappy, energetic little beast). But lately he hadn't had time to care for himself, much less anyone else, and though he'd expected Claire to complain about his late hours and inconsistent schedule and semipermanent state of distraction, she hadn't said a word. In fact, lately she'd been surprisingly nurturing herself. She left notes on the counter about soup or a roasted chicken she'd picked up at Fairway for him and put in the fridge; he'd find PowerBars in his briefcase. When he called to say he'd be working late she always said she understood; she knew what a huge project it was. He showed her his designs, and she responded thoughtfully. She rubbed his shoulders in bed at night, brought him green tea to clear his head, retrieved his shirts from the dry cleaner without complaint.

When Ben really thought about it—which, frankly, he didn't often; he just didn't have the time—there were things that gave him pause. The forced cheer in Claire's voice, flight-attendant polite; the restless tapping of her fingers as they sat together late at night watching TV; the times he'd wake up at 3 A.M. to find her side of the bed empty, and would hear her out in the living room, pacing around. But surely these were normal responses to having a miscarriage. When Claire had gotten pregnant, Ben had envisioned a whole new life stretching ahead for them. Wasn't this the reason for existence—this primal urge to reproduce, to care for young, to continue the species?

But Claire lost the baby. And things got complicated.

He looked up at her now as she came into the bedroom, cradling the cordless phone against her cheek as Charlie told them more details about the accident. Ben caught her eye and she shook her head slowly.

"So terrible," she said. "I just can't believe it."

December 2008

Working on a freelance feature story the week after the dinner party in Rockwell, Claire conducted interviews and did research and had lunch with her editor, and the whole time she was thinking of the skin on Charlie's arm, how it felt like the skin of an apricot, and how he smelled like the floor of a forest, pine needles and moss. She thought of his back, like a mountain lion's, lean and sinuous, with a layer of muscle just under the skin. She was aware of her legs as they crossed under the table, the curve of her own neck, as if those body parts were new to her, not merely newly observed. Men on the street looked at her differently. Sitting on a bench in a small triangle of park on an unseasonably warm day she ate an orange, tearing at the fleshy pulp. The juice ran down her chin and she wiped her hand across her lips, covering a smile. She could feel the power of her desire, an almost palpable strength—the will to seduce and entice and invite.

She thought about Charlie all the time, couldn't stop thinking about him. Conversation with others was a time killer, a way to while away the hours until the two of them might, at last, be together. When her cell phone rang, her nerve endings jerked, as if connected to it by a thread. Her heart beat hard in her chest. She checked her e-mail and text messages constantly; sometimes he had just written, and when she responded he wrote back seconds later. The idea of him sitting in his office writing her was more intoxicating than alcohol.

I have to see you, he wrote.

When.
Friday—didn't B say he'd be away?
Yes—a client in Boston.
A's taking the kids overnight to see a friend upstate. Can you meet?
Yes.
Where.
I'll find a place.
Okay.
I've never done this. Have you?
No.
Never felt like this before. Sorry—cliché.
All the clichés are true. Nothing new to say.
So say it anyway. It doesn't have to be new.
What did Pascal say? "There are reasons of the heart about which reason knows nothing. . . ."

In the dim lobby of the discreet Midtown hotel, the crowd around them blurred; only Charlie was in focus. "I got a room," Claire said. He took a swallow of his Scotch and set it down. Claire tipped up her gin and tonic and finished it, the ice avalanching toward her mouth.

He ran his finger along the hem of her short black skirt, brushing her thigh.

The elevator was tiny, and it took forever, stopping at each floor, the doors sliding open silently, no one there. When it got to eleven they stepped out and made their way to the room. Charlie fumbled with the card and the door handle, but neither of them made a joke of it, as they might have done. Claire felt oddly detached, as if she were in a trance.

In some clear corner of her brain she acknowledged that this might just be her conscience mounting an insanity defense, but she didn't want to think, so she willed herself to stop.

The hotel room was small and dark and stylish, a jewel box. Its one window had a postcard view of Broadway, miniature yellow cabs and neon lights and pedestrians. Claire sat on the chocolate brown velvet bedcover and smoothed it with her hand. Cold light on pale skin; no candles, no music. They were awkward with each other, not knowing how to begin. She looked at Charlie and started unbuttoning her blouse, and he came over to the bed and knelt beside her. He slipped his hand between her legs and pushed up her skirt. She leaned back with her eyes open, feeling his slippery fingers inside her, his breath hot on her thigh.

Afterward, they took the elevator to the ground floor in silence. The hotel was busier than it had been earlier in the evening; the elevator stopped three times before they reached the lobby. Claire looked at Charlie, his cheeks flushed and hair still damp from the shower, and wondered if anyone could guess. Of course, she thought; people do this all the time, don't they? Step across invisible lines, reach over and touch the forbidden. It was easier than she'd imagined.

"I didn't ask for this," she whispered to Charlie, but of course she did, one way or another. What attracted her to Charlie was indefinable, a feeling in the pit of her stomach. She felt wild with him, spontaneous. But Charlie wasn't inherently this way; if anything, he was more conventional than she was—leading a comfortable suburban life, shouldering the burdens of domestic responsibility without complaint. It was only the two of them together that felt unpredictable.

Why did she want this? Why did she need it?

Only two months ago, she had been pregnant. The miscarriage had been terrible, but when it was over she'd been strangely relieved. Ben was the one who had pushed for the baby—he wanted them to be a family, he'd said. She had gone along with it, but secretly she'd been ambivalent. Afraid of losing her autonomy, her ambition. Afraid of being a bad mother. Afraid of feeling trapped. When he asked, now—which he did every few weeks—and she said she wasn't ready to try again; she didn't know if she'd ever be ready, he half-nodded, chin up, like he was taking a blow without flinching. She knew that he would wait a while and try again. He believed his patience would trump her unreasonableness. What he didn't know—and what she barely understood herself—was that she wanted to hurt him in small ways to toughen herself for hurting him worse.

Standing outside by the revolving door, Claire wrapped her coat tightly around her, though it wasn't cold.

"How do you feel?" Charlie asked.

"Crazy. Guilty. Do you feel guilty?"

"This is between us. It has nothing to do with them."

But of course it had everything to do with them.

Claire remembered falling in love with Ben—how unfettered they were, how young. Now she felt old and jaundiced. Cruel. She would have liked to talk to her best friend about it, but her best friend was Alison. She would have liked to talk to her husband, but that, too, was impossible. The only one she could talk to was Charlie, and he was as culpable as she was. They were bound together by deception, like two thieves on the run. Fleetingly she wondered if the passion she felt for him was merely a manifestation of her restlessness, if she had transferred the anxiety she felt about getting settled, stale, becoming her mother, perhaps, into this feeling propelling her into another kind of life, terrifyingly open-ended, the dissolution of everything good and proper and right.

"Oh, Lord, Alison. How terrible," her mother gasped when Alison called to tell her parents about the accident.

"Yes," she said grimly.

"That poor family," her mother said. "How awful. Just awful."

Alison could feel a surge of tears against the dam of her rib cage.

"Are the police . . . Are you being charged with anything?" her father asked.

"DWI. I was just barely over the legal limit." Alison cringed at her own need to say this. "I'm not—technically at fault, apparently."

"Uhh," her father said, as if he'd been hit in the stomach.

"I really should have said something last night," her mother said. "You were so rushed and harried on the phone. I just—I had a *feeling*. Call it mother's intuition, I don't know—I could tell something was going to happen. I was pacing around all night. Wasn't I, Ed? Don't you remember telling me to relax and sit down?"

"I always tell you that," Alison's father said.

"No, but this was different. I feel sick about it. I should have—could have—"

"Mom, don't," Alison said. It was just like her mother to insist that her witchy powers might have saved the day.

"Well, okay, but I regret not saying something. I knew you were in no state to be driving into New York by yourself. You seemed absolutely overwhelmed."

Did I? Alison wondered, unable, as usual, to connect her mother's interpretation of her mental state with how she'd felt. She had certainly been harried when her mother called the night before, but only because she was trying to get out the door at the last minute. Or was her mother right? Was it something more?

"Driving into the city by yourself on a rainy night—and to a party. You don't even like to drive," her mother fretted.

"June, take it easy," Alison's father said. "It was a party for Claire's book. Alison had to go."

"Well. Don't even get me started on that book. It is a slap in the face to poor Lucinda, whether or not she realizes it. That girl should be ashamed of herself."

"June," Alison's father implored.

Alison's mother went on, ignoring him. Here it was, in a nutshell: their dynamic. "I have never, ever trusted Claire Ellis—there was *always* something devious about her. Why you've stayed friends with her, I'll never understand. Haven't I been saying that, Edward, for years?"

She had, in fact, been saying it for years. Perhaps in part because they were so much alike, June and Claire had never liked each other. Claire thought that Alison's mother was a self-absorbed drama queen; her mother thought that Claire was up to no good. Of course, they were both right. What Alison resisted in her mother—the arrogance of her opinions, the calculated impulsiveness, the stubborn refusal to abide by others' conventions, her narcissistic charm—she had always admired in Claire, in whom these traits were manifested as sly subversion.

"Alison," her father broke in. His voice was grave. "What can we do?"

"There's nothing you can do," she said numbly.

"How is Charlie handling all this?" her mother asked.

"Fine. I mean, he's been . . . helpful. He took the kids out for the morning."

"How are Annie and Noah?"

"Why are you crying, Mommy?" Annie had wanted to know, standing next to the bed, her voice already, first thing in the morning, a needling, needy whine. Alison knew that her daughter's concern was all about her own fear and discomfort, and she'd had to fight the urge to

turn away. Instead, she pulled her close, under the covers. (Sometimes, Alison was aware, she expressed the strongest affection for her children when she was least sure of her own response.) Annie had stiffened against Alison's embrace, pulling away to peer in her face. "Your eyes are all puffy, Mommy," she'd said, her face scrunched in alarm.

"They know I was in an accident," Alison said now. "Not the rest."

"How are you going to tell them?"

"She doesn't have to tell them," her father said, at the same time that Alison said, "I don't know."

"Oh, Alison." Her mother sighed. "We should fly up there. You're in no shape to handle the kids right now. And as long as I'm being honest here I should tell you that I don't like that babysitter of yours—what's her name, Roberta."

"Dolores."

"Dolores. She's snippy with me whenever I call there, and I'm pretty sure she doesn't give you all my messages, either. I get the distinct impression that she is not nurturing to those children."

Alison closed her eyes and shifted the cordless phone to her other ear, as if it might also somehow shift the topic. It was true that Dolores, a former English nanny who for mysterious reasons had been reduced to babysitting by the hour, was imperious and controlling, but Alison didn't know what to do about it. Frankly, she was intimidated. And she didn't want to think about that right now. She took a deep breath, calibrating words and tone in her head, and then said, "Mom, I appreciate the offer, but I think we're okay."

"Honey, you're not okay. You're not okay at all," her mother said.

Alison had been a curious child. When she was ten or eleven she would read her mother's correspondence and her friends' diaries as well as eavesdrop on conversations for a mention of her name. She wanted to learn who she was, reflected in the eyes of others. And then something happened: one day when she was in the eighth grade she read one supposed friend's note to another in school—*Alison G. wears such weird clothes*—with the scrawled reply, *Yeah, and she's not as pretty as she thinks she is*—and Alison took the words to heart. *I wear weird clothes and I'm not as pretty as I think I am.* After that she stopped wanting to know.

"You're right. I'm not okay," she said now.

Her mother was full of questions: How fast was the other car going? Was it a licensed vehicle? Was the road wet? Was Alison speeding? What in the world was that mother *thinking,* in this day and age, having the child on her lap?

After Alison hung up the phone she felt raw and light-headed. She'd been crying on and off for hours, but now her eyes were dry. It reminded her of how she'd felt after Annie's birth: drained, bloodless, almost transparent, as if her body were little more than the empty husk of a cocoon.

WHEN SHE HEARD the knock at the back door, Alison was standing in the kitchen looking around at the detritus of Charlie's effort to feed the kids breakfast—half-crushed Cheerios scattered across the floor, spilled milk on the table, the plastic jug open on the counter with its plug missing, sections of the Friday *Times* in piles, an apple with two small bites already turning brown on a chair. The coffeemaker was on, but the carafe was empty. She could hear Charlie and the kids in the playroom.

Somehow Alison had never gotten used to this. When she was with the kids, she was constantly picking up—wiping countertops, sweeping the floor, loading the dishwasher, folding mounds of laundry. Charlie just—played. And she came in later and cleaned up the mess.

Alison could see Robin's curly blond hair through the small glass panes at the top of the door. She felt a quick panic—the last thing she wanted to do was talk to her neighbor. But it was too late; Robin had seen her and was tentatively waving the fingers of one hand, anemone-like, through the glass.

Alison took a deep breath and opened the door.

"Here. I made banana bread," Robin said, handing Alison a foil-wrapped loaf. "It was all I could think of to do."

The loaf was still warm, and somehow comforting in Alison's hands: the solid heft of it, its mammal warmth. "Robin—thank you." How kind. Alison felt a tickle in the bridge of her nose.

Oh no; she was going to cry.

"I won't stay. I just—" Robin said.

Alison shook her head, clenching her jaw. Despite her efforts, her eyes filled with tears.

Robin took the loaf from Alison and placed it on the counter. Then she clasped her hand and led her to the table. "How about some coffee?" she said gently.

Alison nodded, unable to speak. She watched as Robin rummaged in the cabinet for filters, washed out the carafe, spooned coffee grounds from the bag on the counter into the filter, and then filled the carafe with water and poured it into the pot. Normally she would have talked to fill the silence, protested about being served, worried after her neighbor's feelings, but she did none of this. She still felt hollowed out. Her eyes, her skin, her mouth and ears only an epidermal shell, the bones providing structure. Her brain reptilian, merely recording movement, sensing light and dark.

How could she go on?

Miraculously, Robin seemed to know exactly what Alison needed. She was quiet, watching the coffeemaker, glancing over to smile at her every now and then.

Robin was not Alison's type. She was in the Junior League; her twin ten-year-old boys played golf; she and her husband belonged to the tony country club on the edge of town (though Alison knew, through the neighborhood grapevine, that Robin's husband, a banker, had lost his job twice in the past three years). She was probably a Republican. Alison's friends tended to be other women who felt adrift in some way, who'd gone freelance and were having trouble drumming up work, who found themselves unexpectedly pregnant again

69

after a baby or two, who were as conflicted as she was about being a stay-at-home mother. Alison had often marveled at Robin's seemingly unambivalent feelings about motherhood and work. She seemed preternaturally content—busy, involved in the schools (endlessly planning book fairs, movie nights, class parties), on the executive board of the PTA. Alison had not-so-secretly wondered what deep well of need Robin had that was so readily filled by the quotidian details of domestic life.

But now she was merely grateful.

Robin found a coffee mug, filled it, brought it to the table along with the milk. "Sugar? Sweetener?"

Alison shook her head. She poured milk into her coffee and took a long sip.

"Do you want to talk about it?" Robin asked. She fished a knife from the block on the counter and cut into the banana bread. Steam rose from the plate. She put it in front of Alison, who pinched off a bite. She couldn't even taste it; the bread was like Styrofoam in her mouth. She had an impulse to spit it out but forced herself to swallow. "No," she said.

Robin nodded. She sat down in the chair across from Alison.

"The boy died," Alison said.

"Oh," Robin exclaimed. "Oh, Alison"—putting her hand to her mouth.

"I . . . really . . . don't want to talk about it."

"All right." After a moment Robin reached out and put her cool fingers on Alison's forearm. "I'm here when you need me. Okay?"

She started to get up, but Alison said, "Please—don't leave. Stay for a minute."

"Sure. Of course." Robin sank back into her seat.

Alison forced herself to smile. It felt as if her mouth were smiling on its own, a purely mechanical activity. Then she started to cry.

Robin sat at the table with Alison as tears streamed down her face. She cried and cried, until the fluid seemed to have been drained from her. Then she cried some more. Robin got up; even through her tears, Alison was aware that she was looking for a box of tissues, but she didn't find one and ended up tearing off some paper towels and handing Alison a big wad.

Charlie came into the kitchen. He was clearly startled to see Alison sobbing wordlessly into a white muff, and Robin sitting there. "Oh, goodness," he said, patting Alison's shoulder. "Honey, can we let Robin get back to her family? I'm sure she has things she needs to do this morning."

"Do you want me to stay?" she asked Alison.

Alison shook her head. She did want Robin to stay but was ashamed of being so inappropriately needy.

"Anytime at all," Robin said. "Just call me."

She gave Charlie a sympathetic smile, which Alison understood as: *we will both take care of this person. No man should have to shoulder this alone; I can help.*

And she wondered: Why didn't Charlie marry someone like Robin? His life would be so much easier.

After Robin left, Charlie sat at the table with his entire hand covering the bottom half of his face. Alison recognized this as a rare but significant gesture in Charlie's repertoire, signaling that he was flummoxed.

"I called a lawyer," he said after a while. "Ben's roommate from Harvard. Nice guy. Lives in Bergen County."

Alison nodded.

"He said it sounds fairly straightforward. He needs—everything."

She sniffed and cleared her throat. "Today?"

"No. Tomorrow is soon enough. The police report. Etcetera."

She nodded again.

"We'll get through this, Alison."

"Will we?"

He looked her in the eyes, but his gaze was opaque; she couldn't read what he was telling her.

She took a deep breath. "When I called you last night, the first thing you said was, 'What did you do?'"

Charlie sat back. "Well. It was a shock, getting that phone call."

"You were so—cold."

"I was asleep, Alison," he said tetchily. "You woke me up."

"Still." She could feel the tears gathering inside her again.

He wiped some crumbs into a pile.

"'What did you do?'" she repeated in a self-pitying whisper.

"Look, I'm sorry," he said.

But she couldn't let it go. "I don't understand. I don't understand where that came from."

"There's nothing to understand," he said. "Don't read too much into it. In fact, don't read anything into it."

She looked at him dully. She didn't want to read too much into it. She didn't want to read anything into it. But his halfhearted protestations weren't helping much.

"We need to be thinking about the next steps," he was saying.

Next steps. Baby steps, she thought. One foot after another, toddler steps. Phantom steps—steps the three-year-old boy who died would never take. Here I am, going to that place, the most maudlin place, she thought. But she didn't care. She lived in that place now.

72

Early December

When Alison called to invite Claire and Ben to dinner in Rockwell, Claire recognized it for what it was: a peace offering, of sorts. Things had been strained between the two women for some time. It was hard to pinpoint what had happened, exactly; it was a matter of slipped confidences and injured egos, Claire thought, that reinforced the sense that they had little in common anymore. Alison always seemed so busy, in a breathless sort of way. Claire couldn't fathom what she did all day at home with the kids, but whatever it was made it impossible for her to have a sustained conversation. After several maddening phone calls (with children yowling in the background or tugging on Alison's sleeve, and Alison repeating questions she'd already asked), Claire gave up. Alison hadn't called her, either.

And there were other things. When Claire had called—as a courtesy to Alison—to let her know that there were certain places and events from their childhood that Alison might recognize in her novel, though they were camouflaged— Alison had been irritatingly literal-minded about the whole thing. She'd paused for a moment and then asked, pointedly, "Am I in it?" Not, "How interesting, what are you learning about yourself?" or even "Good for you, what an ambitious project." Claire had explained patiently that nobody was "in" it exactly; like any creative work, the book incorporated bits and pieces of memories and impressions and events and transformed them into something else.

"So I'm not in it, then," Alison said stolidly.

"No. Not really. I mean, parts of you might be. My main character has a friend named Jill that might seem familiar to you. But it's not really 'you,' if you know what I mean."

"I don't," Alison said.

Claire sighed. "The friend has blond hair, for one thing," she said. "And other details have been altered."

"But what you're saying, basically, is that she is me."

"Alison," Claire said, "come on. You know what a novel is."

"Of course I do. But this doesn't sound like a novel to me, Claire."

"Look, we're arguing semantics. The essence of it is true," Claire said. "The emotional reality. My emotional reality. But places and names have been changed and some events combined and rearranged beyond recognition."

"Uh-huh," Alison said.

And then, apparently in retaliation, Alison had rejected an article, without warning, that Claire had written—as a favor to her—for the women's magazine she worked for. Claire was paid a kill fee, but she was annoyed by Alison's insinuation that the piece was slapdash and ill-conceived.

So they hadn't spoken in ages. Until now.

At first, when Claire and Ben arrived, all of them behaved a little awkwardly, as if they didn't know one another well. But within a few minutes, merlot and candlelight and soft music had smoothed their conversational edges. The kids were upstairs, apparently with a babysitter, and Alison had actually set the dining room table in advance and prepared hors d'oeuvres in the living room. (They weren't always so formal; on several occasions Claire and Ben had trekked out to Rockwell for take-out Chinese or empty-the-fridge pasta medleys at the island in the kitchen.) Claire was surprised to find herself a little nervous; as they made small talk before dinner she drank one glass of wine quickly, and Charlie rose to get the bottle. When he came over to refill her glass, he mouthed, "I miss you."

Startled, she looked into his eyes.

He held her gaze.

She felt herself flush.

They were all sitting at the dining room table eating baby lettuce with blue cheese and pears when Claire turned toward Charlie—she was next to him, diagonally across from Ben, in their customary foursquare configuration—and inadvertently knocked her wineglass into his lap. Red wine seeped through his khakis, dark like a period stain, and both of them sat there stunned for a moment before the other two figured out what was happening. Charlie sat back and Claire started laughing; she couldn't help it, and then she took her napkin and began to blot. It was wildly inappropriate, her face hovering over his lap, and he pushed her away, embarrassed, as Alison went to the fridge for some club soda (which of course they had in there somewhere: the well-stocked suburban refrigerator). But as Charlie pushed Claire back, he held her wrist. She could feel it, though no one else could see.

For the rest of the evening she sat at the table, watching the others but not listening. Yes, she nodded, yes, and smiled slightly, a vague, all-purpose response. Alison glanced at her sharply a few times, but she was accustomed to Claire's moods. Her way of compensating was to natter on. "There's a big sale at the ABC outlet in Hoboken," she said, "and you know, Charlie, we really need a rug for the

75

bedroom. I can't stand stepping on that cold floor every morning. What about sisal, not the scratchy kind, wool, maybe in a neutral or something? Do you guys have a rug in your bedroom? I can't remember."

"Just an old Oriental that's falling apart," Ben said. "We could use a new one. What do you think, Claire? Should we brave the sale this weekend?"

All Claire could think about was the feel of Charlie's thigh under his khakis, the long stretch of muscle, the thin, taut skin. "We could do that," she said.

Ben launched into a story Claire had already heard about a guy in his office who was dating Miss New York. "I'll clear," she said, getting up from the table. She gathered empty glasses and a serving plate and attempted to arrange them in her arms.

"Be careful," Alison said.

Charlie stood up and took a wineglass from Claire. "I'll help."

Ben caught her eye. She could tell that he was annoyed and a little hurt that Charlie wasn't listening.

"You sit," she told Charlie. "I've got it."

"I need to stretch anyway," he said.

At the swinging door to the kitchen she turned around and pushed through backward, and Charlie looked at her with a funny smile the other two couldn't see.

"What?" she said when they were in the kitchen, the door squeaking on its hinges behind them.

"Escape," he mouthed.

"It's actually a funny story," she said, turning her back to him and opening the dishwasher. "It's just that I've heard it before."

"They get old, don't they?"

She didn't answer. Then she said, "Can you get the

plates?" When he left the room she found someone's half-finished glass of wine, and took a long swallow.

He came back in with the plates. She was rinsing a bowl in the sink. For a moment they didn't talk. "I want to touch you," he said quietly, and though he had never said it before, she nodded without surprise, as if she'd been expecting it. He ran his hand down her neck and she arched her back. Fingers on skin: the contact was an electric shock. Her body stung where he touched her—cheek, shoulder, upper arm, hand. For so long she'd avoided looking him in the eye for this very reason: as she looked into them now, cerulean blue, she saw her own need reflected back. He kissed her neck and she felt the roughness of his lips, chapped by the wind. Without shutting off the faucet she turned to face him, touching his scaly lip with her tongue. He pushed against her, opening to her, his mouth, his hands, his legs. She felt pulled in, like something she had seen once on a nature special, a rabbit being swallowed by a snake, the serpent's jaw unlocking, mouth open wide, neck muscles constricting as it eased the rabbit in.

"We should go out there," Ben said, pacing back and forth in front of the living room window. "We could take their kids for the afternoon or something. I feel so damn—helpless." He sighed. "You know, I handed her a second martini. I *forced* it on her."

After the phone call from Charlie, Ben had gotten out of bed and gone down to the French Roast on the corner for two lattes, coming back with a newspaper, several morning glory muffins, a bag of clementines. Since returning from his errand he'd been restless, jumpy, miserable. Somehow Ben's hand-wringing had the opposite effect on Claire, making her withdraw. She recognized her father in this: his own unresponsiveness in the face of her mother's volubility. Ben's messy emotions were so big it was hard to find a place for her own, admittedly more complicated, feelings.

"I think she might've had more than two," Claire said. She was sitting on the couch, distractedly leafing through the *New York Times Book Review*. She put it down. "Anyway, our going out there today is not going to help. I'm sure there are plenty of people looking after the kids and bringing casseroles and all that. We'd be in the way. And besides, Ben, I'm leaving for two weeks tomorrow. I've got a lot to do."

Ben stopped pacing and looked at her. "You're still holding a grudge, aren't you?"

It took her a moment to realize what he was talking about. "What? No. I just think we should give them space. She needs some time alone, and they need time as a family."

The thought of seeing Alison and Charlie together like this filled her with dread.

"It's just—appalling. Unbelievable," Ben fretted. "There has to be something we can do."

"You did find them a lawyer," Claire said.

He shook his head. That wasn't enough.

"We could send flowers," Claire said. She wanted to be alone, away from Ben's needy articulation of disbelief. She was desperate to talk to Charlie, to find out what he was thinking and feeling, but she didn't know how or when she might get a chance. What was going to happen now? Alison must be shattered. Charlie would, of course, have to attend to her. And what then? Matters that had seemed relatively simple yesterday—the deception, the affair, feelings that had been reawakened after so many years—now felt immensely complex.

"Flowers . . . I don't know," Ben said. "Aren't they a bit—funereal? Or falsely cheerful? It seems like the wrong message, somehow."

"Of course, you're right," she murmured, and Ben went off to call Zabar's, to see if they would send a gift basket to the hinterland, and then trekked over to the store to handpick the items. A task, an errand, was exactly what Ben needed. Faced with being able to do nothing, he needed something to do.

He'd always been that way. The evening of their first real date— they'd made a plan to go out for Thai in the Village a few days after the party where they'd met—Claire had sat on a bench in Washington Square Park and watched him walk toward her, alone with his backpack and a paper cone of flowers: a tall, gangly, dark-haired Harvard student with a soft smile and little gold glasses that were too round for his face. She could tell that he felt a bit exposed coming toward her like that. Even then, before she knew him, she saw through his thin veneer of self-assurance to the insecurity lurking beneath, instantly identifying in him what she recognized in herself.

"Hello, Claire Ellis," he'd said when he reached her. His voice was deep, croaky. He handed her the flowers—black-eyed Susans (what guy brought black-eyed Susans?), eased the backpack off his shoulder, and pulled out a bottle of wine, a hunk of cheese, a floury baguette, two small juice glasses. "I didn't know what to bring, so I brought all this. Hope you're up for a picnic."

For a long time Claire thought that maybe she could live inside Ben's love, that it would keep her sane. She often wondered, in fact, if Ben, with his erudite good sense, was all that stood between her and a life of manic unpredictability. Sometimes she suspected that Ben was living through her—he didn't have to be impulsive because she was; she enabled him to be the nurturing presence in the background. It was a safe role for him, a comfortable one. But was it good for her? Was he helping her by keeping her from her demons, her own unmanageable feelings? At times she felt like an exotic plant, a bonsai tree, perhaps; he was the custodian who kept her healthy but also tightly pruned.

"I CAN'T DO it. I can't go out there."

"Why not?" Claire's therapist, Dina Bronstein, peered at her over her reading glasses.

Claire pushed her forefinger into the leather seat cushion of the couch, making doughy indentations and watching them disappear.

"What's keeping you from going?" Dina pressed her.

"For one thing, I'm flying to Birmingham tonight."

Dina wrote something on the pad of paper she always had in her lap. "Uh-huh."

"It's my tour. It's important."

"It is." Dina nodded.

"I could have canceled this session, I guess. I could've gone this morning. But I needed to see you. I just—I can't face her like this."

"Like what, Claire?" Dina asked gently.

Claire looked at the oil painting above Dina's head of the Maine coast, a picture so familiar to her that she was sure she could identify every rock. She had asked, once, where it was from, and Dina told her it was Spruce Harbor, the village she disappeared to for four weeks every summer. Beginning in May, it changed, in Claire's mind, from

81

a soothing seascape to a provocation, a reminder that Dina had a life outside the office, far away from here.

"The whole thing is so—ironic."

"In what way?"

"Alison is the most cautious person I know. In high school she was always the designated driver. I was the one who did stupid things."

"Like what?"

"Drinking and driving." Tucking her legs under her, Claire sat back in the deep couch. She took a breath and let it out slowly. "Sleeping with someone else's husband."

"Ah."

"Ah."

Dina placed the notebook on the small round table beside her. "And not just anyone else's husband."

Claire nodded.

"So when you say that you can't face her—"

"It's really awful, isn't it?"

Dina just cocked her head.

Claire looked at the thick slabs of blue and gray in the painting, the bold strokes of green. Orange, red, ochre: how did the artist see all those colors in the rocks? "I guess I feel that, deep down, Alison has to know about Charlie and me, whether it's conscious or not. I introduced them to each other, you know. I set them up. I think she knew that there was kind of a—flirtation between us."

"Were you jealous when she and Charlie got together?"

"No, I don't think so. I saw myself as having given her a gift—the gift of his love."

"So how do you see it now?"

"Uhh." Claire sighed through her nose. "I don't know. Maybe the truth is I wanted to keep him around—and giving him to Alison was the only way I could imagine holding on to him."

Dina shifted in her chair. "That's quite an admission."

"You must think I'm an awful person."

82

"Why do you say that?"

"Because I would, if I were you."

"Why?"

Claire took a deep breath. "Well, for one thing, this accident."

"Do you feel responsible for this accident, Claire?"

"No. I don't know. I mean, maybe partially. Charlie was supposed to meet her at the party and drive home, but he didn't come because—because of the awkwardness of it, I guess. And she had those martinis—and then I wouldn't even let her come to dinner. Ben invited her, but I didn't want her to come."

"And you feel badly about that."

"Yeah. It's just all so—complicated."

"It is," Dina agreed.

The windows rattled, and though the shades were drawn, Claire knew a city bus was going by; she could feel it rumbling under her legs. "I can't stop thinking about this time in high school with Alison, when I was driving drunk."

Dina nodded, picking up the pen again.

"We were at someone's house, and I had a few beers. We decided to go to this swimming hole called Grover's Gulch. I remember Alison asking me if I was okay to drive, and I said, Sure, of course. I did think I was. I was driving a bunch of people, and she was in the car behind me. It was just getting dark. The road went up and down"—Claire demonstrated, gliding her flat hand over imaginary ripples—"with these slow, steep inclines and long, coasting descents. Halfway down a hill I could see these blurry white shapes, stretching across the road. I slowed down, but I was going too fast. I felt this thump under the wheels. Thump thump. It was sickening. Nobody in my car even noticed; they were all laughing about something. But when we got there, I pulled Alison aside and told her I thought I might've hit something. Something white.

"I remember she put her arm around me and said, 'Well, it ain't white anymore.' Then she whispered, 'I won't tell if you won't.'" Claire

83

laughed a little. "'I won't tell if you won't.'" She shook her head. "Alison had this way of making the things I did seem okay, even when we both knew they weren't."

"She was a good friend," Dina said.

"She was."

"And now . . ."

"And now," Claire said.

Going through her dresser drawers later that afternoon and pulling out clothes to pack, watching the neon bars on the digital clock change configuration as the minutes clicked by—4:19, 4:20, 4:21—Claire realized that she couldn't leave without calling Alison. She picked up the phone and held it in both hands. Pressing TALK with her thumb, she watched the small electronic window light up. Then she clicked it off. She pressed it again, the window lit up again, and she dialed Alison and Charlie's number.

No one picked up. The call went straight to voice mail. Prickling with relief, Claire forced herself to leave a message. "Hi, Alison," she said. "I just want you to know that I've been thinking about you constantly and feel terrible about what happened. I'm flying out tonight, but please call me if you want to. I know Ben is coming out there, and I"—she stumbled over the lie—"I really wish I could come, too. Well. I'm sorry I missed you. I'm . . . I'm really sorry."

Now this was true. She was really sorry. But even as she said it, she was pushing Alison out of her mind. Because if she really let herself feel for Alison, she would have to feel all of it: the immensity of her own betrayal, the terrible cruelty of what she and Charlie were doing. And she couldn't do that. Not now. Not yet.

October 2008

When Claire lost the baby, on a windy Monday morning in October, Ben had just arrived at his office. "I'm bleeding," she told him when he picked up the phone.

"Holy shit, what do you mean?"

"I don't know. Jesus, I don't know," she said, sobbing into the phone.

"Call the doctor. Do you want me to call the doctor?"

"Just come home," she said.

He left work without telling anyone, left his sketches scattered on the floor. Took the elevator down forty-seven flights, hailed a cab, got stuck in crosstown traffic, climbed out and found a subway, changed at Forty-second Street and sat on the local watching the stops go by in slow motion: Fifty-ninth, Sixty-sixth, Seventy-second, Eighty-sixth. As he ran up the sidewalk, trash skittered across the street in front of their West Eighty-seventh Street building.

When Ben got to their apartment, Claire was in the bedroom. She wasn't crying. She lay on the bed, facing the wall, wrapped in a blanket. "It's gone," she said.

"Are you sure?"

She didn't answer. Ben went over and sat beside her and touched her shoulder, and she curled toward him, put her head in his lap. Silently he stroked her hair, cresting the waves with the tips of his fingers. After a few moments she said, "I wish we hadn't told anyone."

"I'll take care of it," he said.

She was silent again. Then she said, "Do you think God is punishing us because we weren't sure?"

He looked down at her, lying there in his lap. He couldn't see her eyes. "I was sure," he said.

After a while Ben went to the window. The sky was the same soft white with gray undertones that they'd chosen for the living room from the Benjamin Moore sample chart several months earlier, when they'd moved into this family-friendly building. China White. He looked out the window and glanced back inside. It was as if he could open a window and step into another room, and for a moment he wondered what it would feel like to do it. He looked down at the street, the dirty yellow cabs, their downstairs neighbor in a striped fur coat like a human-size raccoon tapping her foot impatiently as her leashed Pomeranian sniffed the front tire of a parked car, and he closed the window.

He turned back toward Claire, but she seemed to have fallen asleep. Suddenly thirsty, Ben turned and made his way to the kitchen, a narrow alley at the back of the apartment, as streamlined as a ship's galley. Opening the stainless fridge, he found a jar of sun-dried tomatoes, a deli container of Fairway olives, various ludicrous condiments like almond paste and truffle mustard, a half-eaten Belgian chocolate bar, and an expired quart of fresh-squeezed orange juice. He opened the cabinet above the sink and found a pack of organic brown coffee filters, but no coffee. Now that he thought about it, he couldn't remember the last time they'd made coffee at home.

He shut the door and slid down the smooth stainless cabinet until he was crouching on the floor, staring out the large window at the other end of the apartment.

For the next few nights Claire tossed in her sleep. "Where are you?" she cried.

"I'm here."

"Where are you?"

"I'm here. Right here, Claire."

She'd shake her head and turn away.

"Don't you think," Ben said a few weeks later, "don't you think"—he traced the blue lines on her forearm—"we should think about trying again?"

She turned away.

"When you're ready."

"What if I'm never ready?" she said.

"Hey. How is she today?"

"Come in." Charlie held the door open, and Robin did, in fact, stride right in. Over the past few days he had come to admire her forthrightness; it was refreshing not to have to do the dance of "what-do-you-need," "oh-nothing-we're-fine" with people who wrung their hands and offered help but didn't know how to come through. With Robin there was none of that—she just showed up. She didn't ask what they wanted; she just brought what she thought they'd need: milk and bread and a warm lasagna. She whisked Annie and Noah over to her house (a pleasure dome, Charlie saw when he picked them up, their eyes wide with wonder at the Disney-like bounty of video games and animated movies on a theater-size flat-screen TV, gaily colored packaged snacks, impossible-to-get toys of the moment tossed carelessly around the family room). He'd practically had to drag the kids away by their heels.

"It's quiet in here," Robin said.

"She's upstairs with the kids."

"You want to tell her I'm here?"

"Yeah. Just a sec." He bounded up the stairs and rounded the corner to the master bedroom. The door was slightly ajar, and he pushed it open all the way to reveal Alison, in sweatpants and a blue UNC sweatshirt (purchased at her fifteenth reunion last summer), her hair in a stringy ponytail, sitting cross-legged with Annie on the floor playing Sorry. Charlie peered into the dimness; the shades were drawn. Noah was sprawled on the floor with two small Thomas trains, conducting a conversation between them in a high-pitched voice.

"Hey. Robin's downstairs," Charlie said with forced cheer, opening a shade. He felt like a nurse, bustling in to wake up a patient.

Alison looked up, squinting into the cold daylight. "What time is it?"

Charlie gestured with his free hand to the alarm clock, then said, gratuitously, "Four-ten."

"Your turn, Mommy," Annie said.

Alison picked up a card and turned it over.

"Move forward ten or back one," Annie read. "Forward ten is better."

"Should I send 'er up?" Charlie asked.

"I'm disgusting," Alison murmured. "I haven't showered in three days."

"You need a bath," Annie said. "A bubble bath. Go, Mommy."

Dutifully Alison picked up a green plastic Hershey's kiss–shaped pawn and pushed it ten spaces with her index finger.

"You're fine. She doesn't care," Charlie said.

Alison glanced up sharply, and he could tell she'd caught the impatience in his voice. Easy, he thought. He hadn't known how much he wanted Robin to stay until that moment. He was, he suddenly realized, desperate for it.

90

"Hah! *Sorry!*" Annie squealed triumphantly, holding up a card. "Sorry, Mommy. You have to go back to start."

Downstairs in the foyer with Robin, Charlie said, "You can go up."

"You sure?"

"Yeah. She's—it's tough."

Robin nodded. "I can only imagine."

"It means a lot that you stop by. I think—people don't really know what to do. Hell, I don't know what to do."

"Is there any news?"

Charlie wasn't sure whether Alison had told her about the DWI, so he didn't mention it. He said, "The boy's funeral is tomorrow. Alison wants to go."

Robin grimaced. "Do you think that's a good idea?"

"No. But her mind is made up. She said she'll take a bus if I don't drive her."

"A bus?"

Oh shit. So Robin didn't know. "She doesn't feel comfortable driving yet," he said.

"Sure, of course. Where is it?"

"Patterson."

"I could take her," Robin said.

For a moment Charlie was tempted to accept. The last thing in the world he wanted was to go to the funeral—it seemed to him intrusive and inappropriate. What right did they have to share in that family's private grief? And he feared that Alison's presence could be seen as worse than inappropriate—it might come across as callous. The fact was that if Alison hadn't been at that intersection—and perhaps, too, if she hadn't drunk those martinis—the boy would still be alive.

But Charlie knew he couldn't let Robin take his place. A line from the book he'd read to Annie and Noah the night before, *The Bear Went over the Mountain,* came to mind: *Can't go over it. Can't go under it. We have to go through it.*

He shook his head. "Thanks for offering."

"I'll watch the kids."

Charlie smiled in tacit acceptance.

After Robin went upstairs, he unloaded and loaded the dishwasher with breakfast bowls, wiped the counter, picked toys off the kitchen floor. Then he stood in the hall and cocked his head, listening. He could hear the quiet murmur of voices. He took his cell phone out of his pocket and dialed Claire's cell.

"Hey," he whispered. "Where are you?"

"God. I've been waiting for you to call."

"I couldn't."

"I know. I wasn't expecting it. I just—hoped. I did leave a message for Alison a while ago."

"I know. She mentioned it. That was—good of you. So where are you?"

"On the way to LaGuardia. Book tour, remember?"

91

"Oh yeah. Real life," he said.

"Doesn't feel like it."

"Well, this sure doesn't."

She grunted. "What you're going through is as real as it gets, right?"

"Maybe. I don't know. Surreal, I'd say." He suddenly felt very tired. He didn't have the energy to say another word. He wanted to crawl into a hole and go to sleep for a very long time.

"I'm so sorry, Charlie," Claire said.

For the first time since the accident, Charlie felt his throat constrict, his eyes blur with tears. He swallowed hard.

"It's okay," she said softly.

"It's really not." He choked, biting down on the words to keep his voice under control.

"I wanted to come out there, but I just—"

"I know. I didn't—want you here." He almost took it back, fearing that she would take offense at his bluntness.

But all she said was, "That's what I figured. I'm sure it's been hard enough."

"Yeah."

"I just—I wish I could see you."

"I know." His longing for her was so acute that it felt cancerous, deep in his bones.

"Ben wants to come. He'll call."

"Okay."

"How is she?"

"She's okay. I mean, what can I say? She's devastated. She's okay."

"I know."

"Enough about all this. I should be asking about you," he said.

"No, you shouldn't. Not now."

"Later," he whispered.

"Later," she said.

CHARLIE DROPPED ALISON at the door of the funeral home and went off to park, then slipped into the maroon-carpeted chapel right before the doors closed. Alison was sitting alone in the back pew. The song "Tears in Heaven" was playing, an instrumental version heavy on the strings that Charlie guessed the funeral home must have had on a mix tape tailored for children. At the front, flanked by two large, heart-shaped flower forms as tidily patterned as frosting on a supermarket cake, was a small baby blue casket.

"It's tiny," she murmured.

"At least it's not open," Charlie said under his breath.

The chapel was more than half full; there were probably sixty people. When everyone was settled the minister talked about the senselessness of this kind of tragedy, but also about how God had a plan for each of us, and how it was not our place to question that plan. Other people, speaking in tear-choked voices, recalled Marco's love of baseball, his collection of Matchbox cars, his uncanny ability to mimic advertising jingles from TV, the way he insisted on wearing his father's leather tool belt around the house, even though it nearly tipped him over. They talked about how God would watch over Marco, and the angels would play with him, and how his grandfather, already in heaven, would teach him card tricks. Nobody mentioned the accident.

It would have been comforting, Charlie thought, to believe in fate now—that there was a reason for all this grief, that it was a test to soldier through, that the little boy's death wasn't simply a result of ill judgment and heedlessness but part of some kind of larger design, the details of which would become clear as the years unfolded. But it was impossible for him. A child was dead, and his wife was at least partially to blame. This child would never be four, or fourteen, or twenty-six; he would not graduate from high school or earn a driver's license or have children of his own. He would not make his parents proud, or disappoint them. His career would be someone else's career, his wife someone else's wife. He would not take care of his parents in their old age, or continue the family name. His mother would spend the rest of her life wondering what he might have become.

It occurred to Charlie that the last time he had been to a funeral was when his own mother died. It was very different from this, of course; her struggle with cancer had been long and arduous, and though nobody wanted to believe it, they'd all known she was dying. She was cremated, and they scattered her ashes in the pond behind her home.

When the cancer had appeared the first time—she'd discovered a lump in her cervix, and underwent a year of chemo and radiation—Charlie's mother had emerged from the ordeal physically diminished and emotionally transformed. Her thick blond hair, which she'd always worn in a conservative bob, fell out, and when it grew back, fine and gray, she cropped it short. She took trips with fellow cancer survivors to Tucson and Taos and became a devotee of Ashtanga yoga. She kept her food processor permanently on the kitchen counter and drank herbal potions in deep, earthy colors, green and rust and brown. And when the cancer came back, fifteen years later, in every lymph node and several of her bones, it was almost as if she was ready for it. In those years, as she confided to Charlie when he finally came to see her, she had done all the things she wanted to do—the things she'd spent the first forty-one years of her life wondering about: trying marijuana, having sex with a stranger, camping on a mountaintop, feeling the muscles and bones in her body move in ways she hadn't known they could.

Near the end, lying in her hospital bed with tubes in her arms, her face scrubbed free of makeup, she'd grasped his hand and looked in his eyes. "Here's what I have learned," she said. "It's not enough to hope that happiness will find you. You have to seek it. And another thing: no matter how complicated your life seems, you have the power to change it. Don't make the mistake I did and waste precious decades because you're too afraid to act."

At the time the words had seemed to Charlie like New Age bullshit; he was living in New York and, he thought, doing pretty much exactly what he wanted. His mother's middle-aged carpe diem conversion seemed both simplistic and a little unseemly—who was this woman with the short spiky hair and serious gaze, devoid of maternal softness, spouting slogans worthy of the posters for sale in the back of in-flight magazines? But these days her words haunted him. He had an image in his mind of his mother in that hospital bed, sitting up against stiff white pillows, her lips thin and bloodless, almost colorless, her eyes dark and bright. He thought of her like this at random times, when he was standing in line at the ATM machine or buying groceries, and his eyes would fill with tears. His mother had been right. She knew what lay ahead, and she warned him, and he—young, self-absorbed, ignorant of the myriad ways that life can beat you down—had humored, placated, and ultimately dismissed her. What fucking arrogance. If he had listened to her, might his life have been different? Would a courageous decision ten years ago have avoided a mess like this now?

As soon as the boy's funeral was over, and "Wind Beneath My Wings" came on the audio system, Charlie nudged Alison, and they tiptoed out. She had wanted to go up and speak to the parents, but Charlie had convinced her that it would be inappropriate—it was the last thing he'd want, if he were the father of the boy. She lingered for a moment at the back, then followed him out the double doors to the parking lot.

On the way home in the car, she turned to Charlie and said tearfully, "I know you're angry at me."

"I'm not angry, Alison."

"Yes you are. Say the worst things you're thinking. That I'm irresponsible and stupid. A drunk. A murderer." She almost spat the words at him, daring him to agree.

He looked over at her warily. In truth, he *was* angry at her—for the insecurities that he was certain had led her to drink too much at the party, for her poor judgment, even for the anguish she was expressing now.

He had both hands on the steering wheel, and he lifted one to rub his cheek. "You're not a drunk. Or a murderer."

She gasped a little, as if his words had caused her physical pain.

Charlie drove in silence, wondering at his own capacity for inflicting hurt. He felt a stab of regret. But he couldn't shake this anger he felt toward her. And he knew that, really, her culpability wasn't the issue—it was that he'd been on the brink of self-discovery, a quest that had nothing to do with her. It was separate from her, from the children, from their life in Rockwell. But this accident made it impossible for him to pursue it. He felt, now, at the edge of a feeling more powerful, more dangerous than he could ever remember having experienced—a bottomless despair.

October 2001

At dinner with Claire and Ben one evening in New York, Alison and Charlie made plans to go away with them for an October fall foliage bed-and-breakfast weekend upstate. Charlie made reservations at what turned out to be a dilapidated bed-and-breakfast he'd chosen from an out-of-date guidebook he'd found remaindered at the Strand—typical of him, as Claire said when they got there. "Charlie's such a cheapskate," she grumbled to Alison as they followed the ancient proprietor up the rickety stairs to their rooms. "We should never let him make the plans." (Charlie was a cheapskate, but Alison knew that he felt acutely the difference between his nonprofit job and Ben's salary as a corporate architect.)

Charlie had left work early and taken the subway to a bus to the least expensive car rental place he could find, near the river on Thirty-first Street. He secured a shiny white Ford Focus and drove up West End Avenue to pick up Alison. Meanwhile, she had packed their bag. He had left a sloppy pile of clothes on his dresser—khakis and a moss green sweater, boxer shorts and socks and a few white T-shirts, a leather utility case containing a frayed toothbrush, a flattened tube of toothpaste, and a sample-size yellow moisturizer from a makeup promotion. She scanned her closet for something, anything, that wasn't black. They were going upstate. People wore colors there.

Alison was standing in the lobby, chatting with Frank, the part-time doorman, when Charlie pulled up in front of the building. It was a cold, windy day. Frank carried her bag despite her protests, and she rolled her eyes at Charlie as he watched them coming to let him know that she had no choice. Charlie was sensitive about treating their doorman like a serf.

"Frank," he said, scrolling down the passenger's window and leaning across the seat, "you didn't have to—"

"It's a pleasure to serve such a lovely young couple, sir, a pleasure. A good weekend to you."

Frank was from the old school, and all you could do was nod. Even Charlie realized this, and he waved good-bye with a pained smile, which Frank returned with a brisk salute.

"I suppose when we have a baby we'll actually need a doorman," Alison said as Charlie pulled into traffic.

"Umm," he said.

"But I like it now, too," she said. "It makes me feel safe. And packages—it's useful for packages."

"Actually," he said, slowing to a stop at a red light, "I was reading that people in doorman buildings get lulled into complacency. Anyone can talk their way in, or slip past when the doorman isn't looking."

"It's green," Alison said. They picked up speed over the next few blocks—Seventy-fourth, Seventy-third, Seventy-second, down into the Sixties, until they hit a snarl of traffic around Lincoln Center. "I don't care if it's an illusion," she said as they sat stalled at an intersection. "I like to feel safe."

He looked over at her with an amused smile. "Well, aren't you conventional all of a sudden. Next you'll be wanting a white picket fence in Connecticut." This was a game they played, accusing each other of bourgeois aspirations. It was their way of dealing with the legitimate fear that their lives were becoming demographically predictable.

"Let's not rush things," she said. "First the Jack Russell. Then the baby. Then the house."

He glanced at the digital clock. "I can't believe you told Claire we'd pick them up, Al. They could easily have met me at the lot. It's adding an hour to our travel time."

"So?" she said. "It gives us some quality time together, right?"

"Quantity time, maybe," he said.

Charlie was right; it took twenty-five minutes just to get through Midtown traffic. There was much to talk about, but little was said. Sighs and mutterings, attention to traffic. As they passed through Times Square, neon rinsed the dashboard, splashed in their eyes.

When they got to the warehouse on Seventeenth Street, Charlie jumped out and rang the buzzer.

"Benjamin, sir," he said with exaggerated formality, "the car and driver are downstairs."

Charlie got back in the car. He and Alison sat in silence for a few minutes, waiting. She adjusted some knobs on the dashboard, turning down the heat. The street was quiet. Cars were double-parked on one side, sharking for a space; every time a truck came along, Charlie had to circle the block.

Alison put her hand on Charlie's leg, just above the knee, a peace offering of sorts, though she wasn't quite sure why she felt she needed to offer one. "What," he said in a neutral voice, neither a question nor a demand.

She pulled her hand away.

"Did you pack my green sweater?"

She nodded.

"Good. It's going to be cold."

"I love you," she said.

After a moment he said, "I know." Then, as if realizing that wasn't enough, he said, "Love you, too. Here they are."

There was a hard rap on her window. "Hey, guys." It was Claire, all sparkly hazel eyes and dangling earrings and big crimson mouth, wearing a black cashmere turtleneck and modishly faded jeans. Alison unlocked the doors, and Claire slid in. Ben rapped on the trunk, a thump that vibrated against Alison's feet, and Charlie triggered the lock. Ben fiddled in the trunk for a moment, then slammed it shut. Alison looked back at Claire, and Claire smiled and squeezed her shoulder. "An adventure," she said. "This is just what we need."

Out of the city, trees were everywhere. The colors reminded Alison of *New York* magazine's fall fashion color palette: sage green, burnt sugar, cinnamon, yellow apple, moss. The fact that she even saw it that way, she thought ruefully, meant that she'd probably been living in the city too long.

Later, Alison framed a snapshot from that weekend of the four of them sitting on the pebbled beach of a lake. It was a cold morning; they all wore mismatched scarves and mittens borrowed from the garrulous proprietor of the bed-and-breakfast. In the photo they're all laughing, but it's as if they've been laughing too long; their smiles are held in place like the afterimage of a bright light in a dark room. You can tell there's been some self-conscious arrangement: Alison is leaning back against Charlie, who has his arm draped over her shoulder, and Claire and Ben are tilting their heads together. It was only when Alison examined the picture closely that she noticed Claire's arm on Charlie's knee, and his fingers touching hers. She might have seen it at the time, but if so it didn't register.

Ben had, of course, been to New Jersey, but he'd never taken the train. Now, in the marble well of New Jersey Transit at Penn Station, he stood, like the other commuters (not many; it was 9 A.M. on Tuesday; almost everyone was going the opposite way) with chins tilted up expectantly, watching the big, black, surprisingly old-fashioned sign overhead to find out which track his train was on. Rockwell, on the Essex County line, was scheduled to leave in ten minutes.

Flip, flip flip—Track 2.

About half a dozen people in the large vestibule now turned, as one, in the same direction. Ben was reminded of how he'd felt traveling in Europe—the unfamiliar rituals, the secret language of commuters, the customs that appeared to be second nature to everyone else. So he did now what he'd always done abroad: he identified the person who seemed most at ease—in this case, a woman with a severe haircut talking into a wireless earpiece—and followed her surreptitiously.

The escalator to the trains wasn't working, so everyone walked down the ribbed steps, strangely unfamiliar in stasis. Trains on both sides. Which one? There was no conductor in sight. Ben followed the wireless woman to the right and up to the front of the train.

Earlier, he had packed his leather satchel with the *Times,* a current *New Yorker,* a bottle of water, an apple. The toy store on his route to the subway was closed, so he'd ducked into Rite Aid and bought shamelessly crowd-pleasing presents for Annie and Noah: Day-Glo lollipops as big as saucers, a Dora the Explorer coloring book for Annie (a wild stab—what did little girls want? He had no idea), a froglike stuffed animal for Noah that apparently came with a code for access to some no-doubt addictive Web site. Charlie and Alison would almost certainly disapprove. Then again, Ben supposed, they had bigger things on their minds.

On the phone, when Ben had asked what he could do and Charlie said, "Really—nothing," Ben realized that he would have to answer that question himself. What he could do was come to them. Claire had left for her book tour yesterday afternoon, as planned—of course she had to go; it would have been unreasonable not to—and Ben had gone into work, though he couldn't shake the feeling that he didn't belong there. That he should somehow do more.

There was no clear etiquette for this. After all, he didn't know (thank God) the child who had died. And it truly appeared that it wasn't Alison's fault. It was a terrible tragedy, but it wasn't his tragedy—it wasn't even *their* tragedy, exactly. So why did he feel compelled to take a day off work and come to Rockwell? How could it possibly help? He thought of Claire's justifications: there's nothing we can do. It's a horrible situation, but really it's no one's fault; nobody should be taking this on themselves. Yes, yes, she was right. Rationally, this was none of his business. But instinctively he felt that coming to see Alison was the right thing to do.

The train was a bit dingy, and altogether too fluorescent—a poor relation to Metro North, the Westchester line that Ben occasionally took to see a client, filled with prosperous mortgage brokers and lawyers talking on cell phones and reading the *Wall Street Journal*. The people around him now seemed comparatively down-market: secretary types, men with shiny, buzzed hair in cheap inky suits; beleaguered mothers with unwieldy strollers. Was it the time of day? It was, to be honest, a little depressing.

The train lurched slightly as it left the station. Ben looked at his watch: 9:37. As he settled into his hard maroon vinyl seat, he was reminded of the many times, as a boy, he had gone with his mother to visit her father in a rest home in upstate New York, an hour from their home. He'd liked those trips—his mother, faced with nothing to do for an hour, relaxed and even seemed to enjoy it, chatting above the steady hum with an intimacy that was rare when they were home. They played card games and read books and talked. Ben liked looking out the window and watching the world glide by. He liked knowing that it might be this easy to leave one place for another. You got on a train, and then you were somewhere else. He particularly liked reading novels on the train; it felt doubly transporting.

For a long time, while Ben was growing up, the world outside his head held little interest. Outside his head, his mother was bustling around in the kitchen, fixing a family dinner his father wouldn't show up for. The dinner would get cold as they sat there, Ben and his mother and his younger brother, Justin, and then his mother would say, in a strained, careful voice, "Well, you two go ahead," and push her own plate away. Ben would struggle to eat the chicken and peas that tasted like dog food in his mouth. His mother would watch them silently for a few minutes, then rise abruptly and start clearing up around them, an angry clatter of dishes reverberating in the still room.

Ben could read anywhere. He read waiting for the bus, sitting on the bus, walking into school. He read at recess and before orchestra. He read at night in the room he shared with his brother after his mother had turned off the overhead light, squinting to see the words by the eerie glow of the night-light in the socket beside his bed. In his world the wizard Merlin was as real as Jim Townsend and Tyler Green, two boys who lived on his block and threw gravel at him when he walked by, hiding in the stairwells of their split-levels. Ben rode the trains with the Boxcar Children; he stepped through a wardrobe into a land where a great lion saved children from an evil witch. He was three inches tall, navigating the perilous terrain behind his house, where sparrows were airplanes and rain puddles lakes. At home Ben often felt helpless, at school he was invisible, but in his head he was a fearless traveler, a brilliant inventor, a hero.

Before Ben knew what an affair was, he sensed that his father was having one. The distraction and irritation, the careless lies—Ben could see that he was tearing away from the family, as slowly and painfully as an animal caught in a steel trap chewing off its own limb. To Ben it made no sense: they were a family, in a house with a yard—a tiny, scrubby patch of yard, but a yard nonetheless—in a neighborhood filled with families, mothers and fathers and kids. The only thing he could fathom was that his father must have another, better, family somewhere else. Later Ben would learn that, essentially, he did. Across town, in a small, second-floor apartment, a mistress and a baby were waiting.

At school, where he got As without even trying, Ben felt like a fraud. He couldn't articulate what he really thought or felt or saw, so mostly he stayed quiet. By the time he was in ninth grade he was drifting through his classes, smoking pot with the stoners behind the school between periods. He joined the chess club, won every match, and then quit; he discovered Nietzsche and shaved his head. It was at this particularly confused point in his midteens that a high school guidance counselor stepped in. Handing Ben a stack of prep-school brochures, he'd given him a thirty-minute seminar on the ins and outs of scholarships and financial aid. A year later, Ben was at a small school in New Hampshire where there were so many smarter, weirder kids that he seemed fairly normal, even ordinary, by comparison.

When, in April of his senior year, he called his mother to tell her that he'd gotten into Harvard, she squeaked and started to cry. He was standing at a pay phone in the student center, using the phone card she'd given him for his birthday. All around him, other kids were opening their college letters, the contents telegraphed by the size of the envelopes. As his mother carried on he watched the faces register a flickering range of emotion. Ben had kept his application to Harvard a secret. There were kids in his class, legacies of legacies, for whom getting in seemed as inevitable as getting a driver's license. He hadn't wanted to set himself up for almost certain humiliation, so he told no one but the college counselor and the teachers he'd asked for references.

"Benjamin," his mother breathed. "This will set you up for life."

His mother's elation was nearly matched by his father's wariness when Ben called him a few days later. "So how's this gonna work? You got a scholarship or something?"

"They're offering me a package," Ben said. "Some money outright, work study, loans—"

"Because I gotta tell you, Ben, I'd like to help you out, but it's not a real good time. I got debts like you wouldn't believe." His father sighed. "Listen, I know you can do this. I had to work my way through school—"

"Dad, you dropped out."

Ben could hear the static on the line between them. "You're a smart kid, Benjamin. Smarter than I was, I guess. Right? I didn't get into fucking Harvard. With that degree you can get any job you want, go into investment banking and make a killing. Jesus. A kid of mine, going to Harvard. I'm starting to like the sound of that."

STEPPING DOWN FROM the train, Ben looked around, trying to get his bearings. The station was located in Rockwell village, across from a bagel shop that Ben recognized and the requisite small-town strip of dry cleaner, post office, bookstore, and coffee shop. Farther down the street were a nail salon and—of course; he should have guessed—a tasteful toy shop with educational wooden toys displayed in the window. It was a lovely day, mild and sunny, and despite the purpose of his visit, Ben felt strangely at peace. This was such a pretty town, Rockwell. Ben could imagine that one day he and Claire might move here, when they had a child, perhaps. It felt quite far from New York, more than the fourteen miles he had traveled to get here.

He went down the steps from the platform to the sidewalk and crossed the street. Bagels—no one would object to that. In the shop he began to order: everything, garlic, pumpernickel, onion—then remembered a time a year or so ago when he and Claire had come out to Rockwell for brunch, bearing smoked sturgeon and lox from Barney

Greengrass, to find that Charlie had purchased only plain and, good lord, cinnamon crunch bagels. "Kids," Charlie had said and smiled apologetically.

"Do you have cinnamon crunch?" Ben asked now.

Their house was easy to find. Clutching the warm, lumpy paper sack of bagels in one hand, the rustling plastic bag of gaudy presents in the other, with his satchel slung over his shoulder, Ben set off into the neighborhood. Though the ground seemed dry, clumps of snow, like errant tufts of cotton, dotted the dead curbside grass. Through the naked trees that lined the sidewalks, the houses along the way were starkly visible. A front porch here, a picture window there, hanging planters, a child's bike: every home contained promise and mystery. As he used to do when he was a child, Ben fantasized about the lives behind each door, ascribing to each a glowing fire, a simmering soup, burbling children—idealized tableaus of domestic tranquility.

Nearing the Granvilles' front walk, Ben slowed. He lingered before the gate of their white picket fence (really! A suburban cliché come to apparently unironic life), wanting to postpone the inevitable rush of feeling. For the first time, he considered the obligation that his presence would impose on Charlie to host him, the sadness and shame that Alison would be forced to express in response to his own unfiltered emotions (Alison—who loved children, who devoted her life to children), the patronizing futility of his sympathy.

He was, he realized in that moment, there for himself, not for them.

Claire was right. He was too myopic to see it until now. He was here to assuage his own guilt, to make himself feel better. To put his own mind at ease. What did he possibly have to say to a woman who'd just been in a fatal accident, to two confused small children, to a friend with whom he had fallen out of touch? What foolish posturing. The Zabar's basket was one thing. Showing up on their doorstep with bagels and cheap toys was quite another.

And yet here he was. He unlatched the gate.

Charlie opened the door as Ben was mounting the steps. "Hey, man," he said, extending his hand for a shake and clapping Ben on the shoulder at the same time, the kind of half-hug Ben associated with pro athletes. "Really appreciate your coming out. How was the train?"

"Oh, fine. Easy," Ben said, following Charlie inside. "How—how is she?"

Charlie nodded, hands on hips. "She's in the kitchen," he said, as if that were an answer. "Al, Ben's here," he called out. "Just go on in," he told Ben. "I've got to get out an e-mail, but I'll be there in a minute."

Ben was surprised to find Alison sitting at the kitchen table, drinking coffee and making a puzzle with Noah. Then he chided himself. What had he expected, that she'd be crumpled in a ball on the floor?

She looked up and smiled, and it was then that he saw the dark circles under her eyes. He went over to her, and she half rose.

"No, no, don't get up," he said.

"I want to." She reached over and hugged him awkwardly, the corner of the table between them. "I can't believe you came out. And on a weekday."

"Oh, goodness, no," he said senselessly, at a loss for words. He ruffled Noah's hair like a jocular uncle. "What are you making here?"

"Lion King," Noah said without looking up. "We're finding the straight edges first."

"That's the way to do it," Ben said, flashing back to his own obsessive puzzle-making days. All those straight edges! "Simba," he said, pulling the knowledge up like a bucket out of some pop-culture well in his brain.

"And Nala. And Mufasa. The picture's on the cover of the box," Noah said, motioning to an upside-down box top at the end of the table. "But Mommy and I don't want to look. That's cheating."

"Oh. Right. Well, you're doing a great job without it. Where's your sister?"

"She's at school, silly. It's *Tuesday*."

" 'Course it is. Silly me."

107

Alison was watching Ben with her steady brown eyes. He caught her eye and smiled, and she, seemingly startled, smiled back.

"Hey, monkey," she said, putting her hand on Noah's shoulder. "Think you can handle this on your own for a few minutes?"

"Why?"

"Ben needs a cup of coffee. Right?" she asked, looking up at him.

"Sure—no, whatever," Ben sputtered. "Don't go to any—"

She waved her hand at him and went over to the coffeemaker.

"I can't do this without you, Mommy," Noah said.

"Just do as much as you can. Or you can take a break."

"Can I watch TV?"

She sighed. "Sure."

"Cartoon Network?"

"PBS."

"But—"

"Oh, all right, but only for half an—"

Before the words were out of her mouth, Noah had slid off his chair and slipped out of the room.

Ben shrugged the leather satchel off his shoulder and set the bag of bagels on the counter. "I wasn't sure what to bring, so I just got these. And here are some godawful things for the kids, from a drugstore, of all places—"

But when he turned back to Alison she was collapsed in a chair, her shoulders heaving, her hands covering her face.

"Oh my God," he said, "Alison." He went over and knelt beside her, stroking her back.

"I'm sorry," she sobbed.

"No, I'm sorry," he said. "I'm so sorry, Alison. I'm so sorry."

September 1998

It was Freud who first proposed convincingly that motives can be hidden from consciousness. Writing this line four months after Alison had gone back to the States and they'd begun a long-distance telephone relationship, Charlie had a revelation. He understood that he'd been prepared to fall in love with Alison not only because he couldn't have Claire, but also because he'd fallen in love with Claire and Ben—the whole idea of them, the way they lived and the way they saw themselves. He liked the person he imagined he was when he was with them; they made him more interesting to himself. Even before he met Alison, he had envisioned a perfect life for the four of them, traveling around Europe by train, staying up late in smoky bars, sharing dog-eared paperbacks, drinking espresso at midmorning in Parisian cafés—every cliché a midwesterner might have about the sophisticated life, joie de vivre and all that.

Claire and Ben would traipse off to Europe for a week on a whim. Days would go by without a word, and then they'd pop up at a master's tea with sunburned noses and announce that they'd been in a seaside town in Andalusia. "The weather was so dismal here," Claire would say, by way of explanation. "We had to do something."

When they finally did invite Charlie along he wasn't given much notice. He was standing outside the university library, thumbing through notes from a lecture, when he felt someone pinch his waist. "We're going to Paris," Claire whispered in his ear. "Wanna come?"

"Hello, Claire," he said. Over the past year Charlie had become accustomed to her abrupt greetings.

"Hello."

"When?"

"Umm . . ." She looked at her watch. "Five hours from now. We're taking the four-twenty train to the ferry."

"I have a tutorial tomorrow," Charlie said.

She tilted her head sympathetically. "I'm so sorry to hear you're not well. There is something going around. I'm sure your tutor will understand. Mine did."

Of course he agreed; how could he not?

They stayed in a sliver of a pension, the three of them in one big room with an in-room sink. They shared a toilet with eight other guests in a closet at one end of the long hallway, and a bathtub at the other end of the hallway that heated water only after you dropped coins in a box. They went out late for Italian in the Marais—the cheapest food in town—and drank Chianti from bulbous straw-covered bottles and ate spaghetti with red sauce. They made their way to the late-night clubs, drifting in and out of the ones without a cover charge, scraping together enough change to get into the Pink Pussycat. Of the three of them, only Ben spoke passable French, so he did the negotiating while Claire and Charlie stood back and let the sounds and smells drift over them, content just to be there, in that moment, where they were.

Strolling back to their pension through deserted cobblestone streets, sleepy and light-headed from the smoke and the noise, they were quiet. Then Claire said, "Remember in middle school, learning about metamorphosis—that stage between cocoon and butterfly? What's it called again?"

Ben glanced at Charlie and smiled, acknowledging their shared tolerance for Claire's non sequiturs. "Instar," he said.

"Yes, that's it!" She clapped her hands together. "That's where we are, the three of us, isn't it? Between one phase and another. Instar."

" 'Isn't it lovely to think so,' " said Ben.

"Quoting Hemingway is not allowed," she said. "Not in Paris, anyway."

Later that evening, as Charlie sat in the badly lit common room of their pension, polishing off a jug of wine and trying to make small talk in his broken Spanish with an Argentinean backpacker, he could hear Claire and Ben in the creaky double bed in their room directly above, thudding arythmically against the floor. Charlie wasn't sure why it made him so uncomfortable—they were often physically affectionate in his presence. Ben would kiss Claire on the forehead when he came back from the library, or Claire might run her hand along Ben's back and squeeze his shoulders, or twine her fingers through his. Of course Charlie knew they had sex. But knowing and hearing were different things.

It dawned on him then that perhaps there was something odd about the fact that he was along on this excursion with them—that they seemed so content to have him around, and that he was so pleased to be included. Sometimes, even in England, he felt as if he were their child, on a family vacation. Sometimes he knew he was there to amuse them. Sometimes it was as if he and Ben were the practical menfolk and Claire was the zany, impulsive female, and at other times Claire and Charlie were the adventurers and Ben was the fey intellectual whom they had to force outdoors for a little fresh air. Charlie couldn't predict what the dynamic would be on any given day—and that, for him, was part of the charm. When he was with them he didn't want to be anywhere else, with anyone else. They insulated one another from the gray weather, the wary English, but most of all from taking their own futures too seriously. While they all complained about the fog and the rain, the heavy food, the incomprehensible rules and the seemingly endless reading and writing, they also knew that a time like this in their lives would probably never come again. Charlie didn't want it to end. And as he sat in that dank common room, chatting with the Argentinean, feeling the vibration against the ceiling, he understood that the only way they might continue like this, together, was to make their group of three a four.

For Alison, now, the world was a different place, and yet it was strangely the same. She was present and not present in her own life. She went through the motions of a routine—getting out of bed in the morning, herding the kids from their bedrooms to the bathroom to the kitchen and then out the front door to the bus and the car, but it was as if she weren't there; she inhabited a shadow. She felt transparent, her mind a blank. She watered houseplants and separated laundry and even went to the grocery store, but she was playing a role; the real Alison was in bed with the shades drawn. She was tired all the time. She fantasized about sleep the way you might dream about a lover, yearning for the bliss of escape.

When, after several days, Alison went to get her wrist examined, Dr. Waldron asked her a series of questions:

"Are you sleeping?" No.

"Are you having trouble getting up in the morning?" Yes.

"Do you blame yourself for this?" Yes. Of course.

"Is your husband providing you with the support you need?" Yes. No. I don't know.

Somehow, in the past few days, they had barely spoken about the accident. It wasn't that they didn't have the time; it was that the time was never right. The kind of talking they needed to do required a level of intimacy and trust that neither of them was sure they shared. Alison used to believe it was mutual respect that kept them from revealing themselves to each other all the time, that each was allowing the other autonomy and space. She didn't think that anymore. Now she believed that there was too much at stake in talking, too much to risk. There was a fault line at the base of their relationship, and both of them were afraid that tapping at the surface would make it worse.

Dr. Waldron wrote out a prescription for Xanax. "We'll monitor this closely," she said. "But Alison, you really should see a therapist."

She nodded.

"I'll give you some names."

Alison had been in therapy only once in her life, when, in college, she went to the women's clinic to talk about a guy she thought she was in love with who made her crazy. The therapist wasn't particularly insightful or even empathetic, and Alison barely lasted the ten sessions her insurance subsidized, but the process itself, as she remembered, was vaguely comforting—it was useful to have a place to go once a week to talk about the stuff she was either too embarrassed to tell her roommates or that they were sick of hearing. One time she said—in what felt like a moment of revelation—"I could make anything up about my life and you'd believe me," and the therapist smiled and said, "And that would reveal something else, wouldn't it?"

114   Whether it was time or therapy, Alison got over the guy. And she'd never had an inclination to go back.

But if ever there was a time to go to a therapist, she knew, this was it. Charlie kept nudging her. She suspected that he just wanted help—someone, anyone, to pull her out of this funk. It would reduce his burden, relieve his stress. But she resisted calling the numbers Dr. Waldron had given her. In some perverse, obstinate way, she wanted Charlie to have to deal with it, with her. She didn't want to make it so easy for him to shake her off.

And perhaps, too, she was afraid of what she might uncover—what the therapeutic process might reveal. Perhaps she wasn't prepared to learn how deep her unhappiness went. Maybe if she started talking about the ways she felt like a failure, how she'd burrowed into a life in which she sometimes didn't even recognize the person she'd become, she would see things she didn't want to face. Articulating the unspoken would make it real.

The drugs did what they were supposed to do. They made her numb. She didn't feel better, exactly; she just didn't feel as much. It didn't help that the late winter sky was gray, opaque; the trees were bare, the streets damp with melting snow and intermittent rain.

In the mornings, after waving good-bye to Annie at the bus stop and dropping Noah at preschool, she'd often go to a nearby coffee shop. Leafing through the communal newspaper basket she'd find a *Times* Living section, then buy a four-dollar latte and sit at a small round table by the window, watching other people get on with their lives: a college kid at the next table, sketching a strange-looking bicycle on graph paper with a pencil, making a few strokes and stopping, resting his chin in his hand. A blind man in a hooded sweatshirt, carrying a gym bag, led by a Seeing Eye dog. An expressionless woman with kohl-rimmed eyes who nodded slightly as the man across from her made an emphatic point. A blond woman in a shiny red Jeep, parallel parking in front of the café. Picketers wearing sandwich-board signs standing on the corner, protesting labor practices at the gourmet grocery on the next block. Everyone appeared to be in a hurry, moving with purpose, except for an old man who wandered aimlessly down the sidewalk, as if he couldn't decide which way to go.

Alison felt alone in a way that she couldn't ever remember having felt, a sense of aloneness so profound that she couldn't breathe. I have done this, she thought—*I deserve this. I deserve to feel this way.*

At night, after everyone else was in bed, Alison wandered from room to room without turning on any lights, pausing at the windows to gaze out at the quiet street. In the dim glow of a streetlight the bare branches of the tree in their front yard looked like the afterimage of a photograph, tangled in relief against the sky. She walked around the silent house and looked at the framed photographs that lined the mantelpiece and cluttered the bookshelves, wondering, Is this really my life? This collage of perfect moments, frozen in time? Every photograph seemed to her now a memento mori—a futile attempt to hold on to the past, a staged declaration of permanence in an impermanent world. They made her queasy.

When she did lie down, Alison replayed the accident over and over in her mind. She thought of the boy in the other car: his skin as soft as a ripe peach, his body solid on his mother's lap. Though Alison had only seen him with his eyes closed, she imagined them wide open, a bittersweet brown. His breath warm and tangy, apple juice and graham crackers, fingers sticky with the lollipop bribe he'd been given to stay in his seat, the bribe that didn't work. His dark, straight hair smelling of baby shampoo, as soft and fine as eyelashes against his mother's cheek.

Alison imagined him leaning back against his mother, her arms enveloping him, offering comfort in the darkness. Squirming now, tired and cranky. He tries to stand and his mother scolds him—"Sit, Marco, stop moving around." His father, distracted, just wants to get home. He has an early day tomorrow; he needs to get up at four-thirty to be at the building site by six. It's a good job and he can't afford to lose it—he needs it, they need it, after that hernia from the last job and no disability. There's a decent foreman on this job; he's a union man and always wanting to sign up the workers. Maybe so, the father thinks, maybe it's time. If the papers come through in the next few months he'll be legal and can get health insurance. It would be nice not to have to worry for a change.

The boy is moving around on the front seat. "Sit still, Marco," the father says sternly. He looks over at his wife with annoyance. Why can't she keep him down? And then his son catches his eye and reaches out, his plump, soft-nailed fingers splayed toward him—"Papa, Pa-pa," he says sweetly, his voice a chiming singsong—and the father's gaze lingers on him with affection. My boy, my only son.

In her mind Alison sees it clearly: the front of the car crumpling like foil, the boy moving forward, slipping from his mother's grasp as she tries to hold on. The mother screams, the father cries out, but the boy is too startled to make a sound. There is just the sickening thud against the windshield, the smashing glass. For a moment there is silence. And then there is a keening wail, the only sound in all of this that Alison actually heard.

The boy hears the impact, feels himself being pulled forward, his mother's hands tightening around his middle and then spreading open as he moves forward, closer to the raindrops on the windshield, the lights of the other car, the streetlights above and the darkness. He sees, out of the corner of his eye, his father turn toward him, and suddenly he is laughing. Daddy is home from work and freshly showered, damp and smelling of soap and toothpaste, wearing a clean, white T-shirt, throwing Marco into the air and letting him fall heavily into his arms, laughing and teasing, throwing him higher. The boy knows that he is in the air now, and he is safe; his daddy will catch him as he always does; the boy will fall into the warm cradle of his father's arms.

part three

That's the way things come clear. All of a sudden. And then
you realize how obvious they've been all along.

—MADELEINE L'ENGLE, *The Arm of the Starfish*

The morning that Alison's parents were scheduled to arrive on a plane from North Carolina, Charlie woke up flooded with relief. He fed the kids breakfast and got Annie ready for school while Alison stayed in bed, flipping channels between talk shows on the tiny television they used for videos in the Volvo on long-distance trips. Noah was sick, with a double ear infection, and at the bus stop Annie threw a screaming fit and refused to get on the school bus—she flung herself on the wet sidewalk and wouldn't get up. In a panic Charlie scraped her off the pavement and tried to shove her up the steps, but she was hysterical, and under the glare of the bus driver he quickly backed down.

Ed and June had planned to take a car service from the airport, but since Charlie had to stay home from work that morning anyway, he strapped the kids into their car seats and drove to Newark.

"What's wrong with this poor child?" was the first thing June said as she got into the front passenger seat. Reaching between the bucket seats, she anxiously touched different parts of Noah's face with the back of her hand.

"I'm thick, Dramma," Noah said.

"Yes, you are. Poor baby. You have a fever. You shouldn't be out in this weather."

"He's on antibiotics," Charlie said, trying not to sound defensive. "It's just an ear infection."

"You know, antibiotics aren't necessarily the best way to treat an ear infection. I sent Alison some information about homeopathic remedies that are less invasive. Maybe you haven't had a chance to look at it. We still don't really know what antibiotics do to young children."

"Yes, we do," Charlie said. "They cure ear infections." Easy, he told himself; let it go.

"Hello, precious," June was saying to Annie over her other shoulder. "Don't you have school today?"

"I hate school. I'm never going to school again!"

"Nonsense. School is very important. Don't you want to be a smart girl?"

"No," Annie said.

June rose slightly and turned around in her seat. "Well, you may not," she said, smiling determinedly at Annie, "but you are six years old. And last I checked, six-year-olds do not get to decide whether or not they want to go to school."

"Listen to your grandma, Anna-banana," Charlie said. "There's been a lot going on, as you know," he said quietly to June.

"Even more reason to stick to routine," she murmured. "Children crave structure."

"June," Ed said from the backseat, "I think you've made your point. Anyway, I seem to recall that we weren't so big on structure ourselves when Alison was a little girl."

"Yeah," June snorted, "and look at what happened."

"June, please," Charlie said, motioning toward the kids.

"No blaming," Ed said. "We said we weren't going to do that. Remember?"

"I remember. I remember. This is not about blame. This is about helping this family get back to normal—if that's even possible."

Charlie shot her an annoyed glance. Did she have to do this in front of the kids?

"I'm thick! I'm thick!" Noah wailed, flailing in his car seat.

When they arrived home, Alison had gotten dressed and was in the kitchen, loading the dishwasher with cereal bowls from breakfast. Her parents dropped their bags and went over to hug her, and she collapsed into their arms. Charlie shuffled the children into the living room and put on a *Shrek* DVD; he knew that June would remark on it, but he

122

didn't care. He looked at his watch: 12:20. If he didn't take the next train into the city his entire workday would be lost. Already the client on his biggest account, the paper conglomerate PMRG, was leaving passive-aggressive messages on his voice mail: "Charles, I'm sure you're a busy man with other things to do, but the clock is ticking on this campaign. We need to hear from you. I tried to reach you by e-mail, but perhaps you haven't gotten my messages. If you can fit me into your schedule, I'd appreciate a call by the end of day today, thanks." When Charlie thought about it, his stomach clenched.

"I need to catch the next train," he said, coming into the kitchen.

"What?" said June. "You're leaving? Is it even worth it at this hour?"

"I've got a three o'clock meeting," he lied, then was immediately irritated at himself. Why should he lie? He had to go to work—he earned the money around here. It was as simple as that. Why did he suddenly feel like he was the one who'd done something wrong?

Alison looked at him blankly. Noah had come in and was whining for juice, sidling through her legs like a cat, but Alison didn't seem to notice. "When will you be home?" she asked.

Charlie looked at his watch. The gesture was a visual signifier; he knew what time it was. "Well, I may need to stay a few hours later," he said, calculating that he might be able to talk to Claire if he had some flexibility. Where was she? Somewhere in the South. All he wanted was to hear her voice, feel a brief connection. That would be enough for now. "I'm dealing with a major account." He turned to Ed, his only potential ally in the room, to explain. "As you might imagine, things have been—difficult here. I've had to take quite a bit of time off."

"I'm sure your colleagues are understanding, given the circumstances," June said.

In fact, Charlie hadn't told his colleagues. They might know about it, but the story hadn't come from him. On Wednesday, having taken off Monday and Tuesday with a supposed stomach flu, Charlie had gone into the office of the senior partner and shut the door. "My wife was in a bad accident," he said. "Someone ran a stop sign and plowed into

123

her car. She's all right, but a person in the other car didn't make it." He didn't reveal that that person was a child. He omitted mention of the police station, the blood-alcohol content, the question of culpability.

"That's terrible, Charles," Bill Trieste had gasped, coming around his desk and putting a hand on Charlie's shoulder. "Alison is all right, though?"

"All right. Shaken up."

"Of course, of course. My God. I'm sure she's needing your support right now."

"We'll get through it," Charlie said automatically. Later he would reflect on his bland responses to expressions of sympathy. We'll get through it. Would they? He wasn't at all sure.

"If you need to take some time off, just let me know," Bill said. "We can make arrangements for your accounts, if it comes to that."

"No, no," Charlie said hastily. The last thing he wanted was to be in the house all day, every day, with Alison. It was hard enough going home at night to face her—the weepy desperation in her eyes, her unspoken need for his absolution, as if he alone had the power to assuage her guilt. And the children, sensing her disconnection from them, were clingy and frantic. No, he didn't want to take time off. He would hire Dolores for more hours; Alison's parents would pitch in. The thought of becoming more enmeshed, just as he was beginning to disengage, made him flush with panic.

"She might want to talk to a grief counselor," Bill said. "I can get you a name, if you want it. When my wife's brother died, she saw this woman for a year, and I believe it helped her tremendously."

"Thanks. That's a good suggestion," Charlie said. He looked at Bill, a trim, handsome man in his late forties, and wondered what he and his wife had been through. As far as Charlie could remember, this was the first time Bill had ever even mentioned a wife.

"Well, listen, take all the time you need," Bill said, patting him on the back as he walked him to the door of his office.

"Thanks," Charlie said. "Bill, I'd appreciate it if you don't share this with anyone. Alison is a pretty private person, and I think she'd prefer to keep this quiet."

"Of course. I understand," Bill assured him.

Actually, Alison hadn't said anything to Charlie about keeping it quiet. He was the one who didn't want people to know. His wife had been drinking, and a small boy had died. A child—a boy like his boy—someone else's son: dead. It was inconceivable. If he had been driving, this wouldn't have happened, he was sure of it. He was more confident on the road, not to mention heavier; he would have absorbed the alcohol differently. Anyway, he wouldn't have drunk two gimmicky blue martinis.

But to go to Claire's party with Alison would have been unbearable.

Before the accident Charlie had wondered if it might be possible for things to continue as they were indefinitely; he and Claire could lead their separate lives and come together in a kind of biospheric space, outside the constraints of real life. Their relationship would exist beyond the realm of everyday concerns. Even at the time Charlie had known that this conceit was foolish; the delicate balance required to sustain such a precarious arrangement was bound to become upset. Either he or Claire would come to feel that it wasn't enough; Alison or Ben would find out. Eventually things would have to change. But now he felt like those prisoners of war he'd read about who were strapped, alive, to the dead bodies of their fallen comrades and thrown into the river. He was bound to Alison in a way that he hadn't been before—he was, or would have to be, the stalwart husband.

125

STANDING ON THE platform an hour later, waiting for the 1:17 train, Charlie pulled out his cell phone.

"Hey there, you," Claire said in a groggy voice.

"Oh God, did I wake you?"

"It's okay. I was napping," she said. "I had to get up at the crack of dawn for a morning show."

"Sorry. Where are you?"

He could hear the rustle of sheets, and he pictured her sitting up, turning on the bedside lamp in the hotel room. "Nashville. The weather is downright balmy. Flowers are blooming."

"How'd the reading go last night?"

"Fine. An old friend from college lives here, so she rustled up a crowd. Otherwise it would've been a homeless man and three old ladies who heard me on Tennessee Public Radio yesterday afternoon."

"How are you?" he asked, impatient with the details.

"Charlie, I'm fine. Fine, fine—it doesn't matter. The question is, how are *you*?"

He inhaled quietly, filling his lungs with the cool spring air. A mile or so away, at the other end of town, the warning horn of the train sounded as it pulled into the station. He should've called her sooner. In a minute the train would be here.

"Ahh. Not so great," he said. Leaving the house, he'd run into Alison's father in the kitchen, sitting at the table eating a tuna sandwich and reading the *Times*. Charlie had said a quick hello and ducked back into the hall to get his laptop bag, but Ed got up and stood in the doorway with his glass of milk.

"I know this is tough," Ed said. "Maybe as tough as it gets."

Charlie had nodded, gathering his keys, BlackBerry, silver iPod from the bowl on the hall table and putting them in various pockets in his bag. "I'm glad you're here, Ed," he said, and he meant it. Charlie liked Ed, liked his quirky sensibility and mild good humor. Ed was the one who constructed elaborate train tracks for Noah, using every odd piece of the Thomas the Tank Engine track that had been collected over the years. During his previous visit, he had made Annie a set of fairy wings out of coat hangers and pink mesh, and took both children to the local museum and ice cream shop for the afternoon. Ed was curious about Charlie's work, in an anthropological way, and sent him books on Thomas Jefferson, in whom they shared an interest—books that Charlie rarely got a chance to finish, but still. Charlie, in turn, had

126

walked Ed through his first computer purchase and set up his e-mail account, and then periodically e-mailed him newsworthy tidbits from the Internet he thought Ed might appreciate.

Charlie's feelings about Alison's mother were more complicated. He didn't like her much, and it wasn't just because he found her self-absorbed and grandiose. June was tuned in to him in a way that made him uncomfortable. She, alone among her husband and daughter, seemed to have sensed from the beginning that Charlie was not entirely engaged, that he had always been, on some level, distracted, even when he didn't yet know it himself. She seemed to be constantly watching him. For a long time he thought it was unfair. He complained to Alison that he didn't think he'd ever be able to please her mother, that she expected the worst from him. "That's nonsense, she thinks you're wonderful," Alison had said (smoothing things over as usual, ignoring the obvious, making peace). Now it occurred to Charlie that June's suspicions—that he was not devoted enough, involved enough with his fledgling family—were in fact dead-on. Perhaps she understood him in a way that no one else did. Ed's generous spirit and Alison's willful denial had kept both of them in the dark. June alone saw him as he really was.

Standing at the station, with Claire on the phone, Charlie looked down the tracks to the train, some distance away, speeding toward the platform. Commuters were folding newspapers, snapping shut cell phones, rummaging for train passes. The whistle sounded, a low, sonorous noise that seemed to hang in the air.

"I can't stop thinking about what happened—how terrible it is," Claire said. "Alison never called me back, and I don't want to bug her. But—"

"She's not calling anybody right now."

"I just want her to know—oh, shit. I guess it doesn't matter."

"No, it does. It matters," he said, not paying attention to the words, trying to put an end to the topic. Charlie didn't want to talk about Alison with Claire. The only way he was getting through this was by keeping the two of them separate in his mind.

127

"I feel like this is my fault . . . ridiculous blue martinis . . . and to tell you the truth I was kind of avoiding her; it just felt—well, you know, we hadn't spoken in a while . . . that dumb article . . . if I'd been more welcoming—if I'd thought about how she might feel . . . And this damn book . . . I know she feels betrayed . . . And *you*. Jesus, Charlie— you. . . ."

Every other word she said was drowned out by the train as it pulled into the station, and Charlie shut his eyes, relieved by the intrusion. "The train's here," he said. Now he felt irritated by Claire—her self-absorption was getting on his nerves. He had forgotten this about her, or maybe he just hadn't noticed lately, overwhelmed as he was by other, more primal concerns: the firm weight of her breasts in his hands, the curve of her naked hip. . . .

"God, I'm a narcissist." It was almost as if she was reading his mind.

"No," he said, stepping on the train and finding a seat. He couldn't bear to reassure her; it was hard enough responding to Alison. And he had his own guilt to deal with, even as he dreamed of escape . . . the baby-soft skin of her inner thigh . . . waited for Claire to return from her book tour.

Or maybe—maybe—could he go to her?

He handed his monthly pass to the conductor, awkwardly cradling the flat phone against his jaw. "Where will you be on Monday?" he asked Claire, nodding at the conductor as he passed.

"Umm . . . Atlanta, I think," she said.

Charlie took a deep breath. "How would you like company for a night?"

"Are you serious? How could you?"

"Her parents are here," he said, finding the pronoun easier than Alison's name. "They're staying for five or six days. Maybe these new clients of mine need some hand-holding."

"Oh, yes," she said. "They do need hand-holding. Come."

May 1998

On a clear Friday evening at seven, the moon a faint night-light in the sky, Charlie locked his bike to the stair rail and pushed the doorbell at Claire and Ben's house. A slim woman opened the door. Her back was half-turned to him, and she was in the middle of a sentence. "I'm sorry," she said, turning back. "You must be Charlie. I'm Alison."

She held out her hand for him to take. It was small and cool, her grip surprisingly strong. Her large eyes were chestnut colored, and her hair was straight and dark brown. She had clear skin and a wide mouth, almost too wide for her face. Her ass, in faded Levi's, was, he noticed, small and firm. "Ben's in there cooking snails, of all things," she said, and now Charlie could detect her soft southern accent, more pronounced than Claire's. She shook her head. "I don't know what this country is doing to you people."

"Turning us into snobs and pedants and raging Europhiles," Charlie said. "It's the Brits' revenge on us for defecting two hundred fifty years ago."

She laughed. "Then I suppose you'll want a sherry."

He followed her inside, where Ben was chopping garlic on a tiny board with a tiny knife, hunched over it like a dressmaker.

"I brought some hard stuff," Charlie said, holding up a paper bag.

"What is it?" Ben paused, looking up, while Charlie

unsheathed a bottle of Dalwhinnie. "'A superior Highland Scotch,'" Ben read off the label. "Ex-cellent. Let the wild rumpus start," and went back to chopping.

Charlie felt a glow of pleasure at having pleased the notoriously exacting Ben. "You, too?" he said to Alison.

She wrinkled her nose, hesitating, and then said, "When in Rome, I suppose," with a shrug.

Opening the cabinet, Charlie found four mismatched glasses and took them down. "And Claire?"

"Better not," Ben said. "I don't know when she'll be back."

"Isn't she coming?"

"Don't know." Ben didn't look up.

Charlie glanced at Alison questioningly. She raised her eyebrows but didn't say anything. They both watched Ben throw the garlic in a pan with some butter. "Almost done," he said, stirring the sizzling beads with a wooden spoon. "Then we can sit down for a few minutes and enjoy that Scotch."

"Straight up, or rocks?" Charlie asked, going to the freezer.

"Straight up. Always straight up," Ben said.

"Bartender's choice," said Alison, smiling.

"Umm—I'll give you rocks," Charlie said. "You might want the water if you nurse this all night."

"Sorry, I'm a total flyweight," she said. "My college experience consisted of keg beer and Sutter Home. And the occasional Sunday morning Bloody Mary."

"Wow, that sounds familiar. Where did you go?" Charlie asked, remembering that Claire had filled him in on Alison's vital statistics, and wishing he'd paid better attention.

"Chapel Hill. University of North Carolina."

"I know what Chapel Hill is." Charlie grinned. "It's practically Ivy."

"So they insist," she said. "And you're from Kansas. Lawrence, right? I've heard it's a great college town."

"Yeah, it's this bizarre oasis. Albeit with a Wal-Mart the size of Delaware."

"How does this compare?" she asked, gesturing vaguely toward Ben, or perhaps toward the university beyond him.

"It doesn't. A whole other world." He handed her a drink, ice clinking in the glass, and looked in her eyes. They were darker now, lively and warm. I could do this, he thought. He wondered, fleetingly, if Claire had stayed away on purpose, to give Alison a fighting chance.

"All right." Ben turned the flame down to low and lifted his Scotch. "Cheers. Here's to public education." He clinked their glasses with his own.

Claire did show up around ten o'clock, after the snails and the salad and the pan-fried trout with a cornmeal crust that Alison had prepared while Ben and Charlie stood around the stove. They were well into the Dalwhinnie at that point, Ben having decided after a few drinks that it would be foolhardy to switch. When Claire walked in, Ben was standing on the table, singing, "I'm just a little black rain cloud," and doing a fair imitation of Winnie-the-Pooh.

131

"Hello," she said coolly.

Ben looked at Charlie. "I say, Piglet. I believe we're in for some stormy weather."

She stared at them for a moment. Then she dropped the bag of books she was carrying and went into the bedroom, shutting the door behind her.

Ben stepped off the table and sank into a chair. He crossed his long limbs, bent and unbent like a grasshopper. His fingers skimmed the tablecloth, tapped his plate, retracted, unfolded. Candlelight flickered on his glasses.

Charlie glanced at Alison, and she glanced back at him.

"Am I the only one who doesn't know what's going on?" he said, forcing a small laugh.

In a soft voice, Ben finished his song. "I'm just float-ing a-round, o-ver the ground, won-der-ing where I will drip."

"So what do you think?" Claire asked Charlie the next day. They were sitting at opposite ends of the living room couch, sipping tea. Ben had gotten up early to attend a Saturday morning lecture a prominent architect was giving at the museum, and Alison had decided at the last minute to ac-company him.

"Of your going AWOL?" The evening had ended with Alison claiming exhaustion and going to bed, and Ben and Charlie finishing the Scotch in silence with the lights off, watching the red-hot coils of the electric heater in the living room. Charlie had slept on the couch. Claire stayed in her room. He was hoping that now she might tell him what was going on.

"God." She shook her head. "No, of Alison."

"I'm more interested in you, at the moment."

"I'm interested in what you think of Alison."

"I'll tell you if you tell me."

"You're impossible," she said, throwing a pillow at him.

He ducked, lifting his cup. "You're the one who didn't show up last night."

"You seemed to do fine without me."

"Come on, Claire."

She took a long sip of tea. "Maybe I was jealous," she said.

"What?" Charlie said incredulously.

"Maybe," she said.

His heart leapt a little and then, just as quickly, sank. It made no sense. "You're the one with the boyfriend. Excuse me, fiancé. And you—you set me up with Alison. She's your friend."

"I know," she said. "But maybe I decided I didn't want to share you." She set down her cup and put her hands over her eyes. "I'm being a baby. Alison is my best friend, and you—you're my closest friend here, besides Ben, of course, and I just realized that if you and Alison got together I'd lose both of you. You'd become obsessed with each other."

"Aren't you moving a little fast? I just met the girl last night. I don't even know if she likes me."

"She does," Claire said matter-of-factly.

"How do you know?"

"I just do. That's why I set you up. I knew she'd like you, and you'd probably like her." She pushed his leg with her bare foot. "So do you?"

"You're a mindfuck, Claire," Charlie said.

She gazed at him for a long time, and he stared steadily back at her. It was the first time they'd looked in each other's eyes, and Charlie refused to look away. What had she just said? That she was jealous, that she wanted him for herself. Did she really mean it? He feared that if he didn't seize this moment it would slip past him like so many others. He had a habit of not taking seriously the choices that were laid in front of him, or perhaps not recognizing their magnitude until too late.

Finally she said, "I love Ben."

"I know," he said.

"He's good for me."

"I know."

"I wish. . . ." She sighed. "I wish I could live two lives."

Charlie shrugged, feeling the weight of rejection pressing on his chest, though until that moment he hadn't imagined that she would ever see it that way—as a choice between him and Ben. "I—"

133

She reached over and put the flat of her hand against his lips. "Don't," she said, and sank back into her corner of the couch. "Don't say anything. I want everything to be the way it was."

He looked at her for a long moment, trying to gauge whether to pursue it. *What are you really saying?* This was the kind of question you didn't ask, or at least that Charlie didn't ask. Midwestern circumspection had been bred in him too well. You accepted what people told you about themselves, even when you knew there was more to the story. You respected their desire to reveal only what they were comfortable with, comfort being the ruling principle.

"Okay," he said.

They sat there for a few minutes, listening to the Bach concerto playing on the portable cassette player in the corner, the ticking of the wind-up clock in the kitchen, the muffled whoosh of cars going by in the rain. Claire seemed closed again, determinedly friendly and distant.

"I like her," he said eventually. "She seems nice. Maybe a little naïve?"

"A little," Claire said. "That's not necessarily a bad thing, you know. Haven't you read Henry James?"

"No," he admitted.

"Well, you should," she said. "Alison is a classic Henry James heroine."

Later, after the rain subsided, Charlie stepped out the back door onto the uneven concrete patio and looked up at the sky, white as skim milk. Trees, heavy with rain, shook their sodden leaves in the wind. He would have liked to see this break in the weather as an omen, but he was finished with omens for now.

Standing at a podium in a small independent bookstore in Raleigh, North Carolina, Claire looked out at the sparse collection of people scattered across the rows of folding chairs, and opened her book to a Post-it-marked page. "Thank you all for coming," she said. "I'm just going to read a few short sections. Then we can talk." She smiled nervously and began:

Emma's college roommate was a girl named Colleen who met her boyfriend, Steve, on the first day of freshman orientation. On a rare evening when Steve wasn't around, Emma asked Colleen how she knew so early that he was the one she wanted to spend the rest of her life with.

"What gave you that idea?" Colleen asked.

"Well, you spend every waking minute with him," Emma said. "Not to mention sleeping. I just figured."

"Look," Colleen said. "I met Steve in the dining hall and we hit it off. We're both pre-med, we run cross-country—we've got a lot in common. But what if I'd taken a year off before college? What if I'd gone to a different school? Well, I know what. I would've met a different Steve. You know—a nice, smart guy who's ambitious enough but a little shy, who's looking for a girlfriend to make him feel secure. There are probably hundreds of them out there—maybe thousands! It all comes down to timing and circumstance. If I had been born in a different town, or a different country—or, for that matter, a different decade—there's no doubt in my mind I'd find the Steve I need."

At the time Emma found Colleen's philosophy shocking, and then, for a while, she was inclined to agree. But experience taught her something else. She came to believe that there was such a thing as true love, and that it was the most important thing in the world—more important than kindness or constancy, more important even than trust.

The reading went pretty well, given that two members of the Raleigh audience appeared to be mentally ill, three were distantly related to Martha Belle Clancy, two were bookstore employees, and one was the media escort. The four remaining people—"civilians," as Suzy, the store clerk, called the audience members who attended out of genuine interest, not obligation or happenstance—had read a review or heard Claire earlier in the day on the radio, or, as one of them told her, stumbled across the novel on Amazon.com, where for a brief cyber-moment it had been a featured selection.

Back in her hotel room later that evening, Claire lay in bed, thinking about how strange it was that she had written those lines more than a year ago. She thought of Ben, of his dark hair slick after a shower, his crisp Thomas Pink shirts and beautiful hands, his attention to detail, his kindness. She thought of him sautéing scallops for dinner, pouring her a glass of wine, saving an article in the *Times* he thought she'd like.

Falling in love with Ben had been easy. Claire was captivated by his intelligence and humor; he was unlike anyone she had ever met. She knew plenty of southern boys with smooth moves and social skills and even, perhaps, brains, but she'd never met anyone with Ben's mordant, deeply sardonic take on life. And he was kind. From the beginning, Ben wanted to protect her, take care of her, send her out into the world with a better sense of who she was—or rather, a sense of her better self.

"I'm not as good as you think I am," she told him once.

"You're not as bad as you think you are, either."

136

"Is that a challenge?"

He looked at her sharply. "I'm not your father."

I'm not your father. Recently Claire had told her therapist about a time when she was eight, skipping rope in the driveway, chanting a song to herself, waiting for her father to get home from work. When he pulled up in his blue Chevy wagon, the first thing he said was, "For Chrissakes, Claire, stop yowling."

She didn't miss a beat. "I'm not yowling, Daddy. I'm singing."

"Well, pipe down. You're bothering the neighbors. And you're filthy," he'd said. "I'll expect you to change that dress before dinner."

His words stung, and she let the jump rope go slack. It was the last time she would ever wait for him after work.

"That's some powerful shame," Dina said.

Ben was the first man Claire had ever met who didn't make her feel neurotic. He told her he loved her energy, her passion and intelligence. For a while it made her doubt him all the more. "I can't be the person you're telling me I am," she'd say. "I'll go crazy if I have to be the person you want me to be."

"I don't want you to be anything. Except yourself."

"What if I don't know who that is?"

It wasn't like Claire had fallen out of love with Ben, she realized. It was more like she had drifted, the way you do on a plastic float in a pool with your eyes closed, moving away from the edge without realizing it. Some minute shift had occurred deep within her, and it altered the way she looked at everything. The peace they shared became interminable. Scrabble bored her; her sleep became restless. It was like waking from amnesia, or some epic dream; her head felt clear for the first time since she could remember. Ben didn't take it seriously, thought it was the miscarriage; a mood, or a phase, part of the natural ebb and flow of their relationship. But Claire knew this was different—something had changed. She had changed. And the life they shared would never look the same to her again.

As she lay in that hotel room bed, staring at the ceiling, a coil of

137

questions unfurled in her head. What kind of happiness is possible? Is it worth risking what I have? What would I give up; what would I gain? She wished she had a crystal ball that would reveal the shape of the years to come—that would tell her what to do. Then she was ashamed of her conventionality, her parochial need for direction. Wasn't that what she had to overcome? That there was no clear path was precisely the point.

And yet . . . she worried about money, worried about the future; she could feel the minutes ticking by. It was as if time had started up again, after years at a standstill. When it seemed that she would be with Ben for the rest of her life, the passing of time had felt fluid, unimportant. But now, suddenly, she was exposed to the possibilities and limitations of a different kind of life.

THE NEXT MORNING, Claire was up at seven. She was supposed to meet the local media escort in the lobby of the Hampton Inn in forty-five minutes. According to the faxed itinerary she'd picked up at the front desk when she checked in the night before, they had a full day planned—two local radio interviews, a lunch interview with the Raleigh *News & Observer*, an interview with the book editor of the UNC campus newspaper. She was also supposed to drop by some of the chain stores to sign piles of books set aside by the managers. These signings were always a little humbling; stores couldn't return autographed books, so the manager calculated sales potential before presenting a writer with a pile of books. Sometimes Claire signed ten, sometimes fifteen, occasionally a discouraging three. The media escort—in Claire's experience, either a nice older woman or a young gay man who'd driven more glamorous and exciting writers around in the past month and was dying to dish every detail—would be chatty and charming, and she was expected to be the same. When an interview didn't work out or if only four people showed up at a reading, Claire felt guilty, as if she'd let the escort down or wasn't worth the trouble.

After a few interviews and signings, she realized that she was being asked the same questions over and over: How much of this novel is based on your life? Was your mother an alcoholic? What do your parents think of the book? Now and then there'd be an interviewer, usually from a local National Public Radio station, who had actually read the book and asked questions that were a pleasure to answer, about the writing process, structural decisions, themes or connections that Claire might not even have been aware of herself. But these were rare. More often, she felt that she was running an obstacle course, trying to avoid pitfalls without making a fool of herself, or of the person who asked the question.

As the tour progressed, she'd begun to sense that the serendipitous things that happen to some authors—splashy reviews in national publications, the public endorsement of the book by a celebrity writer (or any type of celebrity, for that matter), some kind of controversy, a Zeitgeisty appeal that tapped into a general feeling or national mood—weren't happening to her, though nobody would tell her that directly. The cognitive dissonance of this experience—the need to promote the book by conveying a sense of its popularity (Dreamworks! *Entertainment Weekly*!) while getting the distinct impression that this popularity was artificially hyped—was unsettling. It was hard to discern what was real and what was propaganda, and perhaps even harder because she wasn't sure she really wanted to know.

She called Jami, back in New York, for a reality check, and got a party line instead—"Everyone's really happy with the book! National reviews don't matter, it's the local reviews people read! And besides, your book is all over the Internet. It's still early, relax!" But she knew it wasn't really true. First novels have the shelf life of Wonder Bread, and what she was beginning to understand was that for most books the sell-by date was actually the publication date. The important time was before that, when bookstores placed their orders and long-lead glossy magazines decided whether your book was worth ink. Buzz was created then. If not, the publisher picked up and moved on to the next promising first novel. Unless a book got a lucky break, it was old news a month after it came out.

It had been three weeks since the publication date. There were two national reviews, in *People* and *Entertainment Weekly*; the *New York Times* hadn't bothered. The southern papers were enthusiastic; they ran profiles and reviews and included Claire's book in roundups with other first novelists writing about the South. Bluestone didn't have an independent bookstore, but there was a Borders, with a Starbucks, no less, the next town over. The book had been featured in the *Bluestone Record*—a profile and review, side by side, with a big publicity photo of Claire and flattering references to Bluestone's "hometown girl." The profile was little more than a whitewashed account of Claire's years in Bluestone and a verbatim recitation of the half-truths and puffery of her publicity release. The review, on the other hand, by a snarky former high school classmate, was full of insinuations about her motives, cast in a dimly positive light. It was clear that the reviewer had been told she needed to be nice but couldn't resist getting in a few jabs: "One wonders why Ms. Ellis felt the need to confirm northern liberals' stereotypes of southerners. Just for the record, not every southern matron is an alcoholic, and not every southern teenage girl is a rebellious slut. But despite the novel's weaknesses. . . ."

Claire had been on the radio, three different stations, the morning of her homecoming, and she'd spoken at the high school, a semi-honest testament to the instruction she'd received there that enabled her to excel, get out, move to New York, and write a book about her hometown. Many of the students were curious about meeting someone who'd grown up in Bluestone and actually left; a few, seeing in her the idealized fulfillment of their own longing, hung on her every word. It was flattering. Claire felt famous, for once. These students didn't ask her to explain why she'd called Bluestone—Hatfield, in the book—a "small, dying mill town," or any of the other mildly critical descriptions in the book of the town's landscape or social milieu. The hypocrisy and racism she'd depicted, the inclusion of which some of her mother's friends found deeply offensive, came across to these kids as an interesting history lesson.

Claire had sent her mother a copy of the galleys months earlier, after scrawling a lighthearted disclaimer on the title page—"Remember, Mother, it's a *novel!*" —but all Lucinda ever said about it was, "You always did have a peculiar way of looking at things," and "It's probably just as well your father isn't around to see what you have to say about him." At the book party in New York, Lucinda had seemed flattered by the attention people paid her, even as the ones who'd actually read the book lingered on her face a little too long (searching for signs of melancholy or perhaps the Alzheimer's that, as Claire had written, ran in the family) or scrutinized her now-veiny hands (at sixteen she'd been a hand model for Joy dishwashing liquid).

They never discussed the specific incidents that Claire had dredged out of the well of her past and laid to dry on the exposed pages of her book—the time her father had hit her mother across the face and Claire called 911; the time Lucinda had gotten sloshed on those blue martinis and went skinny-dipping in a neighbor's pool with a golfing buddy of her husband's; the time Lucinda walked in on Claire, at seventeen, having sex in the master bedroom with a minor league baseball player she'd met at a bar. It was as if Lucinda had decided that Claire was a sculptor and she'd created a book that was just a physical object—with its sturdy spine and splashy cover and sans serif typeface—and not what was inside.

Actually, the book was beginning to seem like an object to Claire, too. When she was writing it she couldn't imagine how she would ever talk about it. Even fictionalized, the revelations felt so intensely personal that she had to pretend to herself that she was writing in a journal; otherwise she'd never have said the things she did. But now that these moments from her life were contained in discrete, tidy chapters, she felt like any salesperson shilling a product. In interviews she said the same things over and over, wavering between candor and subterfuge. She acknowledged painful secrets as if they were someone else's.

And in some ways it felt as if they were—not her secrets anymore, just stories she'd overheard or read or seen on TV.

About a hundred people from Bluestone showed up at the Borders reading that night, an exponentially larger number than Claire had drawn anywhere else. Her mother was there with her sidekick, Martha Belle, and again Claire was struck by the power of her mother's denial, her steadfast desire to see the book as a thing, a product, rather than the sardonic, barely disguised recollections of a still-wounded daughter. As people filed in, Lucinda situated herself by Claire's side at the front, greeting friends with the benevolent smile of a proud grandparent: "Come see the baby!" She ignored curious looks and answered insinuating questions with bland responses: "I raised her to have her own opinions," Lucinda said to anyone who would listen, and, "She's been her own boss since she was three years old."

For a lot of reasons, Claire was nervous. There'd be people in the audience who appeared, in one guise or another, in her book; they might have reason to be hostile. Since leaving home for college, Claire had returned as infrequently as possible. When her parents' marriage dissolved and her father, at the age of fifty-five, married a local woman two years older than Claire and had another child, Claire had been aghast and her mother devastated. Claire had had little contact with her father in the past decade; they exchanged Christmas cards, and on the few occasions Claire had visited her mother in Bluestone she had dutifully spent several awkward afternoons with him and his new wife, Mandy, and their daughter Brianna, Claire's half-sister.

Claire felt fairly certain that her father wouldn't come that evening, and as she scanned the crowd she was sure she'd been right. Only after the reading was over—three carefully chosen, self-deprecating passages that touched on nothing more serious than the death of a pet guinea pig and her capricious destruction of her mother's prize flower bed (an incident she depicted with far more frivolity than it had occasioned at the time)—did Claire look up and see her father standing alone at the back, a tall man with distinguished gray hair, his impassive expression a bracing shock above the indulgent smiles of the audience she had charmed, clapping politely in their seats.

When the inevitable question arose about her parents' response to the book, Claire gestured toward Lucinda, sitting with Martha Belle, and then to her father—but he was gone. Even as the question was being asked, he had slipped out.

AS THE QUESTION-AND-ANSWER period was winding down, a balding, paunchy, vaguely familiar man in a red windbreaker stood up.

"Hey, Claire, don't know if you remember me. I was in the class behind you at Bluestone High. Terry Shaw. How're you doing." He held his hand shyly in a half-wave, hitched up his pants, and cleared his throat. "Just wondering what 'Jill' thinks about all this."

Claire had known that she might get a question like this, but somehow it caught her off guard. She took a breath. "Well," she said, "this book is a novel, which means, as you know, that the characters are made up. Some are composites, so you might recognize bits of people here and there. But Jill isn't based on any one specific person." Cool it, she thought; you're lecturing—and worse, you sound defensive. Anyway, Terry didn't look convinced. Claire saw him raise his eyebrows at someone a few rows over. She smiled weakly. "Next question?"

Terry raised a half-curled index finger. "She sure seems a lot like Alison Gray."

Claire felt her chest constrict. It was hard to breathe. "Really?" she squeaked. "Huh, that's interesting. Maybe a little, I guess."

Alison. Claire didn't know what she thought of her book. She didn't even know if she'd read it. And now it didn't matter, did it? Real life had taken precedence, relegating Claire's small book to an appropriately minor place in Alison's mind. If she thought of it at all.

143

May 1998

When Alison opened the door at 32 Barton Road to find
Charlie standing there, the first thing she noticed was his
blond wavy hair. The second was that he looked unabashedly American, tan and robust, with a white T-shirt under
his frayed oxford, sleeves rolled to the elbows. His shoulders were broad, though he was quite thin, and his face
was a little soft, as if he hadn't outgrown the last traces of
baby fat. His eyebrows were blond caterpillars over light
blue eyes.

145

At dinner that night she watched him. He and Ben were
a study in contrasts: Ben lanky and angular and slightly
awkward, with his glasses and dark hair and air of sup-
pressed whimsy, Charlie as loose-limbed and sandy haired
as a golden retriever. Right away she was suspicious: easy
charm like his tended to come wrapped around a roguish
core. This M.O. was prevalent in southerners of a certain
type—affluent, entitled, fraternity bred—and it wasn't a type
she usually went for. But as they started talking she realized that there was something else, something in his character that she couldn't pin down. He wasn't cocky, and his
humor was gentle. He had a mild confidence, a lack of self-
consciousness, an ironic take on the world that wasn't caus-
tic or bitter. Despite his social ease, he had a solitary air.

At one point, when Ben was gesturing animatedly, Charlie leaned back in his chair, laughing, and caught Alison's eye. She knew he'd seen her studying him.

"What?" he said, an expectant half smile on his face. It was an expression she would come to know well—seemingly guileless, more guarded than it appeared.

"Nothing," she said.

"Tell me."

He seemed familiar to her, like a fond memory or a recurring dream. "I feel like I've met you somewhere before."

"Ever been to Kansas?" he asked jokingly.

"He's like that, Alison," Ben said. "Not just with you. He has this protean face, or something—I don't know. It's misleading. You think you know him and then you make assumptions about his likes and dislikes, and more times than not you're wrong; you've misjudged him. It's bloody annoying."

"I don't know what he's talking about," Charlie said.

146

Falling in love with Charlie was like traveling to a foreign country and feeling unexpectedly at home. It surprised Alison to discover that he didn't wear deodorant; he showered every day and that was enough, he said, and it was. He had a clean midwestern smell, as sweet as hay. He didn't like pills or lotions or creams; he washed his face once a day, in the shower, with shampoo. He toweled off quickly, like a dog shaking off after running through a sprinkler. Like a dog, too, he was refreshingly unneurotic—he ate what he liked until he was full, and then he stopped; he worked on a paper until he decided he was done, and then he put it aside. He didn't second-guess everything. He once told Alison that he couldn't remember being picked on as a kid. She imagined that he had been raised like an ear of corn in a big field out there in Kansas, ripening on the stalk until he was ready to leave.

From the first time Alison touched him, Charlie's skin was a welcoming place—a warm place, a refuge. It smelled familiar, like her own skin or the skin of a child she might someday give birth to. Falling in love with Charlie was as easy as breathing. Years later, when he started to pull away and Alison finally, stupidly, belatedly, realized that something was wrong, it was still incomprehensible to her that they might ever be separate, that a time would come when his sandpapery face and sinewy arms would be off-limits.

At Cambridge Charlie had studied the early church philosopher Augustine, who believed that although true happiness is possible, most people will never experience it. You cannot be happy if you don't possess what you love—or, possessing it, you realize that it is bad or harmful—or if you don't love what you have, no matter how objectively good it is. True happiness exists only when you have what you love, and when what you love is good for you.

Charlie believed he was in love with Alison when he married her—even if it was clear to him later that what he thought was love was nothing like true happiness, not the barest shadow of it. He saw Claire's delight in Alison's smile, the sparkle in their eyes when they told a story together, their habit of finishing each other's sentences like sisters. The truth was, he had such strong feelings for Claire that he didn't know what to do with them. Sharing some of them with Alison seemed as reasonable a strategy as any. For a time this transfer of emotion was effective enough to fool both of them into thinking that it might be theirs alone.

But in the past few months, since reconnecting with Claire, Charlie had begun to recapture the way he felt at Cambridge. He didn't know what it was, exactly, only that it was transformative. The boredom, his sense of going through the motions—all of that had dissipated.

WHEN CHARLIE GOT home from work that evening, June was in the kitchen, chopping organic vegetables for a stir-fry he knew the kids wouldn't eat.

"You're home early," she said with surprise when he opened the back door.

Having booked an e-ticket to Atlanta for Monday afternoon, Charlie had taken Bill Trieste up on his offer and shunted his biggest account, with its irksome client, off on a colleague. Then he took an earlier train home than he'd said he would. Now that he had a plan, he felt a surge of warm feelings toward Alison and her parents that was directly proportional to the guilt he felt for leaving, the anxiety he felt about lying to them, and the fear that his plan might somehow be foiled. "I wanted to get home as soon as I could. How is she?" He gestured vaguely upward.

June, chopping bok choy, lifted her shoulders slightly. "She's not in bed, at least. She's in the playroom with Ed and Annie."

"How are her spirits?"

"Hard to tell." She stopped chopping and held the knife aloft in apparent contemplation. "I don't think this is the kind of thing you can get over easily. Not if you're Alison, at least. She's going to need a lot of support—a *lot*—in the next few months. Years, maybe."

Charlie nodded, shrugging off his coat. He felt as if she'd gently slipped the knife under his skin. His conversations with June had always seemed this way to him, with the subtext italicized and partially exposed. You don't fool me. We both know that you are absent here, disengaged. You need to change your attitude.

"We're looking for a good therapist," he said, which wasn't exactly true. Dr. Waldron had given Alison some names, but the blue prescription slip with the contact information was somewhere in a pile of receipts and business cards on Charlie's dresser.

"That's a start, but I'm really talking about what Alison needs from you," June said, spelling it out in case he hadn't gotten it.

Charlie turned and hung his jacket on a hook in the hall, then came back into the kitchen. "I know. It's going to be a long road," he said, striving for a bland metaphor to close the conversation and realizing too late that it was exactly wrong.

"Well," June said briskly, "that's not how I would have put it, but yes." Gesturing toward the pile of vegetables under her knife, she said, "I thought it might be time to introduce the children to something a little more interesting than baby carrots and frozen corn."

"Good luck," Charlie said. "What's the backup plan?"

He found Alison sprawled on the floor of the playroom with Ed and Annie, watching them build a castle out of blocks. "Hi," she said, looking up with a wan smile. "I heard you come in."

"I was talking to your mother," Charlie said, kissing Annie on the top of the head and squeezing Alison's shoulder, then sinking down beside her. "Why haven't the kids eaten yet?"

"We had a late lunch. Mom wants us all to eat together tonight."

He raised his eyebrows at her. "It looks like nuggets are off the menu. You sure this is going to fly?"

"They can have toast, if it comes to that," Alison said. "Bless her for trying, right?"

Charlie knew Alison was peacemaking; she was probably as skeptical as he was. The seething indignation he'd felt at June's bullying insistence on what their kids should eat melted away. Alison was right—her mother meant well. Peace, love. Warm feelings, remember?

151

"How go the crusades? Doth the enemy lie vanquished?" Ed asked Charlie. He sat up, crowning a pile of blocks with a conical turret. Having worked in education all his life, Ed made no secret of his disdain for and utter ignorance of corporate America. It wasn't personal, and Charlie didn't take offense. Ed tended to equate working for a corporation—any corporation—with going to war, and Charlie had to admit that he wasn't half wrong.

"The enemy lies, yet is not vanquished," Charlie said, playing along. "But it appears that I have been summoned to the king's court."

Alison pulled herself up to a sitting position. "What do you mean?"

Charlie winced exaggeratedly, trying to convey his own displeasure at this news and his awareness of hers to come. "I need to meet with the client next week," he said. "They're feeling undervalued."

"When?"

"Tuesday morning. Which means I have to fly out on Monday, I'm afraid."

"I thought they were in Philadelphia. Can't you just take an early morning train?"

Clearly, he'd told Alison more about PMRG than he'd remembered. "Ahh—their creative offices are in Chicago." Creative offices? Chicago? It made no sense, even to him. And now he'd have to be sure to keep his flight itinerary from her—and hell, what if she wanted the hotel number? "But, actually, they're on a company retreat in Atlanta, and they want me to go there." He shifted uncomfortably. His ears felt hot.

Ed rolled his eyes and shook his head—further confirmation, in his mind, of corporate waste and stupidity—but Alison just said, "Oh. When do you get back?"

"I'll get a flight that afternoon. I'll be home Tuesday evening. As soon as I can, honey." Three months ago it would have been unfathomable to Charlie that he could lie to his wife like this, with her father and their daughter listening in. The shocking thing was how easy it was, how readily their lifestyle accommodated his deception.

That night, after a predictably disastrous dinner, with Annie moaning about the unfamiliar vegetables and rudely shoving her plate to the middle of the table and Noah chewing bok choy and spitting it out in viscous lumps on his Blues Clues place mat, and then toast and bath time and five renditions of *The Very Hungry Caterpillar*, with Noah successively supplying more and more of the words, Charlie stood at the foot of the bed he shared with Alison, listening in the stillness to the sound of her crying through the bathroom door. The water was running and it was hard to hear, but occasional whimpers and the faint sounds of her sniffling confirmed his suspicions.

"Al," he said, leaning his forehead against the doorframe.

After a moment she said, "I'll be right out."

"Are you all right?"

He heard the faucet shut off. The door opened, and she said, "Yeah." She was wearing a lilac tank top and floral pajama bottoms, and her face was damp and pink. She sniffed and rubbed her nose with the back of her hand, like a child. Her ability to rally like this, to act resolute and self-possessed when she clearly wanted to fall apart, was a trait he'd always admired. One of the things that had attracted him to her at the start.

"Your parents are being helpful." He phrased this as a statement, not a question, to show Alison that he was giving them the benefit of the doubt.

"Mostly." She turned to pluck a sweater from the clothes piled on her dresser, shaking it out and folding it against her chest.

This was what passed for small talk between them these days— Charlie encouraging and slightly disingenuous, Alison only partly willing to play along.

"That stir-fry was actually pretty good. And it probably *is* reasonable every now and then to force the kids to deal with grown-up food, don't you think?"

She held another sweater against the length of her body, draping the sleeve along her own arm and then folding it across the sweater, as if she were teaching it to dance. After a moment Charlie realized she wasn't going to answer. He unbuttoned his shirt and took off his pants. He went to the closet and folded the pants on a hanger, then stuffed the shirt in a dry-cleaning bag that hung on a hook on the back of the door. In his white T-shirt and gray jersey shorts, he went into the bathroom to brush his teeth, leaving the door ajar.

153

"What time is your flight on Monday?" she asked.

He answered with a mouth full of toothpaste, and she went to the door. "What? I couldn't understand you."

"Midday," he said, spitting into the sink with a studied casualness. "I'll leave from work."

She nodded, went back to folding. When she was done she shut all the drawers of her dresser and the closet door. Then she sat on the bed, squirted Kiehl's lotion into her hand, and rubbed it into her hands, elbows, shins.

"I love that smell," he said, trying to fill the silence.

"It's unscented."

"That's just marketing. Everything has a scent." He sprawled on the bed behind her.

"Oh, you're an expert?"

"As a matter of fact."

She turned toward him, nudged him with her shoulder.

This was what passed for flirting between them these days.

He put his hand up the back of her T-shirt, and she leaned against him. It was the first time since the accident that she'd shown any interest in him at all.

She sank back farther, the full weight of her body on his, and he felt himself beginning to stir. He moved his hand around to her warm stomach and then higher, the stretchy fabric of her shirt tight against his knuckles as he spanned his fingers between her small breasts, then cupped each one. She arched her back, her neck against his cheek, and he kissed her jawbone, her chin, the corner of her mouth before she turned her head to his and kissed him full on the lips, her tongue already in his mouth.

154

The lights were on, two bedside lamps and one overhead, and the bed was still made. It was only nine o'clock. It had probably been years, Charlie thought, since they'd had sex like this, at this hour, with the lights on. The door wasn't even fully shut. Alison's parents were downstairs puttering around; Alison hadn't folded out the couch in the TV room for them yet, as she normally did each night. Annie was in bed, but probably not asleep.

These were the thoughts running through Charlie's mind as Alison slid her finger under the waistband of his shorts, slipped them down, pushed him back against the pillows. Straddling him, she took his nipple between her teeth, running her tongue back and forth over it as it stiffened, and he shut his eyes and tried not to think of anything at all.

Concentrate. Pure physical sensation.

Slowly she moved down his body, her breath hot on his stomach, and then, finally, took him in her mouth. He was hard now, and she ran her tongue up and down his length, brushed her lips across the head, put her whole mouth around him. Light-headed, he opened his eyes, winced at the brightness, saw his wife's silky dark hair spread out across his abdomen—her own eyes shut, her tongue curling around him—and closed them again. Now it was Claire's tongue encircling him, her hand moving up his flank, her wavy hair against his skin. . . .

Charlie reached down and held Alison under the arm, urging her up. "Let's fuck," he whispered.

"No," she said.

"I want to. I want to be inside you."

"No." She wouldn't look up.

"Alison—"

"I want you to come in my mouth."

Charlie was startled—though of course she'd gone down on him plenty of times over the years, as far as he could remember she'd never said those words before. It was vaguely unsettling: Was this some kind of self-flagellating impulse? Did she want to feel degraded? Did she feel him pulling away; was this a calculated gesture, a competitive move? Was she trying to control him? It might have been any of these things, or it might have been none. At that point, lying on the down comforter in a T-shirt and nothing else, Charlie decided he didn't much care.

He closed his eyes and consciously tried to relax, pushing away the images in his mind, concentrating only on the opaque orange light through his eyelids, a thick, glowing sea of light, warm as summer. As she sucked steadily he felt a gathering wave of pleasure, and then the stronger pull of an undertow, blood orange, bleeding into the orange of the wave. His body shuddered and stiffened; he stifled a groan, and then felt a sudden, dissipating release.

After a moment he looked down. Alison was wiping her mouth on a corner of her T-shirt. She laid her head against his thigh. Then she moved back up the bed toward him.

"That was amazing," he said, turning onto his side to make room.

"Umhh," she said.

155

He got up and shut the bedroom door, turned off the lights, then went to the bathroom. When he came back to bed she was curved away from him, her hair half covering her face, with her eyes closed.

He wanted to tell her that he loved her—it seemed like the right thing to say. *I love you* isn't much, he thought; it's just what a husband says to his wife in bed in the dark, an automatic reflex, an acknowledgment of the bond between them. It isn't like saying it for the first time to a girlfriend. It's a touchstone, tacitly understood and only spoken aloud out of a desire to connect.

A few weeks ago, putting Annie to bed, Charlie had said, "Do you know how much I love you?" and she looked him straight in the eye and said, "Yes, because you tell me all the time." Her lack of sentimentality had surprised him, and he wondered if she sensed that he'd said it automatically, almost glibly. Was the power of the phrase diminished through repetition?

Now, with Alison, he stayed quiet. In three days he was getting on a plane to Atlanta; by Monday night he'd be with Claire. He didn't want to make any promises that he couldn't keep.

May 1998

In modern society, Charlie wrote, *the psychoanalyst Erich Fromm contended, instinct, which guides us and keeps us safe, has been replaced by reason and imagination. At the same time that we have become more self-reliant, independent, and critical, we are also increasingly fearful, isolated, and alone. We have two alternatives, Fromm believed. We can use escape mechanisms such as authoritarianism and self-aggrandizement to try to reestablish the primary bonds, though these mechanisms will erase our individuality and integrity. Or we can try to relate to the world spontaneously and creatively.*

The phone rang in the hall Charlie shared with seven other expatriate grad students, a shrill, insistent British telecom tone that startled him out of his chair. He put down his pen and hurried out of his room onto the landing. "Hello?" he said into the heavy black receiver. He had to stand close to the phone box; the receiver was tethered to it by a short metal rope.

"It's Claire. What are you doing?"

Charlie was startled. He still wasn't used to her habit of forgoing pleasantries. "Uh—working on a paper. Erich Fromm."

"Wasn't he completely nuts?"

"Not completely," Charlie said. "Well, no more than the rest of them."

"I guess you have to be nuts to state the obvious as if it were the answer to the universe," Claire said.

"Or a genius," Charlie said. He tried to lean against

the wall but was yanked back by the cord. The landing was drafty, and he looked longingly at his open door and electric heater, its red coils visible from the hallway. "So what's up?"

"Are you free Friday evening?" she asked. "We want you to come to dinner."

Charlie had gotten used to the "we," though he was always disappointed when she used it. He suspected it was a way of keeping him at a safe distance. Even worse was when she would say *Ben thinks* or *Ben believes,* or when she expressed a tender feeling for him in the course of their conversation: *Ben is working so hard right now. I have to get back or Ben will worry.*

A few days earlier, standing in the mist on Grange Road, saying good-bye at a traffic light, Claire had suddenly reached out and held Charlie's arm. "I'm so glad you and Ben are friends," she said. "I like you both so much." It was at once a casual understatement of her feelings for Ben and, Charlie thought, a flattering revelation of her feelings for him. *Both so much.* That one phrase made him and Ben the same.

"I think I'm available," Charlie said now. He'd been going to their house for dinner once or twice a week—whenever they invited him—since they'd met. It was better than sitting in a long, formal row and eating boiled peas in the Downing College Hall, and it definitely beat what he could come up with in the cramped kitchen he shared with the other grad students. "What can I bring?"

"Just some grog," she said.

"How many people?"

"Four. You, me, Ben, and a friend of mine. Alison."

"Really?" He was surprised. Their dinner parties were usually large and riotous, peopled with all manner of boisterous Americans and tolerant Europeans.

"Alison is my best friend from home. From North Carolina. She's flying in on Thursday for a little visit. I don't want to overwhelm her."

"How did I make the short list?" Charlie asked, not so subtly seeking a compliment.

"Male, single, straight," she said without hesitation.

"Flattered."

"It's our good fortune that you also happen to be charming, intelligent, and handsome."

"Now you're just making nice."

"Whatever it takes," she said. "So you'll come?"

The truth was, he would have done anything for her. He would've hitchhiked to Siberia if she'd asked him to. To Charlie, reading Rossetti and Swinburne and Robert Browning for the first time, Claire seemed to have stepped out of the nineteenth century, with her translucent skin and full lips, the shapely curve of tummy and breasts under those tiny cashmere cardigans in olive greens and deep reds, her searching gaze and unpredictable smile and wild hair. The expression in her eyes was a peculiar mix of innocence and knowingness; her curves were babylike, and sometimes she seemed so guileless that he wanted instinctively to protect her. She was often late, and sometimes she didn't show up at all; if she did, she would be apologetic, usually bringing a peace offering of some kind—a coffee or Cadbury bar, with a long, involved story about where she'd been and why she was unable to tear herself away. It was frustrating to wait for her—all the more because he wanted desperately to be with her—but he never got the feeling that her lapses of civility were malicious, and he rarely got angry. He made allowances for Claire that he wouldn't have made for anyone else.

Claire was constantly introducing him to someone new

159

by saying, "Charlie, have you met my good friend so-and-so?" It was rare that he went somewhere she hadn't already been, or learned something about Cambridge that she hadn't already discovered. She knew the shortcuts, the back alleys, the restaurant that had half-price dinner specials on Tuesdays and the bakery where you could get free day-old muffins. They'd stroll through the outdoor mall downtown and she'd greet cross-dressers and vagrants, whom she knew from volunteering at the soup kitchen on weekends, like old friends. No matter how much she told him about herself, he never felt as if he had the whole story.

This is what it was: she surprised him. Whatever she did was different from what he would have done, or what he might have predicted. She could be formal one moment and irreverent, even crude, the next. She pulled a sweater over her head like a five-year-old, arms akimbo, hair snarling across her face. She laughed loudly and unabashedly at movies. One evening they got caught in a rainstorm coming back from a farmers' market and ran to wait it out under the sloping roof of a locked boathouse beside the Cam. Standing there, soaking wet, Claire looked him in the eye and slipped her seaweed-slick stockings off under her skirt. At the time Charlie couldn't tell whether it was flirtatious or ingenuous. It seemed simply impulsive, though her movements were graceful and adult.

"So. Alison and Charlie," Claire said a few days later, squeezing Ben's toe. It was late afternoon, and the three of them were in Claire and Ben's living room, ostensibly studying. Charlie was taking notes at the too-small desk in the corner, and Ben and Claire were reading on the couch. "What do you think? She likes the country-bumpkin type."

160

"That's because she's a country bumpkin," Ben said, not looking up from his book.

"She is not!" Claire said, sitting up. "She's not," she assured Charlie.

"Oh, it's fine to call me a bumpkin, but not her?" Charlie said.

"I'm not sure girls can be bumpkins," she mused. "Is there a female ending?"

"Bumpkiss," Ben said from behind his paperback. "Bumpkina."

"Anyway, she isn't one. She's quite cosmopolitan and lovely. Don't you think, Ben?"

"What?"

"That Alison is perfect for Charlie."

Ben looked over at Charlie, as if to assess his qualities, and then began reading aloud. " 'The man who desires something desires what is not available to him, and what he doesn't already have in his possession. And what he neither has nor himself is—that which he lacks—that is what he wants and desires.' "

"Oh, for God's sake. What is that?" Claire asked.

"Socrates. You know, Charlie, this philosophy is good stuff. It applies to architecture in the most interesting ways. Just think about the kinds of structures people get jazzed about."

"Yeah," Charlie said. "But surely you read all those ancient Greeks at Harvard."

"No, actually. I was pre-med for far too long. Chem labs and bio and physics—I never had time to study philosophy. Now I could read this stuff all day."

Charlie envied Ben's ability to immerse himself in a book as if it were as real as the world. Sometimes he'd find Ben studying in a library carrel deep in the stacks, his

161

head over his book, his whole body hunched forward in concentration. Ben rarely noticed his approach, even when he came from the front; when Charlie touched his shoulder he'd flinch, as if awakened from a deep sleep. He was interested in what he was interested in, without any sense that he should be more or less interested in anything else. He didn't seem to need to impress people with his knowledge, though he enjoyed sharing it. Charlie had the sense that Ben had been an unusual child, quiet and bookish and particular, and that someone—his mother, perhaps— had let him be that way without making him feel odd. He took himself seriously in ways that Charlie wasn't confident enough to do, and for that reason he could laugh at himself in ways that Charlie never could. Charlie was insecure; his sense of himself in the world was too precarious to make light of.

Ben kept a violin in a black case propped in the front hall, and sometimes he'd take it out and disappear upstairs into a bedroom to practice—first scales, and then a haunting series of melodies. Charlie had never learned to play an instrument (unless you counted the tambourine he was assigned in middle-school band), and Ben's obvious mastery was one more thing that impressed and intimidated him. Now and then, on a Friday night, Ben would take his violin to the White Horse Tavern, a pub on the edge of town, and play fiddle with a ragtag bunch of guys from Cambridge Tech. Charlie would tag along with Claire and a random collection of friends and strangers she'd pulled off the street. She'd sing along and drink Guinness and, after a while, get up and dance. Sometimes she'd be the only one up there, dancing in front of the band, her reddish brown hair backlit like a rock star's, wearing a long flowing skirt and a black tank top, her skin pearly under the strobe.

Now, sitting on the couch, Claire was quiet for a moment, twisting a strand of hair across her mouth and sucking on the end, one of several odd habits of hers that Charlie had tucked away in his mind for future contemplation. "Maybe Socrates was right," she said. "If Charlie is a hick and Alison is worldly, and the man who desires something desires that which he lacks—"

"She is rather pretty," Ben said to Charlie, closing his book. "But let's not oversell her, Claire. The girl has left North Carolina twice in her entire life; sharing an apartment in New York for six months hardly makes her worldly. And calling Charlie a hick is a bit low, isn't it? Particularly to his face."

"Oh, he doesn't mind, do you, Charlie?"

"I'd hate to hear what you call me behind my back," he said.

"Behind your back she raves about you," Ben said. "That's the funny thing about Claire—she's meaner as a friend than as a gossip."

"Stop," she said, waving her fingers at him. "All I meant is that I thought they'd get along."

"Anyone can get along with anyone, as long as they have decent manners," Ben said.

163

"Tell me a story," Noah said, settling deep into Alison's lap. His hair was damp from the bath, his plump cheeks flushed and warm. He was wearing his favorite footy pajamas, navy blue with an airplane embroidered on one side of his chest like a badge. Clutching Bankie, a ratty scrap of baby blanket with satin trim, he stuck his thumb in his mouth.

Alison knew she should try to break the thumb habit before he got much older. She also needed to curtail warm milk at bedtime, Noah's tendency to creep into their bed in the middle of the night, his insistence on having his sandwiches cut into stars and hearts (something she'd done on a whim one day when he was cranky, and he now demanded every day), his refusal to sit in the front basket of the shopping cart at the grocery store, instead running up and down the aisles at full throttle—and many other newly acquired behaviors. Annie, too, had become, as Alison's mother observed, "spoiled." She wouldn't go to bed at night when Alison told her to, instead sitting wrapped in her comforter on the middle landing of the stairs, reading a pile of books. She plotted and schemed to get whatever dolls and toys happened to be heavily advertised on TV at that moment, using a range of tactics to make her case, from comparison—"But *Lauren* has one!"—to false promises—"I'll be really, really good and do everything you ever want for the rest of my life if you get me the Glitter Gloria doll, I *mean it*"—to threats—"I'll hate you forever if you don't let me!"—to outright lies—"Daddy said he'd get me one, but he's never home." (That last part wasn't a lie.) This arsenal of strategies, typical of addicts and savvy children, ordinarily wouldn't have held much sway; Alison was a seasoned pro at child wrangling. But since the accident she felt powerless to resist; she couldn't bear the inevitable cries and complaints.

"It's a short-term solution," her mother said, sizing things up with her usual bluntness. "You can't bring that little boy back, Alison. And letting your kids run roughshod over you isn't going to help."

Maybe it wouldn't help, Alison thought, but what did it hurt? She wanted desperately to show her children how much she loved them; she brought them presents and treats like a lovesick suitor. She wanted— what? To be the best mother in the universe, the most adored, beyond reproach. The gratitude of her children would quiet the voices in her head that told her she was a bad person, a bad mother, accursed, unworthy. That having taken a life, she didn't deserve to have children of her own; she didn't deserve to be loved by them.

But her children didn't seem particularly grateful for her generosity; they didn't seem to care much at all. The more she gave, the more they took, with a growing sense of entitlement. If the slightest detail didn't please them, their voices became smug and haughty; they erupted in tantrums. Annie would get a new doll, tear it out of its packaging, play with it for a few minutes, and toss it on the floor. At the Stop & Shop Noah lay on his back in the cereal aisle, his arms and legs pumping like an upended beetle, and bawled at the top of his lungs until Alison put Cap'n Crunch in the cart.

"They're going to turn into monsters," her mother said, and her father, who rarely had anything negative to say, added dryly, "They already are."

Now, sitting with Noah on her lap in the old rocking chair in his room, Alison shut her eyes and breathed in his baby smells: aloe-scented baby wipes, antibacterial ointment and a Band-Aid she'd put on a paper cut on his index finger, Oreo cookie. He kicked his furry foot against her leg. "Story, Mommy," he said impatiently.

It was their custom for her to tell him a story about himself: Noah the hero, conqueror of bad guys, who celebrated his birthday every week and for whom broccoli was a Super Food that gave him special powers.

Without opening her eyes Alison said, "Once upon a time there was a little boy who was three years old."

That afternoon, while Alison's parents were downstairs with Noah, and Annie was still at school, Alison had gone to her room to lie down. A headache had lingered for days. It seemed to be wrapped around her brain like a caul, tightening and loosening according to its own erratic whims. Since the accident she had taken Aleve every morning with her birth control pill, a tiny pink tablet and an oblong baby blue tablet in the same gulp of water, an eradicating broth—no baby, no pain.

In the bedroom she had lowered the shades, one by one, a ritual that felt almost religious, then pulled back the covers and slipped between the cool sheets, wearing her jeans and bra and socks. What kind of person goes to bed in the middle of the afternoon, in her clothes? She felt as if she were pretending to be sick, as if she were trying to fool someone. She fluffed and scrunched the pillows, lay on her stomach, curled on her side, but she couldn't get comfortable. She shut her eyes and opened them again.

Her restless glance fell on her bedside table, where in a stack of unread books she spied a slim purple and white paperback: e. e. cummings, *Poems*. She reached over to pick it up. She'd ordered the volume from an online bookseller several weeks earlier; her book club was reading it for April. Judy Liefert, whose turn it was to choose, had explained that she'd read it in high school and it had changed her life, and she wanted to see how it held up.

Several dissenters, primarily Marly Peters and Jan O'Hara, had argued that poetry wasn't appropriate for a book club. "It's so . . . inscrutable," Jan said, wrinkling her nose with distaste. "Poets never say what they *mean,* they just expect you to figure it out. And there isn't even a plot. Why don't we do the latest Jodi Picoult?"

But the lit majors and the intellectually defensive in the group rose up to defeat them. We aren't just a bunch of beach-reading housewives, damn it! We can analyze poetry!

Still, Alison thought, e. e. cummings. It wasn't exactly Pound.

167

She leafed through the volume, drifting in and out of the poems, and alighted on one that immediately felt so close to her own experience it was almost painful to read. It was from a man to his lover; it had nothing to do with Alison's life, and yet it stirred something in her.

Somewhere I have never traveled, gladly beyond
any experience, your eyes have their silence:

For Alison the boy who had died was present in these words, his innocence and potential, her connection to him. She read the poem aloud in a whisper. A chant, a eulogy.

Once upon a time there was a little boy who was three years old.

"Who was it?" Noah said.
"I don't know his name."
"Where did he live?"
"I don't know."

Somewhere I have never traveled, gladly beyond any experience. . .

"What happened to him?"
"He stayed three years old forever."
"He never turned four?"

in your most frail gesture are things which enclose me,
or which I cannot touch because they are too near. . .

"No. He never turned four."
"Why not?"
"I don't know. He didn't want to. He liked being three, I guess."
"Oh." Noah stretched out, wiggled his feet, turned over and buried

his head in her armpit. "That's not a very good story, Mommy," he said, his voice muffled in her shirt.

"Why not?"

He looked up, his expression far away, as if he'd been thinking about something important and had come to a momentous conclusion. "Teletubbies are not people," he said.

She nodded.

"Why aren't they people?" he wondered.

nobody, not even the rain, has such small hands

"Because they don't have hands," she said. She gathered him up, lifting the bottom-heavy weight of him in her arms, and cradled him like a baby. "Did you ever notice that? Did you ever notice they don't have hands?"

"Yes, they do," he said. "They just don't have fingers."

"You're right," she said, laughing.

"Their hands are mittens."

"Yes, they are."

"Why? Why are their hands mittens?"

nothing which we are to perceive in this world equals
the power of your intense fragility: whose texture
compels me with the colour of its countries,
rendering death and forever with each breathing . . .

The words were magical in their strangeness, vibrating with loss and hope and wonder, a rubric for her own tangled emotion. She could not have expressed, out loud, to Charlie or her parents or anybody, what she was feeling, but these words gave her access to it.

"But why?" Noah persisted.

"That's just how they're made," she said. "Why do you have brown eyes and brown hair?"

169

"Because I look like you."

"Oh," she said with surprise. It was true—he did look like her. "Well—right. And the mommy Teletubbie has mitten hands, too," she said, pleased with herself for following his logic.

He nodded. "But where is the mommy Teletubbie?"

"She's there," Alison said. "We just don't see her."

"Why?"

"Why do you think?" she asked, resorting to a default tactic familiar to parents and schoolteachers.

"I think because . . . umm . . . because the mommy has a headache. The mommy is sleeping."

nobody, not even the rain . . .

"Yes, she's sleeping," Alison said. She looked at the boy settled bean-baglike in her lap, staring up at her, and she thought about how dependent and trusting he was, how aware and yet blessedly ignorant. This boy, here, now, in her lap, breathing with his entire body, like a puppy, every fiber of him quivering with life—this child who needed her.

"Big hug," she said in a Teletubbie voice. He reached up and sang, "B-i-i-ig hug," holding her as tightly as a three-year-old could, his hot sweet breath on her neck, his fingers in her hair.

"SO HOW ARE things with Charlie?" her mother asked the next day. She and Alison were at a local park with Noah, sitting on a park bench watching him go down a tall slide, run around to the steps, scamper up the narrow staircase and go down again. Charlie had been up and out of the house before anyone else was awake that morning. By now he was probably on a plane to Atlanta; he'd taken a taxi to the airport from work.

"Oh, you know." Alison shrugged. "Careful, Noah!" she called, half rising off the bench.

"I am," Noah grunted as he slid to the bottom and trudged around the slide to the stairs.

Her mother, looking intently at Alison, didn't even glance over at Noah. "Actually, I don't."

"Things are—fine. As well as can be . . ." *expected.* Everything she could think of to say sounded trite. *It's a hard time for both of us, but we'll get through it.* "He's been very supportive," she said finally. And hadn't he? He'd gone to the boy's funeral, held her in his arms while she cried, let her crawl into bed as soon as he got home from work. Twice he'd brought her Sleepy Time tea in bed. He'd rubbed her shoulders. They'd only had sex once since the accident, but he seemed to be following her cues, and except for that one time she had been uninterested, unresponsive.

But last night, before he left, in a rare moment of clarity Alison had suddenly realized—what?—that he wasn't fully present. Over the course of the evening she had watched him, talking to her parents with the least amount of effort or interest possible not to seem rude, dealing with the kids on a superficial level. It seemed as if he was biding his time, waiting for something. For what?

So how were things with Charlie? Fine, good, okay. She really had no idea. How long had it been since they'd engaged in a real conversation? In the evenings, preparing food together in the kitchen or watching TV, they made small talk, or didn't talk at all. Now that she focused on it, she remembered little things: Charlie's quick impatience that rose seemingly out of nowhere and disappeared as suddenly, a Loch Ness monster of emotion, its appearance fleeting enough that Alison thought she might have imagined it. Alison had never been suspicious, but something about his behavior was off-kilter. Or was it? How would she know?

"Maybe it's none of my business," her mother said, "but he seems—I don't know. Out of it."

"The accident has been a lot to deal with," Alison said.

"Yes it has," her mother agreed. She was silent for a moment, as if considering how to proceed. "But it seems like there's something more. I don't really know Charlie that well, Alison, so this could just be—I don't know—the way he is. But." She took a deep breath.

"Mommy, look a' me!" Noah yelled. He had hauled himself up on top of the molded plastic sunshade covering the slide and was balanced there on his stomach like a surfer.

"Ohmigod, Noah," Alison said, jumping up. She ran over to the slide. Other mothers and grandmothers and babysitters looked over with concern. Bad mother. "Noah, stay right where you are. I'm coming up." She sprinted up the steep steps to the slide, holding on to both metal railings, and grabbed his feet. "Okay, back up," she said.

"No!" He tried to inch forward, and she grasped his legs harder. "Mommy, you're *bothering* me. Leggo!"

"Noah, stop it," she said. He thrashed and turned, trying to get her off. It was like wrestling a Komodo dragon. As he wrenched himself to one side he lost his balance and slid halfway down the side of the canopy, his head about ten feet from the ground.

Alison could feel her hands slipping, his shoes loosening on his feet, his legs sliding out of her grasp. "Help, Mommy," he said, alarm in his voice now, a whimper in his throat. She let go with one hand and grabbed his pants leg, then wrapped the other arm tightly around both legs and slowly pulled him toward her. When she got his stomach to the edge, she grabbed around his waist and lifted him off, turning him around. He grasped her tightly with his arms and legs, nearly making her lose her balance on the small platform, but she braced herself and leaned against the railing.

"Oh, thank God," her mother said from below, holding up her arms absurdly, as if she might have tried to catch them both.

"That child's too young to be unsupervised on that slide," one babysitter clucked loudly to another, who nodded and said, "Um hmm."

All at once Alison was filled with rage—at the babysitters, who had no right to judge her; at her mother, whose distant, critical stance toward her grandchildren and son-in-law had precipitated this; at herself for neglecting her child. He could have fallen ten feet onto his head, he might have been killed.

She was a bad mother, a terrible mother—she didn't deserve to have children of her own.

It was then that she realized she was furious with Charlie. Things between them were terrible, and had been for some time. When was the last time Charlie had told her he loved her? For months he'd been distant; he'd gone through the motions of being a good husband and father without actually engaging with her or with their children. And she overcompensated; she'd done half the work for him of pulling away. She made excuses for his absences; she'd given him every possible benefit of the doubt. He had a lot on his mind. He was stressed, he was tired. In some ways she had even appreciated Charlie's distractedness, which gave her a little breathing room. The children were so close, sometimes suffocatingly close; it was nice—wasn't it?—to have some space to herself.

But something was wrong. Deeply wrong. The fog of sadness that had enveloped Alison since the accident had obscured the trouble between them, but her blindness went deeper than that. She had feared from the beginning that Charlie was not truly in love with her, that she fit his idea of what he wanted in a wife but didn't actually fit him. And what about her? The first time she'd seen Charlie, with his broad shoulders and good bone structure, Alison had thought: this man is good husband material; he will age well. Was he really the one person in the world for her, or had she just convinced herself that he was the closest she would get?

Before the accident, Alison would have said that she was happy, that her life was just as she wanted it. Charlie worked hard, brought home a paycheck, tucked the children into bed at night. Yes, he was distracted, but he also brought her flowers; he may have snapped at her with little provocation, but then he kissed her on the back of the neck. So many things happened moment to moment, day to day, good and

173

bad—how was she to sift through, to separate the significant from the inconsequential? Marriage was hard enough—preposterous enough—in the best of circumstances. Two people, from different backgrounds, whose eating habits and tastes and educations and ambitions might be vastly dissimilar, choose to live in the same house, sleep in the same bed, eat the same foods. They have to agree on everything from where to live to how many children to have. It was sheer lunacy, when you thought about it. Alison's marriage didn't look that different from her friends' marriages—husbands and wives in two distinct camps, their lives largely separate. Long fallow periods of coexisting interlaced with rare moments of connection. Everybody joked about it; everybody knew. Maybe they were all unhappy, and maybe all of the marriages would end in divorce.

If not, why not?

As Noah clung to Alison, sobbing, she made her way down the steep metal stairs to the bottom of the slide, falling into her mother's ineffectual if vaguely comforting embrace. They walked most of the way home in silence, Noah still holding on tight. As they got close to the house, Alison's mother turned to her and said, "I don't blame you. For what happened."

Alison's stomach tightened. She nodded.

"But I wonder . . . ," her mother said.

"Mother—"

"Alison, let me finish. Your going alone to the party—and drinking too much—"

"Please," Alison pleaded. "Please stop. Noah is right here."

"Oh, he doesn't know what we're talking about. Do you, Noah?" her mother said, bending to look in his face.

"Mommy drinking too much."

"Too much what?"

"Too much juice."

"See?" Alison's mother said.

"Too much juice make a tummy ache."

"Yes, it does. Your mommy had a big tummy ache."

"Yeah. She was sad."

"Yes, she was. She still is a little sad."

"Yeah."

"That's why you need to be especially nice to your mommy right now."

"Oh, for God's sake," Alison snapped.

"Yeah," Noah said. "For God's sake."

Alison's mother smiled at her, wanting to share the joke, but Alison looked away.

"Anyway, I don't know what's going on with Charlie," her mother said, "but something *is* going on with Charlie, isn't it?"

"Yes," Alison said. She held Noah tight, tighter than he wanted; he squirmed and wriggled down. "I think he's going to leave me." As soon as she said the words, she knew they were true.

"Oh, Alison," her mother said. She put her arm around her shoulders and Alison started to cry. Her mother pulled her close, the way she had sometimes when Alison was a child, and Alison felt both the desire to resist and the desire to submit, to be held, to let go.

"Why Mommy crying?" Noah asked, looking up at the two of them, his arms around their knees. When he got no answer he mumbled, "Juice make a tummy ache," and nodded his head. Juice make a tummy ache; a tummy ache make Mommy sad. It wasn't so hard to understand if you really thought about it.

175

part four

Do I dare
Disturb the universe?
In a minute there is time
For decisions and revisions which a minute will reverse.

—T. S. Eliot,
"The Love Song of J. Alfred Prufrock"

Sitting at a table in a Barnes & Noble in Atlanta at eight-thirty Monday evening, after her reading, making small talk with the staff and signing books for a few stragglers, Claire felt a rising impatience. Earlier, between appointments, she had called Charlie's cell phone to give him the name of the hotel. His flight had been scheduled to land at 7:49 P.M., too late to make the reading, so he was taking a cab to the hotel, and would meet her in the bar. Now he's in the cab, now he's arriving at the hotel, now he's ordering a drink. . . . She imagined running her hand down the front of his pants, feeling him stiffen in anticipation as he unzipped her jeans and slid his finger inside her. . . .

"Can you just write 'To my good friend Ursula'—that's *U-R-S-U-L-A*—and, oh, I don't know, 'Good luck with your own novel,'" said the woman standing in front of Claire, holding out a copy of *Blue Martinis*.

Claire blinked. She took the book and opened it to the title page.

"It's five hundred pages, Times New Roman double spaced. I was wondering if you can recommend an agent? I'm gonna need one soon. Everybody who's read it says my book has 'best seller' written all over it, so I need someone who really knows the biz. By the way, can I have your e-mail address? I can send it to you as an attachment, and maybe you could look it over, tell me what you think."

No, no, and no, Claire was thinking as she dutifully transcribed onto the title page exactly what the woman had dictated. "Uh—there are a lot of great resources for writers on the Internet," she said, skirting Ursula's requests as she closed the book and handed it back. "Try literarymarketplace.com, for starters. You could also check the acknowledgments of books you think are like yours, to see if those authors thank their agents. Then you can Google those names to get their addresses."

Ursula frowned. Clearly, she expected more for her twenty-four dollars. "But what about *your* agent?"

"Oh. She says she's not accepting any new clients at the moment," Claire said, parroting the words her agent had said to her when she left on tour. ("Under no circumstances will you give any would-be writer who comes to your reading my e-mail address!")

"Well, I know that's not true," Ursula said, adopting a mock-jovial air. "I have a subscription to *Writer's Digest*. I know how it goes down. Agents are always looking for new clients. Just because I don't live in New York City doesn't mean I can't string two sentences together, you know. I was listed in the *Encyclopedia of American Writers* last year, by the way. Not to brag. Just to make my point."

Claire had seen ads for the *Encyclopedia of American Writers*; they charged seventy-nine dollars to list your name and bio, and then you had to pay ninety-nine dollars for the tome itself. She was suddenly bone weary; all she wanted to do was flee. It had been too long a day. She'd smiled and chitchatted with too many random people, and now she just wanted to get back to her hotel and meet Charlie at the bar and fuck him in her king-size bed.

She willed herself to smile at Ursula. "Wow, congratulations!" she said brightly. "I'm sure you're very talented, and I'm sorry I can't be more helpful. But feel free to contact me through my Web site if you have other questions."

By this time Gary, the media escort, and Alan, a store clerk with a weedy goatee, had descended on the table, sensing a situation. "Can I assist you with anything else this evening?" Alan asked Ursula in a sugary singsong.

Stuffing Claire's book in her bag with a frown, Ursula said, "No, thank you. And I just want to say one more thing to Claire Ellis. Irregardless of what that critic said, I don't think your book is tedious navel-gazing masquerading as fiction. At least from what you read to-night. So good luck. I hope the reviews get better."

"What is she talking about?" Claire asked Gary when Ursula was gone.

"Lord knows. She clearly has a screw loose. She probably made it up." He flapped his hand dismissively.

Alan, stacking chairs against a bookcase, called over, "Actually, I saw that one. It's the newest customer review on Amazon, right at the top. One star."

"Oh, well, then," Gary scoffed. "Customer review. Nobody pays any attention to those anyway."

A tiny dark cloud was forming behind Claire's eyes, meeting up with other clouds, gathering size and heft by the minute. She felt an achy exhaustion that had become familiar over the past week, the re-sult of erratic surges and ebbs of adrenaline that occurred throughout the day as she moved from one appearance to another.

"Hey, you two want to go out for a drink?" Alan asked, rolling a heavy bookcase back to its customary place. "I can show you around 'happening' downtown Atlanta."

"Fine by me," Gary said. "We could have a few beers on the pub-lisher." He looked expectantly at Claire. "I'll bet you could use a cosmo right about now."

"I'd love to," Claire said, "but I'm going to have to pass. I'm wiped. Thank you, though."

"You don't have to get up in the morning," Gary said, leafing through Claire's typed schedule. "Your flight to Richmond isn't until two."

"I need to take a bubble bath and go to bed," she said, pulling on her coat. "I'm sorry. I'm a boring old lady."

I'd love to. I'm sorry. I'm sure you're very talented. I'm sorry I can't be more helpful. Thank you, thank you, I'm sorry. Claire felt as if she were choking on her own white lies. She just wanted to go back to her hotel, damn it; was that too much to ask? She felt horribly guilty, but she hated this part of it—the endless expectation that one be grateful and polite. As he drove Claire around in his Prius all day, Gary had regaled her with stories of difficult writers: minor celebrities hawking kiss-and-tell memoirs, querulous old historians, bitchy divas with outrageous requests. So-and-so demanded total silence. Another requested, via the publisher, that Gary never look her in the eye. Another wanted to stop at every fast-food restaurant he came across and sample the fries. Still another dropped Gary in front of a mall and took off in his car for three hours, never bothering to explain where he'd gone. These people were obnoxious, she had to agree. But secretly she was beginning to have a tiny bit of sympathy for them.

"I'm coming back to Atlanta in a few months with my husband to visit his family," she told Gary and Alan, lying brazenly now, "so I'll get to explore a little then."

This seemed to satisfy them. They made plans to meet up later by themselves. Was Alan gay, too? Of course, she realized—that was it. She was just the stage prop to get them together.

In front of the hotel, sitting in Gary's car, Claire said that she wouldn't need him to ferry her to the airport the next day; she'd take the hotel shuttle.

"I've got to get you on that plane," Gary said with alarm. "If you don't get to Richmond on time my ass will be grass."

"Your ass will not be grass," Claire said. "I'm a big girl. I'm not going to miss my plane."

"Promise?"

"Promise."

When she got out of the car, Gary was checking his reflection in the rearview mirror, rubbing his finger across his teeth, tousling his hair.

"Have fun tonight," she said.

"Oh, honey, you know I will," he said. "You have a nice bubble bath."

"I plan to," she said, feeling a flush of anticipation.

WALKING INTO THE dim bar from the hotel lobby, Claire was momentarily blinded. The first thing she saw, when her eyes adjusted, was the whiteness of Charlie's shirt. He was sitting at the far end of the bar, nursing a beer and chatting with the bartender. It was as if she'd conjured him just by wishing. It didn't seem possible that he was actually here—the bar might as well have been in a distant solar system, light-years from Earth.

Then he saw her. "At last," he said, rising with a grin.

She moved toward him. "Sorry I'm late."

"No, don't be," he said quickly, grasping her hand, threading his fingers through hers. "It was nice. The anticipation. Knowing you were coming."

She leaned over and kissed him on the mouth. She felt the weight of his sadness, like a blanket over his shoulders, and she put her arms around him.

"Oh," he breathed. She could hear his heartbeat, or at least she thought it was his heartbeat—it might have been the percussive undercurrent of the music, a Carrie Underwood song she recognized from the radio.

After a moment Claire pulled back. She lifted his glass, which was half full, and took a swallow.

"You need a drink," he said.

She shrugged. "You've been here a while. What do you want to do?"

"I don't care. I just want to be with you."

She slid onto the vinyl stool beside him. "Charlie—the accident . . . . it's all so awful."

"It is."

"How is she?"

"Not so good."

"What does she—what do they . . ." Claire stopped, unsure how to continue.

"There will be a hearing in a few weeks," he said. "Mandatory sentencing for DWI—she'll lose her license for three months and has to

183

take some classes. Thank God, though—it doesn't look like she was at fault in the accident. Technically."

"Technically." Claire repeated the word flatly, without affect, but it was a question. Did Charlie think that Alison was at fault?

"She shouldn't have been driving in that condition," he said.

"She had a couple of drinks. I'm sure she felt she was fine to drive."

"Her judgment was impaired, yes."

"Come on, Charlie," Claire said, finding herself in the odd position of defending her lover's wife to him. "You've never driven anywhere on a few drinks?"

"Yeah, I probably have. But I can absorb more, I have faster reflexes. . . ."

"Basically, you think your judgment is better."

He didn't answer. He lifted the glass of beer and drained it.

Claire shook her head. "It could've happened to any of us. The other car ran a stop sign, for God's sake! And I've never understood the rules of a four-way stop—when to go, when to stop. . . . It can be ambiguous."

This wasn't how she had envisioned their evening together— arguing about Alison. She was suddenly aware again of the headache lurking behind her eyes. Her shoulders felt tight; her feet were sore. Steaming water, a fluffy terry cloth robe, a stream of pink liquid frothing into bubbles . . . "Charlie," she said, capitulating to his stronger emotions, "I don't want to get into this with you. It's really none of my business."

"Of course it is," he said wearily. "It's my business, it's your business. I wish it weren't. I wish it had nothing to do with us. But it does, and— Jesus." He put his head in his hands, his elbows on the bar. "Alison is depressed—her parents—the kids. And being with you is suddenly. . . ." He sighed heavily, almost theatrically. "It's not like this thing between us is just a fling, and everything will go back to normal. It isn't, it won't. At least not for me." He looked up, and Claire nodded, not wanting to respond until he was finished. "I don't know. I don't know, Claire. I just don't know. Alison is usually such a careful person. To a fault. Right? Haven't we always joked about that? She gave up coffee the minute she found out she was pregnant—didn't touch alcohol once in the whole nine months, or when she was nursing. Always wears a seat belt. She insisted that the two of us finish our will before we went away together overnight for the first time after Annie was born. I know she's not at fault—I know she didn't kill that kid. But this accident has fucked up everything. I feel—I feel like she's ruined my life."

"Imagine what she must be feeling about her own life," Claire said.

"Of course, of course I do," he said edgily. "That's the point—her own life is a wreck. She's a wreck. And I'm married to her. How can I—how can we possibly—"

"Stop," Claire said abruptly, putting a finger to his lips. "These questions are way too big to settle in Atlanta on a Monday night." She slid off her stool, put her hand on his thigh. "I suggest that for the next twelve hours we pretend that we're alone in the world. Nobody else. Just us, right now, here." She glanced around. "In this lame bar."

"Yeah. In this anonymous office park," he said. "In this random city."

"Tomorrow we'll be gone."

"What's your name again?"

It was already happening, she thought; the past was indistinct. "No names," she said. She reached into her bag and pulled out a room card, held it up between two fingers. "You know what I'm craving?"

"Can I guess?"

"A bath. With you. What do you think about that?"

"No thinking," he said. "Remember?"

Maybe they were at their best like this—pretending they were strangers, with no history between them, drawn together only in lust. In the hotel room they had sex in a frenzy, with their clothes half on, standing up against the door, then took a long bath together, reveling in the luxury of time. Later they made love again, stretched out across the huge bed, their movements slow and deliberate. Though it was exciting to pretend that Charlie was unknown to her, when Claire finally came (it took a while; she'd been so tense) she felt stripped of this pretense, revealed; his fingers and tongue knew her so well. Their years of friendship and flirtation, the low flame of desire—it was all in his eyes and the way he touched her. *I know you.*

The next morning, when Charlie was in the shower, Claire called Ben. They made small talk for a few minutes—*How'd it go last night? I'm tired of being on the road. Any calls or mail I need to deal with?*—until Charlie came out in a towel and Claire cut the conversation short, tugging off his towel as she snapped the cell phone shut. Lying back against the pillows, she let the phone drop to the floor as Charlie stretched across her, seal-damp, his wet hair brushing against her face, his minty lips on her mouth.

Room service arrived after a while, and they drank coffee and ate English muffins like a long-married couple, exchanging information about their flights. They left for the airport together—Charlie had coordinated his flight time with hers—and went through security before realizing they'd have to split up; she was flying to a different hub.

They were early. Airport security in Atlanta was more relaxed than in New York; they'd allotted more time than necessary. So they found a corner booth in an Au Bon Pain and bought a coffee to share. Sitting in a public place, in the bright light of midmorning, they were suddenly self-conscious with each other. What had been thrilling the night before, now, under threat of exposure, felt a little furtive. If someone they knew stumbled on them and asked what they were doing, it would be easy enough to lie—Charlie on a business trip, Claire on a book tour, a chance meeting in line for the security machines at the airport—but it would be bad. They weren't ready to be stumbled on.

Thoughts hung in the air between them, unspoken. What are we doing? Where is this going? How can it possibly work?

"I want to wake up beside you every morning," Charlie whispered after a while, abandoning protocol. He leaned forward, folding his arms on the marble tabletop. "I want to go to movies with you. I want to build a life together."

She took a sip of coffee.

"I need to know if you want that, too."

"How could it ever work?" Claire said. "Your children, your house—Alison. You're so deeply"—she cast around for the right word—"embedded."

"Yes." Charlie nodded. "But that's my problem, isn't it? What I'm asking is if you're ready to do what it would take to make this work for you."

She swished lukewarm coffee around in the paper cup. "I'm afraid."

"Of what?"

"This is going to sound ridiculous, but it's scary to have such strong feelings. To feel so . . . out of control."

"I feel that way, too."

"I know. I mean, that's part of it. Your emotions are so—boundless. It's hard to trust that they're real."

"Look," he said, "I've spent my whole life doing the right thing, and it hasn't gotten me very far. I figured if I got a steady job and married a good girl and lived in a nice house, I could keep it all together. And look at me now—I'm bored with my job. I'm not in love with my wife. Is that any way to live? Is that the answer? I want to take a chance, before it's too late. I am in love with you, Claire." He laid his hand on her thigh under the table.

"Charlie," she said.

"I want to be with you."

"It would be terrible for everyone."

"Except us."

She nodded slowly.

"When do we stop worrying about what everyone else wants? When do we start thinking about ourselves?" Charlie said.

"I think we've already started," Claire said. "I mean, here we are. Lying to everyone." She pushed the cup away. "Though I hate it. I hate that part of it."

"I hate it, too," he said, but she wondered at the quickness of his reply. On one level she felt as if she knew Charlie intimately, better than she'd ever known anyone. And yet in another way Charlie was opaque to her. There was a paradoxical openness and secrecy about him—was it midwestern? Maybe she was reading between the lines, filling in the gaps with her own assumptions and opinions—and, in doing so, creating an idealized version of what this relationship was, who Charlie was.

Why had she not simply broken up with Ben in England and gone out with Charlie, if they were so perfect for each other?

She knew what it was: Charlie had seemed like a much bigger risk. Back then an emotional risk was the last thing she was looking for. Ben was a sure thing—he loved her without question, without ambiguity; Charlie, she thought, was merely infatuated. She liked the heat and the drama, but she'd never been sure how much of it had to do with her and how much was about him—his boyish insecurity and competitiveness with Ben, his sadness about his dead mother, his craving for a female who might be strong enough to contain him, to hold the sadness, who might comprehend the unarticulated depth of his own loss.

Claire had been in love with Ben; she had wanted to spend the rest of her life with him. But she felt differently now. A life with Charlie probably wouldn't be as calm, and it wouldn't be easy, but it would be exciting. To feel this turmoil in her stomach—a feeling she had never experienced—was astonishing. She was thirty-four years old, and she wanted to feel completely alive, whatever the cost. She and Charlie were being reckless and selfish, but they were also being true to themselves, and in that way, she thought, they were being brave. If she didn't make a choice that was right for her, she would regret it for the rest of her life. And wouldn't that be far worse?

An hour later, sitting in a coach seat next to a man in a cheap suit reeking of drugstore aftershave, Claire sat back and closed her eyes. Her brain was skittish and wandering; it skipped off the point and had trouble finding it again. All through school Alison had been her best friend—the skinny girl with dark eyes, elfin face, and warm smile.

They'd weathered middle-school taunting and high school comparisons; they'd been maid and matron of honor at each other's weddings. They had been friends for nearly thirty years. Moving to New York ten years ago had smoothed Alison's rough edges, but when Claire looked at her she still saw a bird-boned ten-year-old with long skinny legs, dark kelpy hair tucked behind her ears, freckles baked across her nose, and crusty scabs on her shins from sliding into first during kickball games at recess. When they were kids, Alison had reminded Claire of one of those plucky heroines of young adult novels, the kind who doesn't let the calamitous things that keep happening to her dim her sunny worldview.

When Claire and Charlie had parted at the airport, he'd grasped her hands. "I mean what I said. I want to spend the rest of my life with you."

"I don't think you can propose to a married woman," she said. "A few other things have to happen first."

But those things were terrifying. Claire thought of Ben—dear Ben—completely in the dark. What was she supposed to do now—go home and tell him she was in love with Charlie? It was inconceivable, impossible. And Alison she couldn't even think about. The rift between them now was essentially meaningless, Claire had to admit, a cover for her betrayal, nothing more. How could she do this to Alison? Alison would never have done this to her.

Claire was in love with Charlie, yes, but how much did that matter, really, in the grand scheme of things? Maybe, she thought, we are on our way to ruining everything: the two of us and the four of us.

She didn't know what she was going to do.

She felt the plane beneath her lumber down the runway, a heavy body on tiny wheels, gathering speed and then, incomprehensibly, lifting into the air, all forty tons of steel and metal and flesh and blood, rising up to soar through the clouds. It made no sense, it made no sense—and yet here they were, taking flight.

189

February 1998

Alison, Claire had written in her lazy scrawl, *you must come visit us at Cambridge. It's cold and gray and horrifically overpriced here—and Ben has a chronic sinus infection—but we are having an incredible time.*

Alison glanced up at the gray cubicles that spread out around her like an enormous maze. Out of the corner of her eye she could see her boss, Renee Chevarak, through the glass wall of her office, talking loudly in the general direction of the speakerphone, filing her nails, and checking her lipstick in the hand mirror she kept propped on her desk. She caught Alison's eye and pushed the intercom button. "Al, would you come in here?" the box on Alison's desk blared. Alison got up, grabbing a spiral notebook, and went to the door.

"I need to talk to you. Shut," Renee said, waving her nail file at the door. "So," she said when Alison had complied. "I want you to be the first to know. But this is. . . ." She ran the nail file across her closed mouth, simulating, Alison was to understand, a zipper.

Alison nodded.

"I'm in negotiation with another magazine." Renee sat back, dropped the file, and ran her hands through her short blond hair. "It's time for me to move on. You understand."

Alison nodded again, feigning empathy. She was twenty-three years old, less than a year out of UNC, living with three other girls in an illegal sublet on the Lower East Side, and barely covering her part of the rent. After temping all over New York for four months she had finally landed a job, this job, six weeks ago. It wasn't the most exciting position of all time—assistant to the beauty editor of a middlebrow women's magazine—but it was a start. All she could think about was that in a week she'd be back to answering phones at Smith Barney.

The summer before, when Alison had been living with her parents in Bluestone after college, writing obituaries for the local newspaper and wondering what she was going to do with her life, Claire came home for a visit and persuaded her to move to New York. "If you really want to be an editor, New York is where you have to be," she declared. "And I know exactly how to do it. You start as a temp at a magazine or a publishing house, and then you charm your way in."

"I don't even know anybody up there," Alison said doubtfully.

"You know me," Claire said.

"But you're going to England."

"Exactly. So here's my brilliant idea. Why don't you take my spot in my apartment when I go? Then I don't have to sublet to some stranger, and you have a place to live. Honestly, Alison," she added, "you have to get out of Bluestone. Otherwise you're going to end up here forever, like everybody else we know from high school. And trust me—you'll love New York."

But Alison had hated New York at first—the cacophony, the trash in the gutter, the miles of concrete, the closed, expressionless faces of people on the street. As the months passed, though, she began to understand its appeal. She learned something about herself she'd never known before: she liked to be alone. Wandering around the Union Square farmers' market or Central Park on a Saturday morning, she was dependent on no one; nobody knew where she was. It was a strange and magical feeling. After work she'd walk slowly back to her apartment, forty-seven blocks, watching the day turn to evening and the city light up like a Lite-Brite board.

"I'll be frank, Al," Renee was saying. "I don't know what's going to happen to you."

There's a tiny room full of boxes beside the kitchen that's just big enough for a futon, Claire had written. *There's a restaurant down the street called Tatties that serves only baked potatoes. I'm eating sausages and grilled mushrooms for breakfast. And the rain is fabulous for your complexion. Tell that to your beauty editor!*

"I don't think I can bring you with me, at least not yet," Renee said. "So I guess it's okay for you to make an appointment with H.R.—I'll be telling them soon enough. I don't know anyone who's looking for an assistant right now, but of course I'd be happy to give you a reference. I'm sure something will come along." She smiled. "You might want to work on your word-processing skills in the meantime. And hey, like I said, mum's the word." She looked at Alison quizzically, her head cocked to one side. "Where the hell does that expression come from, anyway?"

195

The "Yanks" (anyone with an American accent is a Yank here—what an insult for a Tar Heel!) tend to cluster together, I'm sorry to say, to reminisce about things like college football and decent Mexican food. Ben and I have been hanging out with this one guy, a Kansan on a Fulbright named Charlie Granville, who's funny and charming and smart. A little midwestern for my taste, but not bad to look at. I thought of you. . . . How's your love life? Come over and take him for a test drive. What do you have to lose?

Alison left her soon-to-be-nonexistent job that day with Claire's letter in her black tote bag, an appointment with H.R., and the number for an obscure discount airline she'd found in the newspaper tucked into her day planner.

For the whole afternoon before Charlie got home from Atlanta, Alison's stomach was upset. She couldn't eat; her hands were cold. She moved aimlessly around the house, picking up toys in one room and setting them down in the next, separating laundry into darks and lights and leaving the two heaps in the hall. At one point she set a watering can in the kitchen sink and turned on the faucet to fill it, only to come back ten minutes later and find the water gushing down the sides of the can, splashing all over the floor.

Her parents had left that morning. Her mother wanted to stay, but her father had been anxious to get home. "I'm like a circus elephant. I need a routine," he'd said.

"What are you going to do?" her mother asked as Alison sat on the floor of the TV room, playing with Noah and watching her pack.

"I don't know."

"Do you want my advice?"

"No, I . . ." Alison sighed.

"You need to talk to a lawyer."

"Unh," she grunted.

"Just to find out your options."

"Don't you think it's a little premature?"

"Maybe," her mother said. "Maybe not. It can't hurt."

"I don't know," Alison said. "Maybe it can hurt. Maybe I'm—we're— blowing this whole thing out of proportion."

"That could be," her mother said diplomatically, holding her roller suitcase down with one hand and zipping it up with the other. "But Alison—you're a housewife. If Charlie wants to abandon this marriage, you're not in a strategic position to get what you need."

"I can't believe we're even having this conversation."

"Talk to a lawyer," her mother said. "A good, smart, feminist lawyer. Then whatever happens, you'll be ready."

How had it come to this? All through the afternoon, as she made Noah a sandwich and cut it into stars and hearts, folded a basket of laundry, hung Annie's dresses on hooks in her closet, Alison turned things over in her mind. Nothing about her life at the moment was what she'd envisioned for herself when she got married. For one thing, she and Charlie had always planned on staying in the city. They thought they would raise their children to be like the teenagers they saw on the crosstown buses after school, precocious and watchful and savvy; they'd juggle full-time jobs with the help of a nanny and take their kids with them to restaurants and gallery openings after work and off-Broadway plays on the weekends.

Instead, they had moved to the suburbs. Now Alison felt as if she were inside a giant bubble that moved with her wherever she went, shielding her from extremes, a bubble of middle-class suburban life—a life composed of errands and repairs and strolls to the playground, of chitchat with acquaintances in the grocery store, of scheduling electrician visits and car maintenance, of thumbing through magazines and catalogs that fell through the mail slot every afternoon at two, of her book club and health club and pediatrician appointments, of late-night lovemaking that evolved less from desire than from proximity, of bland kid dinners, fish sticks and chicken nuggets and Annie's macaroni and cheese and Classico sauce with spaghetti on an endless loop.

"You've turned into a nag," Charlie had said one evening several months ago when he announced he planned to go to a Saturday afternoon basketball game in the city, and she said she wished he wouldn't. He was gone all week, she protested; it wasn't fair to leave her with the kids for a whole day alone on the weekend (yes, she loved them fiercely, but enough was enough!). Also, she'd made a list of a few simple chores he needed to do around the house, like repairing a window in the attic and unclogging the basement sink.

Nag. It was such a retro, politically incorrect word that it made Alison seethe. She could not believe he had said it. She felt unfairly typecast as a character in a fifties sitcom: the hausfrau with the commuting husband she scolds and cajoles and manipulates, their gender roles as clearly drawn as the edging cut into the grass along their front walk. (For that matter, how had it come to pass that fixing windows and sinks were his domain; cleaning them was hers?)

"So I'm a nag and you're the henpecked husband, huh?" she said. "Is that how it's going to be?"

"Oh, stop it," he snapped. She knew Charlie couldn't really refute her objection; in her position—and they'd always resolved disputes that way, by trying to see each other's point of view—he'd probably feel the same way. So instead he said, "This is why I didn't want to move out of the city. I feel trapped out here. I can't do a fucking thing on my own without a permission slip."

"What does moving out of the city have to do with it?"

So many of their arguments were about pushing the other person to articulate the things they'd been threatening to say that were just under the surface, wounds that had scabbed over but refused to heal.

197

Not talking about things that matter was one of those surprises of married life that Alison wished someone had told her about in advance. She and Charlie could go for days, weeks even, without discussing anything more important than the phone bill. It wasn't that they didn't have time to talk; it was that the time was never right. Alison's lurking fear was that Charlie's silence masked a fundamental disappointment—that she wasn't interesting or exciting enough for him; that he thought he had "settled." That he felt trapped in a maze of bourgeois concerns and aspirations, that he resented having to work so hard to maintain their way of life.

There was plenty that Alison kept quiet about, too. She didn't feel she had any right to articulate how powerless she sometimes felt as an unsalaried stay-at-home mother, how raising children essentially alone often felt like drudgery, how distant the mundane realities of marriage were from her idealistic girlish notions. She had chosen it, all of it. But with those choices came great anxiety. Together they had constructed a life that was, if not a lie, then some milder form of delusion. Charlie made $130,000 a year, and they could barely make ends meet. They lived on the knife edge of their means; each month they slid further into debt, until February, bonus time, when they could pay off their credit cards. They chose to live in a town with astronomical taxes so that their children would go to reasonable public schools; they chose to buy a "preowned," still-above-their-means Volvo because they wanted a safe car; Alison chose to stay at home. But their fear lurked just under the surface.

Sometimes late at night Alison would whisper, "Maybe we should just leave all this, go somewhere—Kansas, maybe, or North Carolina—"

"But you're the one who wanted this life," he'd say.

"We had to go somewhere. We couldn't afford to stay in the city."

"Not with children, it's true."

"What are you saying? You wanted children. Are you saying you didn't?"

"I'm not saying anything," he'd say. Then it would become about that—about who wanted what kind of life. That was the problem with talking about anything. One of you might say too much, reveal too much, and there would be no going back.

For months Alison had chalked it up to their busy life, the hectic grind of parenthood. It had been ages since Charlie had looked at her—really looked, the way he used to—but she had barely noticed. She wasn't looking at him, either. She was bandaging Annie's feelings and Noah's scraped knees, asking Charlie to hand her the antiseptic cream, *it's on the dresser, honey, in the orange bowl, thanks,* without looking up. After the kids were in bed, Charlie would collect the recycling or the trash, depending on the day, and pour himself a Scotch, and sit down to pay some bills. If Alison made dinner they might eat it standing up at the counter, and ask each other perfunctory questions

198

about their day. With friends, some evenings, over wine and candles, they might laugh about married life—the sex they weren't having, the romance they'd sacrificed to a constant round of dirty diapers and ear infections, the endless repetitive motion of raising kids.

But thinking back now, Alison could see where the cracks had started to form. She hadn't been looking closely enough. She extrapolated from parts to the whole. She built a bridge in her head over the spaces between them. A morning kiss, a bouquet of flowers, a Mother's Day card—it had been enough for her, enough to ignore the gaps in their conversation, the white gully of sheet in the middle of the bed.

WHEN CHARLIE'S CAB pulled into the driveway at dusk, Noah was standing sentinel at the living room window. "Daddy's home!" he shrieked, flushing Annie out of the TV room, where she was watching *SpongeBob SquarePants*. "Mom, Dad's here," Annie called on her way to the front door, sounding remarkably to Alison's ears like a teenager.

199

Alison was in the kitchen, washing lettuce for a salad. She had roasted a chicken and boiled new potatoes and set the table for four. Maybe a normal family dinner—as abnormal as that was—would cure what ailed them: Chicken Soup for the Dysfunctional Marriage. She turned off the faucet and dried her hands on a dish towel.

"Hey, little guy!" she heard Charlie say as he came in the front door.

"I'm not little. I'm *big*," Noah shouted.

"Yes, you are! Hi, Princess," he said to Annie.

"Hi, Dad. Did you bring me anything?"

Alison winced. She went out into the hall. "Annie, that's not very polite. Give your dad some time to get settled."

Charlie looked relieved. He might have anticipated Annie's question, rude as it was, since he usually came home with trinkets or candy from an airport vendor (a model plane with the Continental logo for

Noah, a bracelet or Beanie Baby for Annie). But clearly this time he had forgotten.

"Hey, honey," he said, leaning over and kissing Alison. Not on the lips, exactly, but somewhere close.

"Hey," she said. Her hands were shaking. She clasped them behind her back. "How did the hand-holding go?"

He looked at her quizzically.

"The client."

"Oh, right, right." He emitted an odd little grunt. "It went fine, I think," he said, nodding his head.

"Did you get everything worked out?"

"Yep," he said. "I think so." He was jumpy, as if he'd had too much caffeine.

"Well, that's good."

There might have been an awkward silence then, but Annie was holding up a drawing of a unicorn she'd done in school for Charlie to see, and Noah was tugging on his hand, pulling him toward the play-room and his Thomas the Tank Engine railroad track, saying, "You be Percy and I'll be James." Charlie shrugged and held his free hand up to Alison, as if to say, What can I do?

"I made dinner," she called after him. "A family dinner, for a change."

"Gosh, I wish you'd told me," Charlie said with an exaggerated gri-mace as he headed toward the playroom. "I had a late lunch—and I'm wiped. When I'm done here I thought I might go lie down for a few minutes. If that's okay with you." He disappeared around the corner.

Alison felt as if she'd been slapped. Charlie didn't want to have dinner with his family. He didn't even feel compelled to play along. She took a deep breath and followed him into the playroom. "Actually, it's not okay. I made dinner for the family. The least you can do is sit with us."

Charlie looked aggrieved, as if she had misinterpreted his motives. "Sure," he said. "Whatever you want."

"Meaning . . ."

"Be Percy, Daddy!" Noah demanded, placing the little green engine in Charlie's hand.

"Meaning 'whatever you want.'" Charlie opened his eyes wide in benign agreeableness.

"Meaning it's not what *you* want."

"Daddy, *come on*," Noah said.

"Just a second," Charlie said. "Alison, for Christ's sake."

"Fuck you," Alison said. She turned on her heels and went to the kitchen. She'd folded yellow-checked napkins on four woven yellow place mats set for dinner. Three floating candles in the center of the table, an impulse purchase from Crate and Barrel, bobbed, lit and glowing, in their glass holders. Alison leaned against the counter and closed her eyes. Two, three, four. She opened her eyes. Charlie hadn't followed her. She went over to the table and blew out the candles, then covered the top of the salad bowl with plastic wrap and put it in the fridge—she was really the only one who ate salad, anyway—along with the open bottle of sauvignon blanc. She left the roast chicken and pota-toes where they were, on trivets on the counter.

Standing in the doorway to the playroom, she announced, "Dinner for the kids is in the kitchen. I'm going upstairs."

"Wait a minute," Charlie said.

She waited.

"Why are you doing this?"

"I'm not hungry now."

"Come on, Alison. This is childish."

"Child—issssh!" Noah said, rocking on his heels. "You're funny, Daddy."

"Mom, I'm hungry," Annie said, pushing past her into the play-room.

"Dinner is ready," Alison said. "Daddy's going to get it for you."

"I thought you said it's a family dinner," Annie said.

"I thought it was, but I guess I was wrong."

201

"Christ," Charlie said, climbing to his feet. "If I'd known it was so important to you I wouldn't have said anything."

"That really would've made a difference?"

"Of course."

"Jesus, Charlie," she said. "The point is, it's not important to *you*. Is it?"

Charlie stood in front of her with his arms crossed. "What are you trying to get me to say, Alison?"

"I don't know. You tell me."

He glanced down at Noah, who was sprawled on the floor now, busily running a blue engine around the train track, up a hill and across a bridge and through a green plastic tunnel, murmuring encouragement along the way: "Up the hill, Gordon! Now down the hill and over the bridge, that's right!" Charlie glanced at Annie, who was looking apprehensively from one parent to the other. "We're all a little cranky and hungry, aren't we, Annie?" he said. "I think we'll feel better after dinner, don't you?"

"Maybe," Annie said warily.

"Don't go upstairs," he said to Alison. "Let's be a family tonight. Okay?"

She wanted nothing more than to believe him—that if she didn't go upstairs they would be a family, that everything would be back to normal. But the word *tonight* sounded jarringly provisional to her, as if "family" might be a temporary condition.

Was she losing her mind? Could that be true?

"Come on," Charlie said gently, taking her arm, and she went with him into the kitchen and took the salad out of the fridge and tossed it and set it in the middle of the table. Charlie carved the chicken, taking care to remove the skin and cut the white meat into chunks for the kids, and Alison lit the floating candles again and dimmed the overhead halogens.

Charlie sat at one end of the table and she sat at the other, father and mother with their children between them, sharing an ordinary dinner on an ordinary day, chatting about whether Annie should start ballet and what Noah was learning in his sing-along music class and whether it was time to plant grass seed on the front lawn. It was real life, the way things should be, and even as it was happening it felt to Alison like a distant memory, the moment already slipping into the past.

November 1997

"That guy has a crush on you," Ben told Claire when the
party was over. They were lying in bed in the dark, going
over the evening together.

"What guy?"

"That American from Kansas. Charlie."

"Nah," she said. "He probably has a crush on you."

"I don't think so."

She poked him in the side, teasing him. "Poor guy
doesn't know anyone yet. We should have him to dinner."

"Sure," he said. "All your strays."

"You like it. If it weren't for me, you'd always have your
nose stuck in a book."

"That's an original phrase."

"Shut up and kiss me," she said, turning toward him and
twining her leg around his.

Ben hadn't particularly liked Charlie at first sight. When
he'd opened the door to find him standing awkwardly on
their stoop, in his clothes from the Gap, Ben's first impression was that Charlie looked like every other bland midwesterner he'd met, which admittedly weren't many. Ben's only
prejudice, he liked to say, was against Middle America. As
prejudices went, it was fairly safe: few people at Cambridge
were going to disagree.

"You've never even been to the Midwest," Charlie said

over pints one night when they'd gotten to know each other better. "I'll bet you don't even know where it is on a map."

"Hmm, let me think. This is a tough one. In the middle of the West, maybe?"

"Is Indiana part of it? Ohio? Arizona?"

"I know one thing," Ben said. "Kansas is smack dab in the middle."

"In the middle of what, exactly?"

"Look, you can pretend you don't have any idea what I'm talking about, but we both know I'm right. The American Midwest is a bastion of mediocrity, a sinkhole of consumerism and fast food. I don't think I'm overstating it when I say the Midwest exemplifies American quote-unquote culture at its worst."

"You're a smug prick, you know that?" Charlie took a sip of his beer and laughed. Then he shook his head and laughed some more. "So tell me about—what bumfuck town are you from? Tell me about that cultural Mecca."

"All right," Ben said. "You have a point."

Ben didn't tell many people about his background, but Charlie had been persistent. In a weak moment Ben had divulged that he'd been raised by a single mother in a little town in upstate New York, the kind of place that Manhattanites escape to for the weekend, and escape from on Sunday nights. It had bed-and-breakfasts, but no library. The schools were small and poorly staffed, textbooks out-of-date. The older siblings of Ben's elementary school friends worked at the local drugstore and Burger King, or waited tables at one of the two fancy restaurants in town, places nobody Ben knew ever went to. On weekends the entire town, en masse, attended high school baseball, basketball, or football games, depending on the season.

When Ben left home on a boarding-school scholarship, he had felt paradoxically freer to be himself and determined to invent a self he liked more. He worked hard to shed any vestiges of his past. He conveniently lost his JCPenney fifty-fifty dress shirts in a "laundry mishap," as he told his skeptical mother, and ordered 100 percent cotton replacements from J. Crew. He lost his unsophisticated upstate accent, coating it with various varnishes to see if the finish would take: wry aesthete, cynical rogue, witty everyman. He'd copy a phrase or gesture from someone more self-possessed than he was, and change it just enough to avoid detection.

Over the course of three years of high school and four years of college, he learned how to ingratiate himself with professors (a finely calibrated performance involving earnest inquisitiveness and superficial knowledge of their published work), negotiate sharing a room the size of a jail cell with a mentally unbalanced roommate (tact and avoidance), sign up for the right mix of classes so he wouldn't have a nervous breakdown during exams. Most important, he'd learned that confidence can be faked, and if you fake it long enough you can actually acquire it.

Which is why Charlie's ingenuous provincialism had grated on him at first—it was a reminder of a world he'd left behind. Charlie looked to Ben like a guy who should be catching baseballs in outfields and dating cheerleaders and inheriting the family business (which, in fact, he was—though by the time the business was ready to be inherited, his father had declared bankruptcy). He looked like a guy who'd marry a local beauty contestant, build a cookie-cutter house with cathedral ceilings on a bald tract of land, and raise a passel of towheaded kids. He'd ride a tractor mower around his property every weekend, cutting a wide swath around the spindly saplings he'd planted at even intervals.

He looked like the type who'd either pack on fifteen pounds in the decade after college, or become a fitness freak, running on the broad, quiet streets of his development every morning before work, lifting weights at night in the home gym he'd built in his basement.

But every time Ben thought he had Charlie pegged, he'd do something that surprised him. For one thing, he was smart. Here he was at Cambridge, studying Aquinas and Jung. Here he was taking the train into London to buy cheap tickets to a Beckett play in the West End. Here he was, blond and easygoing, with a shrewd glint in his eye and a dry sense of humor. Ben would never have predicted that they'd become friends, but here they were, sharing beer and conversation in a smoky pub on a foggy night in a foreign country.

Claire had been away for thirteen days, but it felt to Ben as if she'd been gone for months. And maybe in a sense she had. He'd been surprised to find, on the third night, that he was relieved to come home to an empty apartment, that an unhappiness of which he was barely aware had pervaded their shared space, as invisible and enervating as carbon monoxide.

Ben had never been especially good at picking up people's cues—particularly the unhappiness or dissatisfaction of those closest to him. An old girlfriend once speculated that it probably had to do with his mother's melancholy, his father's barely contained rage; at the first sign of trouble, Ben was likely to retreat into computer chess or a crossword puzzle—activities that occupied his mind to the extent that he could be physically present and yet emotionally disengaged. For the first week Claire was gone, it had been a relief for Ben to turn his attention to the Boston commission, which would consume as much time and energy as he allowed.

But the Boston project was now well under way; other people were involved, and Ben no longer felt solely responsible. The plans had been approved and finalized, and ground had been broken. His role had become secondary. And just as he'd done when final exams were over, he took a week to simply breathe—to clear the low-priority papers off his desk, return e-mail and phone calls, sleep late, buy himself some new shoes, get a good haircut (not just a quickie from the barber in the basement of his office building). He called his mother, checked in on his brother, took his two prize hires out for a fancy lunch on Drone Coward's dime, an occasion they used to announce that they were both taking jobs with rival firms. At night he ordered takeout and sat on the couch like any ordinary New Yorker, letting the laugh track from syndicated sitcoms wash over him like warm, sudsy bathwater. He watched *SportsCenter*. He read the Dining In section of the *Times*.

One evening, as he was clicking through channels, a wagging finger caught his eye. "Listen to what people tell you about themselves," a self-help guru was saying. "If they tell you not to trust them, *don't*. If they tell you they're bad news, believe them. It's human nature to want to think the best of others, but if you listen carefully, people will always tell you who they are."

Ben turned off the TV and sat there, staring at his shadow reflected in the black screen. On some subterranean level below consciousness, his brain, ostensibly resting, began to generate data, sifting through unconnected moments—conversations, observations, gestures, and expressions he didn't even know he'd been aware of—to build a hypothesis.

I was just out with a girlfriend. . . . There were no messages—nothing important—I erased all the calls. . . . She likes the country-bumpkin type . . . I'll just be out for a few hours. . . . Honey, I picked up your dry cleaning . . . It's going to be so tedious. One obscure radio station after another. . . .

Do you think God is punishing us because we weren't sure?

And other things: the phone calls with no one there. The silk-corded bag from a pricey lingerie shop Ben had glimpsed in the garbage, with a fleeting thought. Lingerie? When's the last time she wore fancy lingerie?—he promptly dismissed it, his brain swimming with too many other details.

Seemingly out of nowhere, a memory floated up: the first time Claire had met his father. It had been a bitterly cold January weekend in upstate New York. Ben's father, along with his current girlfriend, Paula, met Ben and Claire for lunch at a chain restaurant in the parking lot of a strip mall. After an hour and a half of mediocre food and strained conversation, the two men went to get the cars. "You're in over your head, son," his father said as he and Ben tramped through the snow. "If I were you I'd get out while you can."

Though Ben was accustomed to these kinds of pronouncements

from his father, this one caught him off guard. He'd thought they were all getting along pretty well, despite his father's loutish insinuations about Claire's previous boyfriends and the way he mocked her southern accent. "Why do you say that?" Ben said, trying to keep his voice as neutral as possible.

"I just know. She's a type. Can't trust her."

Ben laughed dryly. "That's rich, coming from you."

"I guess I deserve that," his father said. "But maybe that's part of it. Takes one to know one."

They trudged along in silence.

"Hope I'm wrong," his father said when they reached the cars. "For your sake."

"She's nothing like you, you arrogant prick," Ben had said.

It was the last time he spoke to his father for years. But as he let the pieces, fine as silt, sift through his brain now, a picture began to emerge, the way in a trick painting the background details settle into focus, becoming clearer than those in the foreground, forming an unexpected image—a picture composed of shadows, a wraith, perhaps, or a skull. And suddenly Ben's confused, unanticipated emotions the night of the party—the rush of feeling for Alison, the swell of identification with her, and his own recoiling—began to make a horrible kind of sense.

That boy has a crush on you.

All your strays.

Claire and Charlie.

The night she spilled her wine in his lap and they disappeared into the kitchen, leaving Ben and Alison to make awkward small talk. What were they doing in the kitchen all that time?

The rift with Alison.

Was Ben losing his mind? Was he making this up out of some kind of deep-rooted insecurity?

Ben wasn't a particularly jealous person. He didn't see the point. As a kid he'd witnessed his father's rabid, hypocritical jealous rages at his mother, and they sickened him. Anyway, he was used to people being

211

infatuated with Claire. She was eminently, as a boorish drunk at a party had told him one night, "fuckable." He knew, also, that part of her craved the attention, but this had seemed innocuous to him, a quirk of her psychology that played itself out in harmless flirtations. To be desired was enough, Ben had thought; it fulfilled her need.

It never occurred to him that she might act on it.

All at once, jealousy took root in Ben's stomach like a hardy, noxious flower.

Claire's distractedness, her distance, even her compassion. She'd been unnaturally nice to him lately, both in and out of bed. There was a distance and a cover in that. Sex had never been the primary bond between them; though at first, like most couples, they couldn't keep their hands off each other, over the years their cohabitation had become so siblinglike that when they turned toward each other in the night it sometimes seemed almost inappropriate. Ben had always thought that their connection was based on a deeply felt, shared sense of irony, which tended to quash lust, a decidedly unironic feeling. To make mad love was to take it seriously, to admit to an earnest, naked need that the two of them didn't often confess to. It helped when they were drunk, when self-consciousness was obliterated; after parties, late at night, they could be ravenous for each other.

But lately Claire had been approaching him with a disorienting sincerity—acting out, Ben thought now, a pantomime of desire. Was it pity sex? For the two of them to be ironic together meant that they shared a worldview; they were in sync. Her kindness to him now, on reflection, struck Ben as patronizing. Something was definitely going on. With a heavy heart, he realized he would have to find out what it was.

Or would he? He'd never been good at confronting people; it was so much easier to let things unfold, give emotions time to dissipate. And wasn't it more natural that way? When he'd asked too many questions as a child it usually ended with his mother in tears and his father storming off. Ben had constructed his entire adult life on the premise that people should behave courteously toward each other; in his view, the rules of decorum and the right to privacy were inviolable. He didn't want people

212

poking and prying in the stew of *his* mixed feelings. Who knew what might rise to the surface? Putting Claire on the spot might provoke the issue unnecessarily.

He took so much for granted with her. They got along beautifully day to day; they rarely fought, and when they did, it didn't last long. Claire wasn't necessarily easy to live with—she felt things deeply, acted impulsively; she could be arrogant in her opinions—but these things had never really bothered him. He admired the operatic scale of her emotions. If it was true that, over the years, the passion between them had tapered off, wasn't that normal? Their relationship had grown into a different kind of love, stronger and more mature, a slow simmer rather than a consuming burn.

Maybe she was simply going through a phase, pulling back to focus on her book and other priorities. She was allowed to do that. They weren't joined at the proverbial (or was that literal?) hip. Plenty of unconventional marriages survived, even flourished. Look at Bloomsbury—Virginia Woolf and Vanessa Bell and Duncan Grant. And hadn't he read somewhere that Margaret Drabble and Michael Holroyd lived in the same English cul-de-sac, married to each other but inhabiting separate houses, meeting in the afternoon for tea? He and Claire didn't have to live a conventional life, damn it; he loved her enough to respect her wishes for autonomy and freedom, even if—God forbid—it were sexual.

And if it wasn't a phase, if she was genuinely pulling away? Well, he would find out soon enough.

THE FLOWER SHOP on Eighty-second and Columbus, a narrow space with painted brick walls, was one of Ben's favorite places on the Upper West Side. It was hard to define what set it above ordinary florists—was it the Zen-like simplicity, rare outside SoHo, that showcased the beauty of individual blooms, or the bold colors and combinations, bunched beautifully in old-fashioned tin buckets along one wall, or the floor-to-ceiling display on the opposite wall of bright earthenware pots and exotic glass vases? Whatever the reason, Ben loved it. The florist was part of a neighborhood he'd carefully carved for himself out of the overwhelming variety available within the ten-block radius of his and Claire's apartment. Ben's world was composed of several good restaurants, a dependable dry cleaner and Vietnamese takeout, a twenty-four-hour pharmacy, two coffee shops, a tiny, ancient, used-book shop and a giant Barnes & Noble, and two gourmet grocery stores. If he didn't have to go to work, Ben could imagine living out his life quite contentedly on this mile-long stretch.

Today he wanted something lush and elegant, a bouquet that would convey both congratulations and sincere, old-fashioned love. Claire was coming home. Wouldn't it be wonderful, he thought, if they could both see this as a new beginning? Standing in the flower shop, looking around at the variety—you couldn't go wrong, really, and anyway he'd ask Zoë, the owner, with whom he was on a first-name basis, for her opinion—he basked in the glow of possibility. He felt an odd, unfamiliar excitement, like the buzz of a new relationship. It was as if he and Claire had recently met and then she'd gone away on a long trip, and tonight she was coming back. Would he cook something, or should they go out? Maybe somewhere new, to surprise her—or perhaps it'd be best to stick with an old standard. He'd make several reservations, just to be sure.

He chose an eclectic mix of blue irises, yellow roses, white snapdragons, and purple tulips. "Gorgeous, perfect!" Zoë declared when he explained that Claire was coming home from her book tour. She wrapped the cut ends in a damp organic paper towel and then folded the flowers into a paper cone, as neatly as a midwife swaddling a baby. "*Voilà*," she said, handing it to him with a flourish. "No woman would be able to resist."

It was a sunny day, the first of the season warm enough for people to be out in shirtsleeves. And out they were, breathing in the spring air—parents with baby strollers, joggers in spandex, dogs. Leaving the flower shop Ben took off his jacket and slung it over one arm. He headed down Columbus Avenue, working his way toward Fairway at Seventy-fourth by zigzagging degrees—west on Eightieth to Amsterdam, south on Amsterdam to Seventy-ninth, west over to Broadway. At the entrance to the grocery store he grabbed a basket—carts were impossible on a Saturday; it'd take hours to get through—and roamed up and down the aisles in a sensory fugue. Kumquats, papaya, figs, arugula, kale, skate and salmon and whitefish salad, dark-roasted coffee beans . . . He put milk and fresh orange juice and whole grain bread and coffee into the basket. Yes, they'd go out to dinner, he decided; otherwise, with the flowers, there'd be too much to carry. The decision was a relief. He'd had a momentary flutter of anxiety imagining himself fussing over a salad and sea bass filets while Claire stood back with a glass of wine, watching him. Assessing.

But no—that wasn't going to happen. Only a moment ago he'd been filled with giddy anticipation. He deftly made his way to the shortest line—cash only, mostly baskets—and paid up, adding a Swiss candy bar to his purchase at the last minute. As he left Fairway with his mesh bag, he glanced at his watch: eleven-forty-five. Her plane would land at two. There was plenty of time to tidy up the apartment and send a few e-mails for work. Beyond that, the weekend stretched ahead lazily, full of expectation and promise. Claire was coming home.

215

IN HIS DRESSER drawer, as he was putting away his clothes, Ben came across two pairs of Claire's underwear folded inadvertently in a stack of his T-shirts. White with blue flowers. Little girl underwear. She always wore cotton bras and socks and underwear, cotton T-shirts to bed. Once, early on, he had given her a short silk nightgown, pale blue. She wore it a couple of times, and then she tucked it away. Looking around, he found it now in a pile of clothes on a high shelf in the bedroom closet, along with a bulky wool sweater she'd bought with him on a trip to Scotland, two of his old button-downs she used to wear around the house on weekends, the Barbour jacket he'd gotten her in London. She had been self-conscious about wearing it at first; it was brand-new, and they're supposed to look lived in. Ben took it down and fingered the thick oilskin. It was perfect now, just the way you'd want it. He put it back on the shelf and closed the closet door.

BEN WAS STILL at his laptop, answering one final e-mail, when he heard Claire's key in the lock. According to the tiny clock on his monitor it was 2:51—just about the time he'd figured it would be, given the cab ride from the airport. Quickly he pressed SEND LATER and stood up.

He had arranged the flowers in a Simon Pearce vase on the coffee table in the living room. He'd deliberated over whether to unwrap them—would it be nicer for her to open the package herself? In the end he decided it would be better to come upon them lush and blooming, a visual expression of domestic tranquility.

Claire stepped into the apartment, jangling her keys, balancing a bag on each shoulder and trailing a roller suitcase.

"She's home!" Ben said, leaping to the door to help her, holding it open as she rolled across the threshold. "Is there anything else?" He peered into the hall.

"This is it," she said, setting the keys on the side table and letting the bags drop to the floor. "God I'm glad to be here."

Ben stepped forward and put his arms around her, leaning in to kiss her. She stiffened slightly, and then, as if realizing she was being impolite, relaxed into his embrace.

"I missed you, babe," he said.

"Me, too," she said, her voice muffled against his shoulder.

"You must be exhausted."

"I am. I could sleep for days."

Turning away, she bent down to gather her bags. For a moment they argued over who would carry them into the bedroom—"Stop, let me do that"; "Don't be silly, I'm fine." Then she gave up and let him, following him through the apartment to the back, passing the flowers on the coffee table without comment.

"I got those at Fleur," he said in the wake of her silence, then imme-

216

diately regretted it. He felt like an awkward teenage boy on a first date, trying too hard to impress.

"What?"

"Oh—nothing."

She stopped and looked around, her gaze eventually resting on the flowers. She went over and touched an open yellow rose with the tip of a finger, then crouched down to smell it. "These are lovely," she said, looking up at him. "For me?"

"Of course."

"That's sweet," she murmured. Something about her tone made the hairs on the back of his neck prickle. She was talking to him the way you might talk to a sick child or a very old person, with a mixture of condescension and something else—pity?

"I thought they'd brighten up the place," he said briskly, depositing the bags in a heap on the bedroom floor.

"Umm," she said, stretching her arms over her head. She went to the window and looked out.

There it was again—that awkwardness. He didn't know what to say, and she didn't seem particularly concerned about filling the silence.

"Are you hungry? Thirsty?" he asked.

"I'm fine. Well, maybe some water," she said, still facing the window.

He went into the kitchen, got down two glasses, took a liter of Poland Spring out of the fridge, considered slicing a lemon: no. Too fussy. He filled the glasses, splashing water across the counter and onto the floor. Christ. His hands were shaking. What the fuck? He mopped up the mess, wiped the bottoms of the glasses, and brought them out to the living room, offering her one. She took a long sip.

"The place looks good."

"Maria came yesterday. She said she wanted it to look extra nice for you, 'mi bella señora,'" he said, imitating Maria's melodious voice.

Claire smiled. "How sweet." That word again! "Any mail worth bothering with?"

"I put a pile on your desk. Some invitations. A letter from some southern writers' conference, asking you to be on a panel. I threw out the junk. Paid the bills."

"Kept the engine running."

"I guess. Luckily it's not a very big engine."

"Well. Thank you."

He nodded, shrugged. What else would he have done?

"How's the Boston project?"

"It's going pretty well. Of course there are a million complications."

"Of course."

Small talk, chatter chatter. Why did it feel like such an effort? Claire stood at the window with her water glass, tapping the side with a finger. Tap tap tap. *Tap tap tap.* Ben could feel the tapping on his spine, hear it inside his head. TAP TAP TAP. He thought he might go crazy with the tapping.

He couldn't stand it anymore. "Tell me what's going on," he said suddenly.

She turned around. He could see that she wasn't sure she'd heard what she thought she'd heard—what he had implied. That something was going on, and he knew enough about it—*how much?*—to ask. A range of responses flickered across her features. "What do you mean?" she said.

"You seem uncomfortable."

She smiled. He could see the veins in her neck, visible from the effort. "I'm just really tired. I need a good long rest. Then I'll be right as rain."

It was tempting to let it go. That was all she needed: a good long rest, and she'd be right as rain. (What did that mean, anyway, "right as rain"? It wasn't like her to invoke a cliché. If nothing else, it was an indication of the falseness of the sentiment.) All he wanted was for things to be the way they were—two well-meaning and rational adults living their lives together, devoted to each other. She did love him; he was sure of it. She'd written dozens of cards and letters and e-mails over the years attesting to the depth of her feeling. (Here he was, he thought ruefully, invoking those long-ago letters, as if they proved something!)

He didn't want his fears confirmed. He didn't want to know. But he couldn't live this way (or could he? he wondered in a late, desperate negotiation with himself; *maybe he could*). It would be better, as with a loose tooth, to yank it out quickly, rather than endure the torture of slow detachment. Right?

"Claire—"

"Not now, Ben," she said, as if sensing what he was thinking. "I'm so tired. Can we do this later?"

"Do what?"

"This. This—" She moved her hands in an angry flurry in the air. Stirring things up, Ben understood. Agitating. Opening Pandora's box, allowing the Furies to escape. Once they were out, they could never be put back. Did he want that? Did he really want to do this now?

"Are you sleeping with Charlie?" he asked abruptly.

"What?" she said, her voice rising in a strangled laugh. Her eyes grew bright.

He waited.

"Why do you . . . what do you . . . What makes you think that?"

"Don't do this, Claire."

"I'm sorry, Ben," she said, "I don't think this is the time to. . . ."

"To what?"

"Look," she said, as if she were about to level with him.

He waited.

She bit her bottom lip.

"Look at what," he said finally.

To his surprise, she started to cry. He watched dispassionately as tears welled in her eyes and ran down her cheeks. Her mouth quavered; she let her wavy auburn hair fall across her face. She covered her eyes with her hands and stood there in front of him, her shoulders heaving and legs shaking, muffled cries rising out of her until she was flat out sobbing in a way he'd never seen before.

So this was it, the moment he'd been dreading. Yes. Claire was sleeping with Charlie. It would stand to reason that she was in love with Charlie. She would probably leave him for Charlie. Ben felt as if he were experiencing all this from a great distance, from the ceiling, perhaps, or maybe even farther away. He felt as if it wasn't actually his life that was disintegrating but someone else's, someone he didn't know. He felt sorry for the guy, in a general kind of way—the way you feel sorry for people in earthquakes or other disasters, fire and flood and warfare and car accidents. It would suck to be him, to be that guy whose wife was having an affair with her best friend's husband. But he didn't actually feel sorry for himself. Not yet, anyway. What he felt instead, he realized with dawning comprehension, was relief. Relief that it was out in the open, that he wasn't going crazy, that his instincts had been right. And something else. He didn't know how to define it, exactly; he wasn't sure what it was. But it felt like a larger kind of liberation, an unburdening. He felt free, for the first time since he could remember. He might never have chosen this freedom, but here it was, for the taking.

Watching Claire as she stood in front of him, crying still, Ben felt a rush of tenderness for her, and he went over and took her in his arms. He hated that she felt terrible. He wished there were something he could do. Of course she was in love with Charlie; he understood completely. Hadn't both of them been in love with Charlie, on some level, for all these years?

Later he would feel other things—bitterness, rage, loneliness, loss. He would make mad promises that he would change, that things would be different, that somehow he would become the person Claire had decided she loved more than him. He would become Charlie. But he didn't know the first thing about becoming Charlie. He couldn't have done it if he'd wanted to.

November 1997

"Ah, hello," said the tall, thin, dark-haired man who answered the door. "Careful, we're missing a step. The stone dislodged itself last week and I don't know how the devil to replace it."

How the devil. Another American trying to sound English. "I'm Charlie. Granville." Charlie stuck out his hand.

"Ah, yes, Charles Granville. Benjamin Sayers. Ben." He squeezed Charlie's hand and smiled. "Claire said she'd invited you. Said she found you aimlessly wandering the streets."

"Something like that." He could see Claire inside the house. She was biting the lip of a plastic cup, laughing at something somebody was saying.

"Come in, come in," Ben said, waving him up. "Claire likes to think of us as the Cambridge University Immigration Service for New Americans. Been here long?"

"Two weeks."

"Bit of a culture shock, isn't it? Flats and lifts and all that."

"There's a lot of rain," Charlie said. By now they were standing at a drinks table in the middle of a small living room crowded with people, most of them sitting. Without asking, Ben poured a tiny glass of pale sherry and handed it to him.

"You'll get used to it," he said. "Have you got a bike?"

Charlie took a sip of the sherry and winced at the flame in his throat. He'd only tasted sweet sherry before. "I need to get one."

Ben looked him up and down. "What are you, five nine?"

"Five ten," he said, color rising to his cheeks.

Ben smiled. He'd obviously caught Charlie's sensitivity about his height. "Just a few inches shorter than me," he said. "I have a bike you can use, if you want it. A friend left it behind last spring." Before Charlie could answer, Ben asked, "So where are you from?"

"Kansas."

"Kansas!"

"What about you?" Charlie said, ignoring Ben's response. He was used to it; Americans at Cambridge all seemed to be from the East Coast or California.

"New York," Ben said, confirming Charlie's generalization. "You're not a 'Harvard man.'" He drawled the words with self-conscious irony. "I'd know it if you were—we're a pretty insular group. I'm guessing—Penn?"

"University of Kansas, actually."

Ben raised his eyebrows.

"My mother taught there," Charlie said, hating himself for feeling the need to explain. "Tuition was practically free, so—"

"So you saved your parents a bucket of money and ended up here anyway. That's the way to do it. You on a Marshall?"

"Fulbright."

"Law?"

"Philosophy. You?" Charlie said, struggling to regain some leverage in the conversation.

"Mellon. Architecture. I'm auditing Petrovsky's lectures on ancient Greek philosophy, though. Fascinating stuff. Have you made it to any of those?"

"It'd be a lot less work if you two just exchanged résumés," Claire said, coming up behind Ben and putting her arms around his waist. "Hi, Charlie." She smiled a big, open smile. "So nice of you to come."

He looked at the two of them—Ben tall and lanky, with unruly brown hair and small, round wire-framed glasses, and Claire with those wide-set hazel eyes and high cheekbones and candy apple lips—and suddenly wanted more than anything to be a part of their lives. "Thanks for inviting me," he said.

"Come on. There are people you should meet." Claire flashed a smile at Ben and took Charlie's hand, leading him into another room.

Ever since Charlie had returned from Atlanta, several days ago, Alison had been wary and brittle. She clearly knew something was going on, but as long as she didn't push it there was no reason to initiate a conversation—not yet, at least. Charlie needed time to figure things out. It was funny—when he was with Claire he was certain she was what he wanted: she was the love of his life. But when he was home with Alison and the kids, he felt rooted. He had planted this family here; he was loath to tear it up. He did love Alison—as much as, if not more than, most men love their wives, he thought. And he was crazy about his kids—Annie with her single-minded concentration and pixie chin and a smile just like his, Noah with his mother's dark eyes and trusting gaze. How could he choose to leave them?

And yet in forming the question he had already supplied a phantom answer.

Sunday afternoon he drove into the city to work for a few hours. What with the accident and then his trip to see Claire, he'd been out of the office quite a bit; several deadlines were looming, and he hadn't bothered checking e-mail for days. Alison was suspicious when he told her he needed to go in, and it was a guilty pleasure to be genuinely affronted when she didn't believe he was telling the truth. "It's just a few hours, honey," he said. "I'll be home by six. Let's do a family dinner, okay?"

There were 316 e-mails in his in-box, half of which were spam and half of which had to be dealt with, one way or another.

Let's raise the idea at the staff meeting on Tuesday. I'll get you the proposal by Wednesday.

Delete, delete, delete.

Call my cell phone. We need to talk.

Charlie sat back in his chair. It was an e-mail from Claire, sent a few hours earlier. Why hadn't she called? He looked in his bag and saw that he'd forgotten his cell phone; it was at home in the charger on his dresser. He hadn't bothered to listen to the messages on his blinking office phone.

He dialed her number.

"Charlie," she said breathlessly when she picked up. "I'm so glad you called. I didn't know what to do. I was considering smoke signals to get your attention."

"What's going on?"

"Oh, my God," she breathed. "I—I got home from the airport and Ben just—assaulted me—"

"Assaulted you?" Charlie broke in.

"No, no," she said. "I mean, he confronted me. About us. He knew. He figured it out."

"Oh. Wow," Charlie said.

"Yeah. But then it was weird—he didn't seem upset, really. I mean, I'm sure he is, but—well, you know Ben. He keeps a lot inside."

"Where is he now?"

"I don't know. He went out."

"Are you okay?"

"Yeah. I'm fine. I guess in a way it's a relief. I hated lying to him."

Charlie looked out his office window at a pigeon sitting on the ledge. He reached over and tapped the glass with his finger. Fly away, pigeon. The bird didn't budge.

"So what about Alison?" Claire asked.

In bed that morning, before the kids were awake, Charlie had molded his body around Alison's sleeping form. She stirred, opening her legs slightly, and he found his way in, stroking her until she came, arching back against him, and then he came, too, shuddering quietly and drifting back to sleep. When he woke up a little while later he could hear her downstairs with the kids, making breakfast—pancakes, by the sound of it. Noah was clamoring to crack the eggs, and demanding a dinosaur shape; Annie chimed in asking for a heart.

"I don't know," Charlie said. "She hasn't said anything. But . . . she suspects. Something."

"Umm," said Claire. She was silent for a moment. Then she said, "So what are you going to do?"

That was the question, wasn't it? Charlie had meant every word he'd said to Claire in Atlanta, but—Christ, this was soon. He stared out the window at the pigeon, which, as if sensing the intensity of his gaze, bobbed its head at him and turned away.

"I'm not saying you *should* do anything," Claire continued. "I was just wondering what you were thinking. And also—well—I guess there's a chance Ben might call Alison. He didn't say he was going to, but. You never know."

"Yeah," Charlie said, thinking, Holy shit. This is happening. He thought of the children's fable about the dog with a bone that, seeing his reflection, mistakes it for a dog with a larger bone, and drops his own in pursuit of the illusion. "I need to figure this out," he said. "I guess . . . I'll call you later."

"Listen, Charlie." She sighed. "I didn't mean to set anything in motion prematurely. You should wait until you're ready. If—if you're ready."

He nodded abstractly, then realized she couldn't see him. "I'll give you a call in a few days," he said.

When he hung up the phone he felt a grim foreboding. He stood up and went to the window, leaning his forehead against the cool glass. The bird was gone. Below, on another window ledge, Charlie could see several pigeons huddling together, and he wondered for a moment if one of them was his pigeon; if it had left his ledge in search of company, or if it had flown off to someplace else by itself.

AT ABOUT FIVE-THIRTY, as he was finishing up, Charlie called Alison from his office and asked if he could pick up anything for dinner on the way home.

"I was just about to boil water for pasta," she said.

"No, don't. You should take a break. How about Chinese?"

"All right."

"I can be in Rockwell in forty-five minutes. I'm just about to leave."

"I'll call in the order," she said. "Do you want anything special?"

This was a formality. In fact, their order was always the same: sesame noodles, dumplings, chicken and broccoli for the kids, garlic string beans, and Alison's favorite, spicy shrimp and eggplant. She would call their order in to the least mediocre of the mediocre Chinese restaurants in town (and the only one that served brown rice, as Alison told newcomers to town who asked for a recommendation, though they never actually ordered brown rice themselves), and he would pick it up.

But this time he said, "Maybe so." It hadn't occurred to him until that moment that he wanted something special, but perhaps—yes—he did. "How about—uh—a noodle thing, like chow fun. With pork."

"Instead of shrimp and eggplant?" He could hear the surprise and disapproval in her voice.

"We could do both."

"That's too much food," she said. "And we already have a noodle thing, sesame noodles."

"So cancel the sesame noodles."

"But the kids love them."

"So just order all of it. We can have leftovers."

"That place is never any good on the second day. You know that."

He sighed. "Come on, Alison, it's eight bucks. I'm in the mood for chow fun. Could you just order it, please?"

"Okay," she said tersely.

As he took the elevator down to underground parking, he wondered at Alison's truculence. Though of course she had every reason to be mistrustful, Charlie had no idea whether she actually was. She'd never confronted him with any suspicions; if she had them, she'd done a good job of keeping them to herself. Even if she did think he was up to something, she had no reason to suspect that Claire was involved. Unless . . . what if Ben had called? But surely then they wouldn't be arguing over noodles. No—she didn't know. He was sure of it.

In a way it might have been easier if she did. The idea of being honest with Alison was profoundly unnerving. How was he going to summon the strength to tell her? And what would happen then? Charlie felt as if he were poised on the edge of a cliff, and he could either step back to the safety of land or step forward into a free fall. He knew what was behind him, but had no clue what lay ahead.

AT DINNER ALISON was friendlier. She took some chow fun for herself and exclaimed over how good it was, then urged it on the kids, both of whom refused to try it. Too many unidentifiable green things. "Just take a noodle. A noodle! You love noodles," she said to Annie in the falsely jovial tone of a Mouseketeer.

"I love *sesame* noodles," Annie said. "And only because they have peanut butter on them."

"It's not peanut butter. It's sesame paste," Alison said.

"Eww. Then I don't like them either."

"It's peanut butter," Charlie said quickly. "Mom was kidding." He raised his eyebrows at Alison, who nodded, signaling her complicity.

"Is that true, Mommy?" Annie asked suspiciously.

"Yes."

Annie sniffed the brownish noodles already congealing on her plate. "Okay. Because I do love them," she said, clearly relieved.

Alison glanced at Charlie, who smiled back. Disaster averted. It was these kinds of moments, Charlie realized with a stab in his gut, that he

229

would regret giving up most, the moments he couldn't share with any-one else, embedded in the intimacy of creating a family. He hadn't re-ally thought it through, but suddenly it occurred to him that all of this would be off-limits as soon as he told Alison what was going on.

He looked at Alison, cutting broccoli into Skittles-size pieces on Noah's plastic Tigger plate, furrowing her brow in concentration. There was a fine vertical line between her eyes that seemed to have become permanent in the past few months. In her dark hair he saw glints of gray. She was wearing a long-sleeved purple T-shirt and old Levi's, her "mommy uniform," as she called it, and the holes in her earlobes were empty; she must have forgotten to put earrings in, or maybe she didn't wear them anymore. He had to admit that he didn't know. It had been a long time since he'd noticed much about her. Was that a symptom of the problem, he wondered, or was it, in a larger sense, the problem itself?

After all that fuss about the noodles, Charlie didn't want them. He wasn't hungry. He choked down a few bites, moved the food around on his plate like a cagey anorectic, and went to the fridge for a second Sam Adams. Or maybe a third. Yep—he'd gulped down one right away when he came in, opened a second when they sat down to eat. When everyone else was finished, he scraped and stacked the plates—which Alison had once told him was rude to do at the table, but which he did now anyway—and loaded the dishwasher.

"Do you want to do the dishes, and I'll do the kids?"

"Nah, I'll do the kids," he said. He brought the plates over to the counter, holding his beer by the neck, and then took a long swig. He was beginning to feel a little fuzzy around the edges, and it was so much more appealing than the alternative that he determined to finish this one and have another.

"Okay," Alison said equitably. "I'm reading *On the Banks of Plum Creek* to Annie; she knows which chapter we're on. And Noah gets to choose three books from his shelf."

"Four! Four books," Noah said. "No, five."

"Right," Charlie said, thinking, Wouldn't it be much more efficient to read them both the same book?

"I've tried reading them the same book and it never works," Alison said, divining his thoughts. "But you could try."

"I want to read *Plum Creek*," Annie said, pouting, "not dumb baby books."

"That's it, then, we'll read *Plum Creek*," said Charlie. "And six books for you, Mister."

"Yay!" Noah dashed out of the kitchen and clambered up the stairs in giddy anticipation. Annie slunk out after him.

Charlie finished his beer and put the bottle in the recycling bin under the sink, where it clinked loudly against the others. For a moment he lingered in the doorway. Could he get another beer without Alison noticing? Spying a tub of Country Crock whipped margarine on the counter, he grabbed it as an alibi and opened the fridge. While Alison's back was turned, he slipped a beer into the front right pocket of his khakis. "Well, I'm heading up," he said cheerily, ducking out the door.

The two-socket ceiling light in the upstairs hall was bright, too bright; it made him wince. Why hadn't he noticed it before? The bulbs were probably 100 watt, too strong for the fixture. Charlie turned it off as Noah came tearing out of his bedroom, wearing socks and nothing else.

"I want to take a bath!" he shouted, and against Charlie's feeble protests he ran into the kids' bathroom and turned on the spigot.

"I don't have to take one, do I?" Annie said, coming into the hall in her yellow nightgown with white unicorns frolicking across the bodice and matching yellow slippers. "Anyway, I told Mommy I'm too old to take a bath with a boy."

Reaching into his pocket and shifting the cold beer so it wouldn't make a mark like an iron on his now partially frozen upper thigh, Charlie realized he didn't have a bottle opener. Shit. He couldn't go downstairs; it would be too obvious. "He's not a boy, he's your baby brother," he said absently, going into Annie's room and rummaging around on her little white desk. Plastic ruler? No. Stapler? Scissors? Hmm—no. Finally he came across a claw-shaped staple remover, and positioned it, Jaws of Life–like, over the bottle cap. Twisting and prying, he managed to get the cap off at the expense of the staple remover, which appeared irreparably mangled. He tossed it into Annie's white plastic wastebasket with a thud, and took a long swallow.

"My staple remover!" Annie cried, rushing toward the wastebasket and sifting quickly through the contents. Damn, she must have been watching. Holding the battered item up accusingly, she wailed, "Daddy, you broke it!"

"I know, I know, shhhh," Charlie said, holding his free hand out in front of him and flapping it as if he were dribbling a basketball. "Hush, sweetie. It's not a big deal. It was cheaply made, anyway. I'll get you a better one."

"I don't want a better one. I want *this* one. You ruuuined it!" she sobbed, holding it tightly against her chest.

In the next room, Noah started to howl. "The water's too hot. It bunned my fingas. MOM-MY!"

With both of his children in tears, and his wife already sprinting up the stairs, Charlie took another gulp of his beer, draining it, and set it strategically behind him on the desk, blocking it from Alison's view. What was wrong with these children? Why did everything have to be so dramatic?

"What in the world is going on?" Alison said as she came into the room.

"Daddy broke my staple remover!"

"I bunned my fingas!" Noah said, barreling in behind her, holding up his injured digits.

Alison inspected the chubby splayed hand. Apparently satisfied that Noah would live, she turned to Charlie and asked, "What were you doing with a staple remover?"

"Oh—well—I was just—"

"He was opening a bottle, Mommy, and that is *not* what you're sup-posed to use a staple remover for," Annie said indignantly.

"What kind of bottle?" Alison asked, and Charlie, his ears red-dening slightly, reached behind his back and retrieved the empty Sam Adams. "Another beer?" she said. For a moment they were all silent, listening to the water filling the bathtub in the next room. The children gazed up at both of them with their mouths open. Alison looked at them and then at Charlie, as if to say *let's not do this here.* "Okay, look. You go finish the kitchen. I'll get them to bed."

"Awww, why can't I have a bath?" Noah whined.

"But—" Charlie said.

"Charlie, you're drunk," she said quietly.

"I am not."

"We'll talk about this later," she said.

"It's nice to have the moral upper hand, isn't it?" he said somewhat desperately.

She gave him a look of such cold fury that he stepped backward, bumping against the desk. "You would know," she said.

AFTER FINISHING THE dishes—which were almost done, anyway; Alison was a marvel of efficiency—Charlie sank onto the couch in the TV room and flipped to CNN to watch the news. Unfortunately MarketWatch was on, which made him anxious (the fact that he'd never been particularly interested in the stock market was his secret; he knew it was his masculine duty to care, but now that the market was tanking, taking his 401K with it, he cared even less), so he flipped through channels, skipping from a family comedy from the seventies to a show with contestants eating bugs, before landing on *The Simpsons.*

This was more his speed. He watched the show, prone, with one wary eye. When the episode ended—a complicated story involving Clint Eastwood, mud pies, and the nuclear power plant where Homer worked—Charlie turned off the TV. The house was quiet; the children, he concluded, were in bed. He sat up, feeling groggy. Four beers weren't so many; in college that amount wouldn't have fazed him at all, but he wasn't used to drinking that way anymore. And he hadn't eaten much dinner. All he wanted to do now was go to bed.

He could hear Alison in the room directly above him—their bedroom—padding around. He knew he should go up there, but he didn't want to.

He sat up. Fuck. There was a small mallet in his brain, hammering his cerebral cortex. With each throbbing pulse his head seemed to grow larger.

Lying down again, he closed his eyes. He might have even drifted off.

"So what was all that about?" a blunt, angry voice demanded from above.

Charlie blinked. Groggily he pulled himself onto one elbow and swung his legs over the side of the couch. He squinted up at the shadowy figure looming over him—Alison, wearing blue flannel pajamas (in April? An unseasonably cold April, but still). Her face, free of makeup and damp around the hairline, shiny with moisturizer, seemed strangely exposed, as if she'd not only washed her face but also scrubbed off an epidermal layer.

"What time is it?" he asked.

"Nine-forty-five."

"Oh. Wow." He rubbed his face.

She crossed her arms. "We need to talk."

He frowned, as if surprised. He wasn't surprised, but he didn't want her to think he'd been waiting like a coward for her to make the first move—which was, of course, exactly what he had been doing. "Okay," he said.

She sat down on the couch, close to the edge, as if she might skitter away at any second. She bit the corner of her lip, twisting her mouth into a grimace. "I just realized something," she said. "You have been blaming me since the accident for killing that little boy."

"Alison—"

"Stop. That's not what I realized. What I realized is that I've been blaming myself, too. I've been blaming myself for killing that boy, and for the problems in our marriage, and for the fact that you've essentially absented yourself from our lives. I thought it was all my fault. But you know what?" Her voice rose in a sharp crescendo. "I wasn't the one who ran a red light. I wasn't holding my child on my lap in the front seat. Maybe if I hadn't had two drinks I could've moved out of the way faster—but probably not; I've never had fast reflexes, especially driving, *especially* at night. Believe me, I'll live with that memory for the rest of my life. But I will not live with your judgment and scorn."

"Hey, hey," he said gently, trying to calm her down, "I don't—"

"You're gone most of the time," she snapped. "You're gone emotionally, too. And when you actually do spend some time with us you get drunk. You fucking hypocrite. You've basically checked out, haven't you?"

He waited to see if she had more to say, but she just sat there, looking at the floor, her chest moving rapidly up and down in her flannel pajama top. That old philosophical question flitted through his mind: who breaks the thread, the one who pulls or the one who hangs on?

This is happening. There's no turning back.

"Alison, you're right," he said, putting his hand on her arm. "You're right. About all of it."

An evolving expression slid across her face, like a cloud moving across the sun—relief to mistrust to defensiveness. "What do you mean?"

"I guess . . . I guess I have blamed you. Maybe I thought if I made you into a villain it would be easier."

"What would be easier?"

Shit. "It would be easier to . . . say what I have to say."

She recoiled, pulling her arm away. "I don't understand."

"I don't know how to tell you this."

"Oh God." She put her hands over her eyes.

"I just—It's nothing you've done."

"I knew it," she murmured.

235

"Knew what," he said, trying to sound sympathetic instead of like he was fishing. How much did she know?

"That you weren't—in love with me anymore."

"It's not that," he said. "I do love you. I'll always love you."

"Please," she said, holding up her hand.

"I don't. . . ."

"Just tell me."

There wasn't a single molecule of Charlie that wanted to be having this conversation. He felt as if he had been pushed out onto a tightrope, high above the ground; now all he could do was try to keep his balance and make it across.

"I'm—I think I'm in love with Claire," he said.

He had heard the expression "the blood drained from her face," but he'd never seen it before. Alison actually went white. "Wh-what?" she sputtered.

Charlie shrugged helplessly, deploying an old weapon, the equivalent of a girl flirting to get her way. If he could become a little boy in her eyes, naughty or willful or irresponsible, it might not be so devastating; she might even somehow forgive him. Unfortunately this tactic seemed to have lost all effectiveness.

"Claire *Ellis*? My-best-friend-from-childhood Claire?"

He didn't respond. It hardly seemed necessary.

"You've got to be joking," she said. "You've got to be fucking kidding me. Please tell me this is a joke."

"It isn't a joke."

"What—how—" She shook her head, as if trying to wake from a bad dream.

"I think I've been in love with her since Cambridge," he said haltingly.

She stared at him.

He looked down.

"Go on," she said.

"She—Claire—didn't want me then. I mean, she was already with Ben."

"Jesus." Alison's lip curled in disgust. This, he could tell, was even worse—that Claire had first rejected him and then passed him along to her.

"And I thought the feeling would go away," he continued. "I mean, I had a crush on her, but she was with Ben, and that was that. I liked Ben, too. I liked being with both of them. For a while I thought maybe it was that—I just wanted to be in their life, you know? Their life—their lives—seemed so much more interesting than mine. And then . . . you came."

Alison's body went rigid. She looked straight ahead, at some imaginary point in space halfway across the room.

"And you were so beautiful," he said. "You are—you are so beautiful."

"Don't, Charlie."

"I fell in love with you, I did. I had never met anyone like you. So poised and yet—I don't know—open."

He could see tears welling in her eyes.

"I wanted you. I wanted to marry you."

"You were in love with her."

"No, I—I wasn't then. Or I convinced myself that I wasn't, because there was nothing I could do about it."

"So I was the consolation prize," she said bitterly.

"No. No," he said, "it didn't feel that way." He had intended to be scrupulously honest with Alison—he owed it to her; it was the least he could do. But she was right. The stark truth was that he would not have married her had Claire been free. And even though he did grow to love Alison—he had been, he truly believed, in love with her—a part of him was always thinking about Claire, imagining how things would have been different if he had married Claire instead. "I was happy to be with you."

She looked at him for a long moment. "I don't believe you."

He shifted uncomfortably.

"This whole marriage has been a lie."

237

"No, Alison."

"Just stop the bullshit," she said. "How long have you been fucking her?"

"Al—"

"How long?"

He sighed. "We started seeing each other a few months ago. In the winter."

He could see her calculating the date in her head. "When?"

"Before the holidays."

"Oh, that's lovely," she said, her voice heavy with sarcasm. "Where? Where did you go?"

"The—the first time?"

She made a face.

"A hotel. In Midtown."

"Where was I? Or was this on your lunch hour?"

"No, it was—it was a Friday. You were visiting Pam Thurgood in upstate New York with the kids."

"Aah," she said, nodding slowly, "I remember that weekend. You said you had to work late, right? That was why you couldn't come."

"You know," he said hesitantly, "the actual details are kind of irrelevant."

"Really," she said.

"Yeah. I just think . . . it's not important what happened when, and all that."

"Uh-huh," she said. "So how was it?"

"What do you mean?"

"I mean, was she a good fuck?"

"Come on, Alison."

"What? Is that irrelevant, too? I'm guessing it matters to you."

"I just—I don't think we need to be doing this."

"Ummm." She nodded, parodying amiability. "Yeah, you're right. We don't need to be doing this. You're fucking my best friend—you say you're 'in love with'"—she knifed quote marks in the air with hooked fingers—"my best friend—*my best friend*—but you're right, how rude, how impolite of me to ask you anything about it." She bit down on the words, her voice rising with each syllable until she was practically shouting.

Jesus, she's going to wake the children. Charlie wanted to stifle her somehow; he had to restrain himself from putting his hand over her mouth or telling her to shut the fuck up. He knew he didn't deserve to be impatient with her; he had to hear her out, but *Christ* it was hard. He didn't want to explain, pick over each detail, sit there and take it as the enormity of it sunk in and she got more and more furious.

"Yeah, that would be crass, wouldn't it?" she continued. Now she was on her feet. "You fucking asshole! You low-life. You brought two children into the world, and now you're going to abandon them."

"No I'm not."

"Yes you are."

"I'm not, Alison. I wouldn't do that."

"Oh, okay. I see. Is Claire going to move in with us?"

"Alison, please."

"I have given the best years of my life to you—that fucking cliché, it's true," she cried, spitting the words at him. "I devoted myself to you, to this marriage. To being a family."

"I know, I know," he said, patting the air with his hands, as if trying to tamp down her emotion. "And you are an amazing wife and mother. This may sound crazy, Alison, but I mean it—this is not about you."

"Exactly!" she screeched. "*This is not about me*. It's never been about me, has it?"

"Alison," he said miserably.

"Stop saying my name." She strode out of the room, and for a brief moment Charlie wondered if the conversation was over. Then she came back with a handful of tissues, which she pulled out of her balled fist one after another like a magician with silk scarves. She blew her nose loudly. Tears were streaming down her face. "Does Ben know?"

"I think so."

"You think so?"

"Yes, he does."

"How do you know?"

"Because . . . Claire called me."

She hiccupped. "When?"

"Today."

"When today? When you were 'at work'?"

He nodded.

She shook her head. "I knew you were fucking lying about going to work today," she sobbed.

"I wasn't lying. I really had to go in."

"How convenient, that she knew you 'had to go in.'"

"She didn't know. She called my cell phone."

"Bullshit. Your cell phone was here."

"Right," he said, struggling to keep up with her detective work, "so then she sent me an e-mail on the off chance—Jesus, Al, what does it matter?" he said finally. "I wasn't lying to you about today. I had to go to work. I didn't see Claire. But . . . I have lied to you. I have been lying to you. I hate that part of it—"

"Oh, you hate *that part* of it?"

"Yes, I do. I hate lying to you."

"Why are you doing this?" she screamed. She collapsed onto the couch beside him and doubled over, as if in agony, clutching her stomach with one hand and sobbing into her wadded-up tissues in the other. "Why? *Why?*"

There was really no answer. He was doing this because he could not keep skimming along the surface of his life without one day crashing into something hard and unpleasant, a truth about himself he had long tried to avoid—that his inability to make difficult decisions was what had gotten him into this mess in the first place. He wanted both lives; he didn't want to have to choose. He wanted this life with Alison and a parallel one with Claire, but that didn't seem to be possible. He was doing this because he had finally realized that it took more of an effort to keep the chaos contained than it did to let it go.

And though he did, genuinely, love his children with his whole being, and hated the idea that they, like him—like Alison—would suffer through a divorce, he was convinced that he would only get one chance to feel this kind of passion, to express it, to *live*. In a way, it was as simple as that: you only get one life. And though his children were everything to him, sometimes he closed his eyes and wondered what his life would be like if he had claimed what he wanted from the beginning, if he had not given up so easily, and, as a result, had never made them.

He wouldn't say any of this, of course. He couldn't say it. So he put his hand gently on her back while she cried, and eventually she grew quiet.

November 1997

"Damn. I've forgotten to bring a pen. You don't have an
extra, do you?"

Charlie was standing in a dingy, narrow hallway in
Queens College, waiting for an appointment with the
graduate student advisor, Master Holcombe. It was the girl's
eyes that Charlie noticed first, an unusual greenish amber
in her pale face, the color of a fallen leaf in the snow. She
stared at him expectantly, with a frank intensity he found
unsettling.

"Uh, let me check," he said, rummaging in his bag. He
came up with a fistful of writing implements and presented
them to her on an open palm.

She chose one, and smiled. Her teeth were small and
white. "Thanks," she said. "You're American."

"How can you tell? I've barely said a word."

She laughed. "You're so American."

"Why does that sound like an insult?" he said lightly,
though it did. "You are, too."

She squinted at him. She was wearing a short brown plaid
dress and brown leather sandals. Her skin was pale; a smat-
tering of freckles fell across her nose and chest and arms.
He couldn't tell much about her shape in that dress, which
hung from her shoulders like a sack, but her bare legs were
tanned and strong. She was tallish, and her curly cinnamon

hair was pulled back in a clip. "Everything I say sounds like an insult," she said. "So I've been told."

Just then the door opened and a young man with a receding chin and strips of thin hair plastered to his forehead slipped out. He wore gray slacks and a flimsy white collared shirt, which had taken on a pinkish cast from the skin underneath. "Holcombe said to send in whoever's next," he said.

"I guess that's me. Nice to meet you," the girl said, offering Charlie her hand.

"But we didn't," he said. "Meet. I don't even know your name."

"Claire," she said. "Ellis."

"Charlie Granville."

She smiled. "Why don't you come to drinks after dinner at our place tonight? We're rounding up all the Americans we can find."

"We . . ."

"Ben and I. My boyfriend. Fiancé, actually."

Charlie nodded. He felt a suffusing prick of disappointment, like a bee sting.

"Thirty-two Barton Road," she said. "Eight o'clock."

He looked at her fingers; she wasn't wearing a ring. "Thank you," he said. "I'd like that."

244

When something terrible happens, a lifetime of small events and unremarkable decisions, of unresolved anger and unexplored fears, begins to play itself out in ways you least expect. You've been going along from one day to the next, not realizing that all those disparate words and gestures were adding up to something, a conclusion you didn't anticipate. And later, when you begin to retrace your steps, you see that you will need to reach back further than you could have imagined, beyond words and thoughts and even dreams, perhaps, to make sense of what happened.

Four weeks after the accident, Alison had to go in front of a judge to face the DWI charge. Robin not only offered to accompany her to the hearing, but she also helped Alison prepare papers for her lawyer, Paul Ryan, and wrote a letter of support to give the judge.

The courtroom was in a new municipal building. It was quiet and carpeted—like the funeral home chapel, Alison thought, designed to muffle dissonant expressions of anguish and despair. Its small windows, with short, burnt orange curtains, were set high on the wall, so all you could see were squares of sky and odd angles of other buildings. Alison had only been inside a few courtrooms in her life, one for a magazine article and one to protest a parking ticket. Both were in old buildings, formal, ornate spaces with enormous windows and raised wooden platforms for the judge—nothing like the room in which she now stood.

As Alison walked down the wide center aisle, she was surprised to see the mother and father of the boy sitting in the far corner, on the right. Ahead, on the left, Paul Ryan was talking quietly to a young woman in a navy blue suit—the prosecutor, Alison supposed. Robin put an arm around her shoulder, gently urging her forward.

The court was kind to Alison, kinder than she would have been to herself. The judge revoked her driver's license for three months and assigned her to twelve hours at an Intoxicated Driver Resource Center. There would be nearly $1000 in fines and fees, as well as several thousand dollars in insurance surcharges over the next three years. In her statement, the judge said that while Alison hadn't caused the accident— the investigation revealed that the boy's father had driven through the intersection without applying his brakes—she was nonetheless partially at fault. Her blood-alcohol level grazed the legal limit. Her reflexes were impaired; she might otherwise have reacted more quickly and averted the crash. She would have to live with the knowledge that her drinking may have been a contributing factor in the boy's death.

The judge glanced at Robin, the loyal friend, sitting behind Alison. She looked Alison up and down. She said she hoped Alison had learned a lesson from this. She implored Alison to think, really think, about what she had done. She said that if there was one thing she'd learned as a county judge, it was that life hinges on small moments and seemingly trivial decisions.

Across the aisle sat the father of the boy, wearing a Mets cap and a blue windbreaker, and his wife, with her hair pulled back in a tight bun. At the funeral her hair had been long and flowing. Now she clutched a Ziploc bag of what appeared to be Ritz crackers, and stared straight ahead. The father's arm was stretched across the wooden pew-like bench behind her. The drumming of his fingers was a muted percussion in the quiet room.

Neither of the boy's parents looked at Alison, though she kept glancing at them. She had written a letter to them expressing her regret and sadness, but they'd never responded. She didn't know if they had even received it.

When the hearing ended, Paul Ryan leaned over and said quietly, "Now you can put this behind you."

"Thank you for everything you did," she said.

Robin gave her a hug. "Ready to go?"

"In a minute," Alison said. "I want to speak to the parents."

Paul, stacking papers in his briefcase, grimaced. "I'm not sure that's a good idea."

"I need to," Alison said. As she made her way over to Marco's parents, she caught the husband's eye. He put his arm protectively around his wife, who shrank back against him.

"I am truly sorry," Alison said. "I have two children myself, and I—"

"Okay," the father said, cutting her off, gripping his wife's shoulder. She just stared at Alison, her expression impassive.

"I understand why you came. If there's anything . . ." Alison said helplessly.

"We just wanted to see who you were," he said, and turned away.

Walking across the parking lot to the car—Robin's Honda minivan—Alison looked up. Gray clouds moved fast across a pale blue expanse, and it seemed as if the land under her feet was moving equally fast in the opposite direction. She didn't know which way she was headed. All the things that had seemed solid to her a month ago—a month ago, and all of her life until then—were crumbling. The ground had shifted; she'd lost her balance. She felt as if she were falling off the earth.

FOR WEEKS ALISON felt as if she were underwater, in a deep, murky place, struggling to make her way to the surface. She couldn't believe anything Charlie said, anything Claire said. She didn't know which of her friends were as ignorant as she was, and which might have known all along. She was learning that it was unusual for people to speak plainly to each other about painful or difficult things. We talk to each other, and about each other, but rarely are those conversations the same. We learn through years of living with white lies and self-deception that plain talk can ignite a powder keg of feeling, so we speak in euphemism and metaphor, steering clear of the flinty truth: Your husband doesn't love you. Your best friend has betrayed you. You have been living a lie.

At the drugstore in town one day, Alison observed a young mother holding a child, apparently her daughter, about two years old. The mother was bending to sign a credit card bill at the counter. The girl's legs were wrapped around her mother's waist, her arms around her neck. They were molded together as one, and Alison wished for a moment that she had a camera. Then she realized that her inclination would be to give the woman the photo so that she might see something about her life she might not otherwise have known.

When Alison looked at photographs now of Charlie and her together, she studied them for clues. Is he looking off in the distance? Is she looking down? How close are they sitting, are they touching, is he turning toward her or away? She had taken thousands of pictures in her life, and most of them were collected in photo boxes labeled by year. Occasionally, after some self-contained experience—a trip, their wedding, the birth of a child—she organized the pictures into an album. But what story did those pictures tell? What did they hide or reveal about what was happening now?

It would have been easy to stick to the story of the wife who was betrayed and lied to and left; and some days, for Alison, that was the story of her marriage, the only one that mattered. When something happens in a marriage, everybody wants to blame one person or the other, as if an easy answer might make it more understandable and less sad. He was unfaithful—good riddance. She didn't know how to love him—doesn't he deserve better? But when you are one of the people in that marriage, you know how complicated it is. Perhaps he was unfaithful because you didn't know how to love him, and perhaps you didn't know how to love him because he never fully gave himself to you. Perhaps he was in love with someone else. And maybe you knew that—maybe you knew it long ago, before you were married, and you married him anyway.

❧

CLEARING OUT THE clutter on a bottom shelf one afternoon, not long after Charlie left, Alison came across *Blue Martinis*. Annie was at school and Noah was taking a nap, so Alison sat on the floor, and, for the first time since it had arrived in the mail several months earlier, opened the book. Out fell a slip of paper with "Compliments of the Author" printed on it. On the title page she found an inscription, in Claire's familiar scrawl, which she hadn't known was there. "To Al—" it said, "Maybe the only person in the world who knows which parts of this are true and which ones I made up. I won't tell if you won't. Love, Claire."

The next page held an epigraph: "As if . . . what was actual, as opposed to what was imagined, as opposed to what was believed, made, when you got right down to it, any difference at all." It was from *Charming Billy*, by Alice McDermott.

So it didn't matter, apparently, which parts of Claire's book were true. The story was real and it wasn't real, the facts as arbitrary and malleable as fiction.

Alison had a strong urge to close the book and put it away, but she hesitated. Her unwillingness to face things head-on was, it seemed, part of the problem.

Leaning against the wall, Alison turned to chapter 1 and started reading.

249

The opening of the freezer door. Clink of heavy glass. Ice in a silver shaker. When Emma heard those sounds she pricked up her ears like a cat hearing the grind of a can opener. She wandered downstairs to find her mother pouring blue liquid into two martini glasses, setting the shaker on the Formica countertop and licking her fingers, wiping her hands on a linen towel. Twisting a strip of lemon peel into each glass. Handing one to Emma and raising her own.

Cheers.

Sometimes—Emma could tell by the violent smear of lipstick already present on the rim—her mother would be starting on her second when she invited Emma to join her.

Reading and skimming for the next two hours, Alison entered a world both familiar and foreign, a fun house version of reality. She'd been prepared to dislike the book, but she found herself drawn in, seduced by descriptions of places she recognized and sketches of people she knew.

In a small town there are too many people watching and judging, too many ways to be recognized. Not enough allowances. There is no escape; you are defined and labeled before you're even aware of yourself as a "self"—before you have anything, consciously, to do with it. You make one mistake or two, say one thing to one person, and everybody knows it. Everybody thinks they know who you are, even if you're not sure, yourself.

250

Emma's home was a desolate and lonely place. Cool darkness: heavy drapes pulled shut across sliding-glass doors. Her father was a looming presence, using up all the oxygen, making the air in the house thin and difficult to breathe. Her mother's unhappiness—creeping, etheric—poisoned what air was left. When Emma walked in the front door her father would give her a blank look, her mother peered through the scrim of her five o'clock cocktails, and Emma would become as indistinct to herself as she was to them.

It wasn't a novel in the way Claire insisted it was; the details of their real life were accurate, down to the crumbling stone patio behind Alison's house and the cocktail dress Claire wore to school when she was thirteen to exasperate her mother. The story wasn't so much fictional as it was partial—a piece of their lives, a fragment of the tale.

Emma didn't remember much about life before Jill, and she didn't remember meeting her. All she knew was that when Jill arrived in her life, sometime in the first grade, it was as if she had been there all along.

It was in Jill's attic room, with its twin beds, that their friendship was forged. With the lights out, each girl was in her own narrow confessional; the darkness yielded secrets that daylight hid. On summer nights, under cool sheets, they teased apart jealousies and grudges, analyzed the flirting techniques of boys at school, critiqued other girls' boyfriends. Emma would fall asleep listening to Jill's shallow breathing in the bed beside her, Jill's leg flung over the side like a Raggedy Ann, cherry stains around her mouth.

The next morning, the two of them would stand side by side in front of the oval vanity mirror, so close that their shoulders pressed together, squeezing into the frame.

"You're lucky your hair is straight," Emma would say.

"It's horrible. Dirt brown."

"At least it's not curly. Boiing!" Emma would demonstrate, pulling on a strand and letting it spring back.

"Just be glad you don't have this nose."

"Yeah, thank you Lord for giving me freckles instead."

"My hippo hips don't even fit in the mirror."

They'd continue this litany of self-abasement until one of them said something uncomfortably close to the truth, and the other would feel compelled to reassure her with a painful earnestness: that's not true at all, you're gaw-jess, dah-lin'. This would dispel the illusion that, like witches repelling curses, they might banish these faults and fears by articulating them, and the game would be over.

Emma felt big next to Jill—too tall, with uncontrollable hair and oversize features, freakish, galumphing, too much. Slight and

251

delicate, Jill was the kind of girl even the toughest boys behaved with, as if they sensed that in her reticence, her apparent vulnerability, a fairy tale–like transformation was possible. Emma had always thought that like Snow White or Cinderella, Jill would be the one who'd marry a prince someday.

Did Claire really feel this way about her? If so, Alison had never known. She thought about her mother's reaction, how she'd warned Alison that she wouldn't like the way she was portrayed. It was true that Jill's major attributes appeared to be loyalty, naïveté, and a willingness to pick up the pieces when the main character went too far. If Jill was the innocent maiden, Emma was the savvy heroine whose calculated impulsiveness usually got her what she wanted.

Skipping ahead, to high school, Alison read:

Emma and Jill were sitting together on the brick wall outside the main entrance to the school, waiting for Emma's mother to pick them up. Two guys they didn't know—seniors, probably—were in a car, idling at the curb, looking over at them and smirking.

"That one's cute," one of the guys said loudly, pointing at Jill, "but the other one's a babe."

"Yeah, you might end up marrying her," his friend answered, cocking his finger at Jill, "but she's the one you'd want on the side." He aimed his imaginary gun at Emma and pulled the trigger.

When Noah started calling "Mommy, I wake!" from his darkened bedroom, Alison said, "I'll be right there," and turned from the middle of the book to the end. Emma was eighteen now and had applied to colleges up north in secrecy. The day the acceptance letter came from Barnard, she started packing her bags. Jill was staying behind and going to a college in-state.

On her first night in the city Emma took the subway to Times Square. It was one of those summer evenings when the city seems to shimmer; the air has cooled, the light softened. Everybody's away, in the Hamptons or at the Shore. Restaurants are half empty, taxis sail down Broadway, doormen idle under awnings. New York feels like a secret you're privileged to know.

Wandering up Broadway, she squinted at the tall buildings, dazzled by the lights. If anyone caught her eye she smiled and said hello. She looked like a tourist, though she didn't feel like one. She had only been in New York for six hours, but already it felt like home.

Emma's past—Hatfield and everyone in it—was behind her now. As she walked around the city she could feel it: her past fading into memory. Real life, she knew, was just beginning.

And yet here Claire was, Alison thought, pretending the past back into existence. The difference was that now she could talk about it like an adult; she could look at it with cool and even ironic distance. She could be philosophical. Her past was real and not real, true and imagined. It didn't really matter, did it? It was childhood, long ago.

I won't tell if you won't.

Alison closed the book. She could hear Noah singing the "Open, Shut Them" song to himself in his bed. She got to her feet and put the book back on the shelf, then went to her son, her own real life, in the next room.

part five

The only future we can conceive is built upon the forward shadow of our past.

—MARCEL PROUST

From where Ben is standing, on a hard-packed mound of dirt above the scooped-out dig, the tractors and yellow backhoes below look like toy trucks. It's a boy's fantasy come to life (not his fantasy, exactly, he thinks, but some boy's). As he watches the machines lurch around in the mud Ben spies a bird, probably a sparrow, perched on one of the teeth of a loitering digger. He remembers a story he loved as a child, about a baby bird that falls out of its nest and sets off in search of its mother, though it doesn't know what she looks like. "Are you my mother?" the bird asks everything it comes across—a digger, a crane, a dog, a flower.

This is a little how Ben feels at the moment—lost, without direction, unable to find his way because he doesn't know what he's looking for.

Are you my wife?

It doesn't do any good to recount the details, but Ben can't help it; he keeps running over things in his mind. For all the time he has spent replaying it, he honestly can't make any more sense of what happened than he could in those first slow-motion minutes when he saw the shape of his future, and Claire's, and realized that they were not the same.

He feels as though he's living someone else's life. It's as if he'd been watching a show on TV and then, with the click of a remote, changed the channel. There's no continuity and no flow; it's just a whole different story.

A week or so after Claire left, Ben had called Alison.

"Did you have any idea?" he asked.

"I don't know," she said. "But I didn't want to know."

They were quiet for a moment. Then she said, "They could've saved us both a lot of time."

"And themselves," he said.

There was not much more to say. Each was embarrassed for the other. To be linked in this way was terrible.

It would be easier if Ben could separate the strands of the story, but they remain tangled in his mind in an impossible snarl. There is his marriage to Claire, his relationship with his mother and father, his rural childhood and urban adulthood, his friendship with Charlie and Alison. As he thinks about the past it is as if he is looking too closely at the dots in a pointillist painting but can't step back to see the larger image.

It makes no logical sense to him that Claire would leave him for Charlie. Charlie is a good guy (or at least Ben used to think so), but he possesses little ambition or fire. He is stuck in a job he doesn't like, and seems in no particular hurry to figure out what he wants.

Except, that is, for Claire.

How foolish. How wasteful. Claire hurt two of the few people in the world who truly cared about her, who always wished the best for her, who loved her. And Charlie—Charlie has two children who need him, a house, a yard, a whole conventional adult life that Claire has always seemed happy enough to avoid. When Ben really thinks about it, he gets angry. So he tries not to think about it much.

Since moving to Boston to oversee the construction of the Boyd Arts Center six weeks ago, Ben has been constantly on-site. How he ever tried to oversee this job from New York is hard for him to imagine now. Weekly visits did not permit this kind of access and accountability. When Philippa Boyd decided on a whim that the façade demanded sandstone, not limestone, Ben was able to convince her that limestone was more in keeping with the design, the location, the symbolic import of the whole project. On-site, he could intercede when the chief engineer decided to shift the building 20 percent to the left for vague structural reasons, thereby altering the entire focal point, the meeting of earth and water.

On weekends Ben strolls through Cambridge, revisiting old haunts. Restaurants he frequented as a student, record stores, The Coop—he can lose himself for hours. He has signed on to teach a continuing education class one evening a week in the fall at Harvard—a place he had mixed feelings about as a student but that now feels as comfortably familiar as an ancestral home. Observing the undergraduates— remarkably more diverse, even, than when he was a student—he feels a mixture of nostalgia and envy. Their adult lives are embryonic; they have no idea what's in store.

Boston feels safe, familiar, clean-rinsed by frequent rain. Ben appreciates the New Englandness of it all—the neat, conservative clothing people wear, the discrete provincial villages, even the twee romanticizing of colonial history. He likes the cool evenings and the boats in the harbor. He loves his job, and is happy enough not to feel pulled back to New York, with its clamor and unpredictability. Water finds its own level, his mother likes to say, and Ben thinks that's about right—he has found his level, and it's neither too deep nor too wide.

Sometimes Ben worries that he will end up as one of those persnickety single men in small spectacles and bow ties who make a fetish of neatness and erudition. The other morning, as he ground his coffee and steamed milk and read the *Boston Globe* at the round oak table in his breakfast nook with a piece of buttered whole grain toast, he felt a brief, sudden panic: might his world have permanently narrowed to this?

He has told the other partners at Sloane Howard that he's only in Cambridge to see the project through, but Ben suspects he will stay. A few days ago he called a friend from graduate school, a partner in a small local architecture firm, who set up an exploratory lunch. Besides, he has no home to go back to. He and Claire put the New York apartment on the market, and it sold surprisingly quickly. They divided their lives fairly amicably: Ben took the books, Claire kept most of the wedding presents. Claire and Charlie are already living together, from what he understands, in a friend's apartment downtown.

It seems to Ben that the breakup of his marriage was like a carefully choreographed dance, except he hadn't been taught the steps. All he could do was follow, and try to pick it up as he went along. He'd always thought that when you've been with someone for a long time your feelings are like an iceberg, only a small part of which is visible above the surface. Now he can see that what he thought was the tip of Claire's deeper feeling was in fact all that was left—a shard of intimacy, a nub of desire, the only remaining fragment of a dissolving relationship. She was lost to him before he realized he was losing her.

Ben has come through this experience changed, but he can't say, as he has always said before about times of stress and uncertainty, that it is for the better. He is stronger now. More wary. Less inclined to expect the best, as if it were his due. He has avoided bitterness, and maybe that is the most he can hope for.

As a child, Ben would not do things that hurt too much—look directly into the sun, push his body past endurance, run the water too hot. His goal was to avoid pain. And yet here it is, unavoidable.

ONE DAY, WHEN his life is still in boxes and his head in disarray, Ben answers his cell phone to hear the voice of the girl he hired last fall, Sarah, the one who deserted Drone Coward for a more prestigious job.

"I'm bored at this place," she tells him with characteristic bluntness—a bluntness he finds both alarming and intriguing. "I want to come back, if you'll have me."

"The Boston project is an exception," Ben says. "You really want to design pools and guesthouses?"

"No. But I want to work with you."

"Why?"

"Because you care about your work. I'm finding that's rare."

"Oh, you are, are you," Ben remarks absently, recalling details about the girl—her corn silk hair and thin wrists and unsettling intelligence. Her steady gaze and stone gray eyes. "Where's the boy?" he asks.

"Who? I have no idea. I never liked him much."

When she comes up to Boston on the train he takes her to dinner, and by dessert he has hired her as his associate on the Boyd project. It will be nice, he thinks, to have someone to talk to about work. Not that he hadn't talked to Claire—he just wasn't ever sure she wanted to listen.

"So what do you want to do with your life?" Ben asks Sarah one day, and she answers, "I want to design interesting buildings and I want to have a baby, not necessarily in that order."

I want to have a baby. In his marriage to Claire Ben had begun to give up on the idea, to reconcile himself to the life it appeared they would lead, but now that he has been set free perhaps he can finally admit how important it is to him, how he yearns for a child.

How strange, Ben thinks: I could grow to like this life. Maybe all of us could live several lives, giving some things up and gaining others, assembling different versions of contentment. Here in Boston, it isn't hard to imagine that Claire was simply a part of his life that is over, a stage he went through, a phase, a bloodless leaving—like graduating from college, or quitting one job and starting another, or losing touch with an old friend.

Claire was large, greedy. He was always trying to please her, to make her happy. He appreciates that Sarah is so self-contained; he doesn't have to be the sane, logical one. He can be spontaneous and even offbeat. He can be greedy himself.

After work, now, Ben goes home to a rented loft space on the top floor of an old brick factory building with a half-moon living room window leading to a balcony overlooking a cobblestone street. On clear nights he goes out on the balcony and gazes up at the stars, chips of light, halogen-bright, against the velvety expanse. He plays his child-hood game of searching for ancient constellations, Leo the Lion and Orion the Hunter. He notes the moon's progress from crescent to full, and watches meteors streak across the sky. Standing there, surrounded by stars, he thinks about how easy it would be to believe, as people did for thousands of years, that all the stars and planets move around the earth.

One of the first major purchases Ben makes in his new apartment is a telescope. Setting up the tripod in front of the half-moon window, he thinks of Galileo, who in the early seventeenth century trained his rudimentary telescope (less powerful than modern-day binoculars) on the moons revolving around Jupiter, and made the stunning discovery that the earth is not the center of the universe. Over the next hundred years, astronomers came to believe that all the planets orbited around the sun. Now, of course, they know that the sun is just one of many stars, spinning far from the center of the Milky Way galaxy, which is itself only one of billions of galaxies.

Through his telescope Ben follows the moons of Jupiter and identifies the hazy Orion Nebula. He sees the stars of the Milky Way, Saturn's rings, the spiral arms of the Andromeda galaxy. Sometimes he imagines that he can see his life with Claire like this, from a great distance, the way satellites orbiting above the planet's atmosphere can identify objects on earth as small as cars. Claire was the sun in his solar system; he hadn't questioned whether to revolve around her. But there are other solar systems in the galaxy, other galaxies in the universe. How far does he want to travel? He doesn't know yet, and maybe he doesn't need to know. Maybe it is enough for now to know that other worlds exist.

"It's so—small," Claire says.

"We prefer to say 'charming,'" the Realtor says, holding open the front door. After a moment she peers around the corner into the hallway. "Now where did your husband go?"

"What? Oh. He's not my husband."

"Sorry," the Realtor says, "I just assumed."

Claire nods. Then she says, "Why?"

"Why what?"

"Why did you assume?"

The Realtor gives her a look, as if she's trying to gauge what Claire wants to hear. "You seem—connected," she says. "And of course," she says, tapping her ring finger with her thumb, "the wedding bands."

Claire looks down at the gold ring on her left hand. Four months have passed since she and Ben parted, so why is she still wearing it? For that matter, why is Charlie wearing his? She thinks it has something to do with the fact that everything happened so quickly—the revelation of the affair, the dissolution of their marriages. Maybe the rings are a talismanic symbol of normalcy that neither of them is ready to give up.

For the past few months, ever since Alison asked Charlie to move out and Ben left for Boston, Claire and Charlie have been living in the apartment of a former professor of Claire's, Eva Stokes, who's been on sabbatical in Europe. In her first year at NYU, Claire had taken Professor Stokes's "Intro to Women's Studies," and, predictably, it had changed her life. Eva became Claire's thesis advisor, and they'd stayed in touch. Every few months they had lunch or dinner together; Eva would rail against patriarchal hegemony and Claire would nod in agreement. When it looked as if Claire and Charlie would need a place to stay, Claire contacted Eva and asked about the huge, university-subsidized apartment on Eighth Street that sat empty while she was in Rome. Impressed that Claire was breaking the shackles of institutional oppression (that is, ending her marriage), Eva offered the use of her place until her return in early August.

It is a hot afternoon in July. Claire and Charlie are looking at apartments in their price range and feeling the sting of sticker shock. What they can afford, given Charlie's financial burdens and Claire's sporadic income, turns out to be uniformly cramped, dark, and charmless.

Claire goes to the window and tries to open it, but the sash is broken. This apartment is in the East Thirties near the river, a part of town with which Claire is unfamiliar, and she is fighting a feeling of panic at the idea that they may have to live here, so far from her usual haunts. They would get a better deal in Brooklyn, she knows, but she doesn't want to cross a bridge; the East Side is distant enough. The Realtor calls this an "emerging" neighborhood, but all Claire sees out the dirty window are a parking garage and several dreary buildings, fronted at their bases with locked grille work. They look to her like bared teeth.

But wait—down on the street, now, a woman with dark hair and Jackie O sunglasses is walking by, pushing a baby stroller. From this distance she looks like Alison, and Claire feels a twist in her gut. Alison's hair, as shiny as a blackbird, her eyes watchful like a bird's, hopping down a branch, head cocked to one side. Her maddening deliberation, her hesitation and careful weighing. Her kindness and constancy. Alison was always there, taking what Claire had to offer and giving back more than she probably deserved.

How profound this betrayal is—to hurt the person she once loved best.

Everything is muddy. Claire can't make the fine distinctions; they seem to have escaped her. Alison, the accident, Ben—dear Ben—

264

creating a new life in Boston. She shakes her head. She doesn't want to think about all the repercussions, to contain these other lives in her experience. It's hard enough to know what she feels for herself.

Twelve years is a long time to love someone without acting on it. In a way, Claire thinks, she has been more faithful to Charlie all these years than she was to Ben. Had she been inclined to unfaithfulness, she might have moved from Charlie to other obsessions. Her love for Ben was reinforced by their vows; her love for Charlie was spun out of air, suspended in time. Doesn't she deserve to be happy now? Doesn't she deserve to spend the rest of her life with the one man in the world she has ever truly desired?

"Ah, there he is!" the Realtor exclaims, and Claire turns to see Charlie amble into the room.

"The toilet's broken," he says, coming over to join Claire at the window. "This building is monstrous."

"Yes. It's a big, healthy co-op with a solid financial history," the Realtor says, her voice resolutely chipper, as if she's trying to fix up an unattractive friend on a blind date.

265

Charlie wraps his arms around Claire's shoulders. "You hate it," he whispers.

She shrugs, determined not to be ill-tempered. "What do you think?"

"I'm with you."

"I know that, but what do you think?"

He squeezes, pulling her close.

For a moment she shuts her eyes. These enveloping arms, his grip on her so different from Ben's tentative grasp. Ben never just held her like this, fully in the moment, without worrying about whether he was crushing her or if she wanted to pull away. If she wants to pull away, she'll pull away. Charlie knows this. He has a doglike faith in her ability to push him off her lap.

The apartment isn't really so bad, Charlie thinks, but he knows Claire doesn't like it, and it's pointless to try to talk her into it. He's happy enough to be borne along on the tide of her quest. If anyone can find the perfect apartment in their price range, it will be Claire.

In their price range. Charlie is only beginning to realize what an enormous strain this divorce will put on his finances. Alison has the house, the Volvo, the gym club membership she doesn't even use; he has almost nothing, and yet he has to pay for everything. Alison is returning to work, though; she starts a job on Monday. Apparently her lawyer has apprised her of the fact that Charlie won't support her forever, and that unless she takes action she will probably have to move.

Charlie's favorite shoes are at the house, his favorite chair—the first chair he ever bought with his own money at a real furniture store (not a dorm room La-Z-Boy from the Salvation Army or Goodwill). His grad school papers and the warranties for his camera, his watch, the stereo system. He'd spent hours, weeks, researching and anticipating and hooking up the stereo, threading wires along doorframes, drilling small holes through walls while Alison rolled her eyes in the background. But to take the stereo with him would be absurd; he'd have to dismantle the living room, the speakers in the kitchen. . . . Every day he thinks of things he left behind. Framed sepia photographs of his mild-mannered grandparents and stern-looking great-grandparents, commingled on a hallway wall with pictures of Alison's ancestors. Yearbooks from the University of Kansas. Someday he will get some of these things back— the ones that matter most, perhaps—but he'll have to let most of it go.

With Alison the future had been all promise—scooping up the past and feathering their domestic nest with it. Now the future will be about letting go, watching pieces of the past drift to the ground. All the things Charlie took for granted—his comfortable house, seeing his children every day, the myriad tasks and errands that Alison took care of—are lost. Almost everything has become more complicated. Chalk it up to—what? A learning experience? If nothing else, the past decade yielded Annie and Noah; the years were worth it for that alone.

Two weeks after Charlie left, he'd called Alison and asked if he and

Claire could meet her for coffee to talk. To explain. At first she said no, but then she relented.

They met at a Starbucks in Rockwell. "We never meant to hurt you," Claire said. "I don't want you to take this the wrong way, but it didn't have anything to do with you, Alison."

"'We,'" Alison said. "So you're a 'we' now." Her voice was almost eerily calm. "You can't steal my life and tell me it has nothing to do with me."

"Blame me," Charlie said. "It's not you. Or her. It's me."

"Oh, I know it's you. *Your* betrayal, *your* immaturity, *your* idealization of her," Alison said, almost spitting the words. "Your selfishness. Noah and Annie don't have a father anymore."

"Come on, Alison," Charlie said. "That's not true."

"You've robbed them of their innocence. Their trust. Does that feel good?"

"Please. Aren't you being a little—?"

Claire put her hand lightly on his, as if to stop him from saying more. Then she said, "We're giving you your life back, can't you see that? That life you thought you had—it wasn't real."

Alison's eyes grew wide, and she blinked. "How dare you say that to me."

The whole thing had been excruciating. Only lately has Alison been able to talk to Charlie on the phone without collapsing in tears or shouting and hanging up. Noah, sweet Noah, has been full of questions but is willing enough to treat Charlie's absences and reappearances as if he's a traveling salesman. Annie has been alternately furious and manic, acting out in restaurants, acting as though she doesn't care. Charlie has had to woo her gingerly, careful not to promise too much while at the same time conveying his unconditional love. It is a strategy destined to fail. Whatever he does, short of moving back in, will disappoint her.

Charlie knew it would be hard, and mostly it's worse than he imagined. And yet—and yet. He is happier than he has ever been. He loves waking up to a mass of copper curls on the pillow beside him every morning, listening to the rhythmic rasp of Claire's breathing (heavier than Alison's, who slept as quietly as a cat). It is wondrous to live in New York again, even to hunt for an apartment on a budget. Charlie feels as if he's been thawed out, freed from a block of ice. How bizarre, to say you are leaving and then just . . . leave. He'd never imagined that it would be so easy—that, like a wizard in a legend, speaking the words would make it so. Something this monumental should be more challenging; he should have had to walk through fire, outwit a dragon, hack through thorny brambles. Find his way through a maze before he was allowed to walk out the door.

"I'm getting the sense this place isn't for you," the Realtor says.

"Do you have anything else we can look at?" Claire asks.

The Realtor flips through the file she's carrying. "In this range," she says slowly, as if she's doing them a huge favor by even talking to them, they're so far below her usual price point—"it's going to be hard to find exactly what you want."

"If you don't think you can help us—" Charlie begins.

"No, no," she says quickly, flashing a conciliatory smile. "Actually, there's something here that might have potential. It's near Astor Place. Large, airy, needs a bit of work. It's empty, so I can take you there now, if you want. I just have to call the super for the key."

"Great," Claire says.

Charlie glances at his watch; he should get back to the office. But what's another hour? With all the upheaval in his life, leaving his job seems even less of a possibility these days, but who knows? The impetus to make a change is stronger now. For the first time in years, Charlie has a sense of the inherent potential of each unfolding moment. He feels like a snake that has shed its skin. The skin is still out there, in the tall grass, almost intact, but the snake has left it behind. Sometimes Charlie wonders if Claire is too much for him, the hawk to his snake. Deep down, he fears that she might take him high into the air and drop him. But at least he will see, as Donne described it, "the round earth's imagined corners"; he will embark on a journey. He will take flight.

"This is Alison Gran—shit." She pushes number seven on the phone, waits for three beeps, listens to the commands, and starts again. "This is Alison Gray. Please—shit." She pushes the button. "You have reached Alison Gray at *HomeStyle* magazine. I'm either away from my desk or on another line. Please leave a message." She presses number five and sits back in her chair. Good. Done. Next?

As if on cue, a young woman with wispy blond hair pokes her head around the door. "Alison—great, you're here. Staff meeting in ten minutes in the conference room. We're going over the holiday issue."

Alison smiles—Christmas in July. Welcome to the upside-down world of magazine publishing. In December they'll be testing barbecue sauces and staging a cookout on a California beach. She looks around her office. It is cramped and spare, with a window overlooking the dirty, exposed organs of the short building next door, but she knows she is lucky to have it. Not to mention the job—it isn't a great time in publishing to find a full-time position. Three months ago, when she'd called everyone she knew in the industry to see what was available, it had seemed hopeless. One acquaintance, looking over her e-mailed résumé, essentially told her there was no chance. "Twenty-six-year-olds are being hired at your level," she said. "And the thing is, magazines want to hire young. It keeps things fresh. You have some good experience, but it's a little—well—outdated, isn't it? Unless you work for a parenting magazine, you're kind of out of the loop. Even there, I'd say it's a long shot. Have you considered getting an MBA?"

Great—so she was over the hill *and* underqualified. After going back to bed with a pillow over her head for several hours, she'd flung the covers off and sat up. She had spent ten years in this profession, damn it. She wasn't going to let one snippy—okay, completely demoralizing—comment stop her. She resolved to call everyone she could think of, friends of friends of friends—whatever it took. She needed a job.

In the end it was Renee Chevarak, Alison's old boss, who gave her a break. Renee was now editor in chief of *HomeStyle*, a magazine that was about everything its name implied. "Of course I remember you!" she said when Alison finally convinced Renee's assistant to put her through. "You were the only assistant I ever had who actually knew how to file. Where the hell have you been?"

"I took a little hiatus," Alison said. "Had two kids . . . but now they're older, and—"

"You're going stir-crazy."

"Something like that." Renee's glib tendency to sum people up with one-liners—which Alison had once found irritating—now came as a welcome deflection.

"So what are you looking for?"

270   "I don't know," Alison said frankly. "At this point I'd be willing to consider just about anything." She told Renee about the senior editing jobs she'd held at other magazines, and then the freelance assignments.

"You know," Renee said thoughtfully, "I have something here that might be perfect for you. I'm introducing a new feature called 'Focus' that will have a different theme each month—Focus on Family, Focus on Rituals, whatever. I need an editor who will come up with ideas and commission pieces—see the whole process through, beginning to end, every month. How does that sound?"

Focus on Health Insurance. Focus on Mortgage Payments. "What a great idea," Alison said, remembering Rule No. 1 about Renee: her brilliance needs to be acknowledged before the conversation can move forward. Then she remembered Rule No. 2: parrot her words back to her—it lets her know you're listening, and validates her ideas. "I think that might be perfect for me."

"All right, then," Renee said. "When can you start? Just kidding. There's an editing test you have to do. Not a big deal—you could probably do it in your sleep. And you have to go through several interviews, with human resources and with my staff, before you get to me." She paused. "I should say 'if.' But don't worry—I'm pretty sure you will."

Alison's heart sank. For a fleeting moment it had seemed as if getting this job was going to be miraculously easy. Now it looked as unlikely as any other prospect. She'd get strawberry jam on the take-home exam; the prepubescent staff would take one look at the bags under her eyes and her five-year-old suit and they'd start saying how much they appreciated her coming in and that they'd be in touch.

"Oh, to hell with it," Renee said suddenly. "I'm the boss here. And I'm in a bind. Come in tomorrow to talk to me. I want to make this happen. How soon could you start?"

Bad clothes, old shoes, no babysitter. (Dolores was out of the picture; Alison had reluctantly concluded that her mother was right.) Self-inflicted haircut. In dire need of a total physical makeover. How long would it take to get ready, six months? "When do you need someone?"

"Yesterday. Hey—any chance you'll be in the city this afternoon?"

"Uh—sure," Alison said, flipping through babysitting options in her head: If Robin—dear Robin!—could take Noah and pick Annie up at the bus. . .

"Good. Come by the office at two o'clock; I can carve out a little space then. Now, if this works out I'll have to put you on a one-month contract basis. You understand. Just to hedge my bets."

Alison wanted to jump through the phone and kiss her. After what she'd been through, she appreciated Renee's bluntness. She needed someone who'd be straight with her, who wouldn't make her guess. She'd had more than enough of that.

Now, in her tiny office, Alison glances at the clock, turns on the computer, and opens the manila folder on her desk marked FOCUS. It is full of clipped newspaper articles, fabric swatches, Renee's notes on Post-its—"Focus on Enviro/Mental?"—digital photos, and glossy ads torn out of magazines. Clearly, the Focus section is supposed to be what passes for high concept in the world of shelter magazines, capturing some fairly obvious national trend after it becomes prevalent enough not to seem peculiar, but before it becomes stale. At the same time, the rubric should be broad enough as to be almost generic. And Alison will need to make these "predictions" six months ahead.

She thinks about her own life. What is important to her now? Certainly, her criteria have changed. Six months ago she was a vaguely dissatisfied housewife with young children; now she is a terrified single working mother trying to remake her identity. Focus on Aftercare? Focus on Take-out Pizza?

As an editor at mainstream women's magazines, Alison had always had an uncanny ability to pinpoint what readers wanted. A writer she worked with once turned to her in a meeting and said, "I've never met anyone so in touch with Middle America. Frankly, you freak me out." It was a joke—but it wasn't. Alison could never have passed for one of those tart-tongued New York editors weaned on sushi and cosmopolitans. At the last magazine she'd worked for, she became famous for a quote her boss had posted in the lunchroom: "We're doing a feature on comfort food? I *am* comfort food!"—Alison Granville.

Focus on . . . She looks at her watch again. 3:13, two minutes until the meeting. Right now Annie is switching activities at summer camp—3:15, arts and crafts; Alison has the schedule posted on her bulletin board—and Noah is waking from a nap at the Sunny Side Up Child Care Center. At 5 P.M. Alison will be standing at the elevator, rushing to catch the train home. Leaving early had been her main requirement in taking this job. She didn't quibble too much over salary or benefits; she just wanted to be home by six. A nice girl, Rayonda, a student at the local community college, picks Annie up from the bus at four-thirty and then gets Noah at day care at five. By six o'clock Rayonda has usually put fish sticks in the toaster oven and microwaved frozen peas, so that when Alison walks in the door she and the kids can sit down together.

On weekend mornings in Rockwell, Alison often goes on long walks with Robin—power walks, Robin calls them. Alison drops her kids off to watch cartoons with Robin's kids and groggy, coffee-slurping husband, Robin clips her pedometer to her moisture-wicking T-shirt, and off they go down the street. On these excursions they pass other clusters of power-walking women who call out cheery greetings; Robin seems to know them all by name and asks specific questions such as, "How is Trevor liking St. Luke's?" and "Did Liz come through with the Rangers tickets for the auction?" Clearly Robin has dozens, even hundreds, of friends. A whole world exists in this town, Alison is beginning to realize, that she knew nothing about. Trotting along (Robin walks so fast!), Alison feels vaguely like a wildebeest on the plain encountering other beest from the herd. Once she might have recoiled from such associations, but now she is comforted by the idea. There is a herd, and she is a part of it. Not only a part of it—she is the sidekick of an alpha female. (Alison thinks about high school, where she inhabited the same role. Does nothing ever change?)

Her life isn't perfect. It is far from perfect. But it isn't as awful as Alison had imagined it would be. In some ways it is not only better than she'd feared, but it is also better than it had been when Charlie was home, when she thought things were fine between them. It has been shocking to realize how absent Charlie was from their day-to-day lives; some days, now, the children barely notice his absence. Many of the things Alison thought she needed him for—taking out the trash and recycling, paying the bills, small home repairs, sex—she finds she can do just as well on her own.

Maybe not just as well. But well enough to counterbalance the wrenching loneliness she feels some nights, the tiredness in her bones, and the dull awareness that she has to summon the strength the next morning to do the whole routine all over again—waking before daylight to shower and dress and get the kids to camp and day care and herself to the train, spend a long, stressful day in the city, and come home to two tired children at night. Alison doesn't spoil the kids anymore; she simply doesn't have time. Annie sets the table for dinner, helps clear it while Alison does the dishes, runs the water for bath time, and helps

273

her brother get ready for bed. After bedtime stories and good night kisses, Alison is ready to collapse into bed herself.

Late at night she thinks about the child she never knew, as real to her as the ones she does. Her own anguish is only a small piece of what his parents must suffer, and yet it has taken her on a journey toward something deeper and more profound than she has ever experienced. Each moment of loss, she has come to believe, contains within it the possibility of a new life. When the unimaginable happens, and your life changes irrevocably, you may find along with the pain a kind of grace. And in the place of certainty and fear—the fear of losing what you had—you are left with something startling: a depth of empathy, a quivering sensitivity to the world around you, and the unexpected blessing of gratitude for what remains.

Now, when the children are asleep, the house is quiet. Alison pads around softly in her bare feet, straightening pillows, changing lightbulbs, restoring order, and feels oddly at peace. Charlie's needs, stresses, and preoccupations had taken up so much space. It is lovely not to hear him stomping around upstairs, or to have to think about what to feed him, whether his laundry is clean, whether his seemingly endemic distractedness is a cover for irritability. Will he snap if she asks him a question? For a long time they coexisted in this house without sharing much of anything. Now he's across the river, making a new life for himself with the only other person in the world who knows Alison as well as he does.

It makes her heart lurch, when she thinks about it. And just under the sadness are more complex emotions, anger and jealousy and hurt. So Alison tries to concentrate on the here and now. It is three-fifteen on a Monday afternoon, and she has a new job. In New York, as a senior editor at *HomeStyle* magazine. That's pretty good. Even better, she has a theme, just in time for the meeting: Focus on Quiet. A favorite book, a sleeping child, the tick of a clock in a still room, solitude. Peace. She stands up, closes the folder, and makes her way down the hall to the conference room.

acknowledgments

I am privileged to work with Katherine Nintzel, the kind of editor that writers dream of, and the entire magnificent group at William Morrow. I want to thank Beth Vesel, my longtime agent and friend, for her vision and wise counsel; the English Department at Fordham University for supporting my creative work; and my close tribe of sisters, Cynthia Baker Zeitler, Clara Lester, and Catherine Baker-Pitts, who sustain and inspire me.

The Virginia Center for the Creative Arts and the Geraldine R. Dodge Foundation gave me space and time to write. Anne Burt, Alice Elliott Dark, and Pamela Redmond Satran, who read some or all of the manuscript several times, form the core of my community of writers and friends. Karen Sacks, Executive Director of Volunteer Lawyers for Justice, paved the way for me with New Jersey legal experts, including Marvin Adames, Chief Municipal Prosecutor of the City of Newark; Clyde Otis, a municipal prosecutor; Alix Rubin, a partner at Entwistle & Cappucci; Nicole Masella at Hack, Piro, O'Day, Merklinger, Wallace & McKenna; and Carmela Novi at Casha & Casha. Thanks also to John Cusolito at Liberty Mutual Insurance Company.

I am grateful for the support of my parents, Bill and Tina Baker, and my mother-in-law, Carole Kline. Finally, my husband, David, and sons, Hayden, Will, and Eli, are at the center of everything; they make my life rich.